I0564067

The Blighted Touch

Denise Tanaka

Sasoriza Books
www.sasorizabooks.com

All rights reserved. No part of this book may be reproduced in any form or by any electronic or mechanical means, including information storage and retrieval systems, without written permission from the author, except for the fair use of quotations.

THE BLIGHTED TOUCH

copyright ©2025 by Denise B. Tanaka

Cover design by Fiona Jayde Media

Published in the United States by Sasoriza Books

www.sasorizabooks.com

This is a work of fiction. All of the characters and events portrayed herein are entirely the product of the author's imagination. Any resemblance to actual events, locales in the real world, or persons living or dead, is not intentional and strictly coincidental.

No generative AI tool has been used in the cover art, the conceptualization, development, or drafting of this work. Permission is not given for the use of this material for AI training without specific licensing.

Contents

Other Books in the Series

Dedicated to the late Emily Joan Alward (1935 – 2011) a retired librarian, author, and editor of the "Once Upon A World" anthology. Many years ago, my first short story sale appeared in this publication. That tale involved a woman and her caveman brother defending their sacred mountain from a trespasser. (It is repurposed in this book as a background story for the characters.) Emily sent a very kind personal letter with my author copy that gave me inspiration and encouragement. I felt hope that my dream of becoming a successful fantasy author was on the verge of coming true. But dreams got delayed. A long journey through multiple rewrites, writing critique groups, and life's many hurdles has finally resulted in the book you now hold in your hands.

One

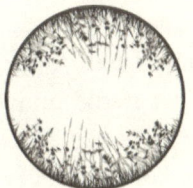

AYA THE VILLAGE herbalist urged her sluggish feet to hasten uphill. Was it too late? Would the contents of her basket be strong enough for the task ahead? Ascending the grassy slope felt harder and farther than should have been. Bur-thistles and prickly weeds snagged on her calf-length skirt. Her heart pounded. Breathing raked her dry throat. She slouched like a woman three times her age. Youthful in years, Aya no longer felt young since inheriting the role following her mother's death the year before.

The midwife had summoned her to come earlier, but Aya had to spend all morning to rummage the forest floor. Mushrooms of all kinds, deep twisted roots, and rare aromatic herbs filled her cloth-lined wicker tub. She had gathered as much as she could carry of unique items that usually eased the sufferings of a woman on the verge of giving birth. The basket's handle creaked with her every step.

"What has taken you so long, Aya!" The midwife called out from the doorway of the thatched cottage at the top of the hill.

"I had to go to the forest."

"Speak louder! I can't hear you!"

Still halfway up the grassy slope, Aya shouted to be heard. "I gathered fresh potent things from the woods."

"Good, good. Hurry, now! The baby is coming out soon!"

This would be the first pregnancy reaching the end of its term in the past four months. Aya feared the worst outcome even though the midwife had expressed hopefulness. It was not the woman's first child, and her last ones delivered easily. All seemed to go well up until now. A child tucked safely in its mother's womb must surely be insulated from the mysterious affliction that everyone else suffered.

A mother should be able to embrace her own newborn child without the blight flaring up. *What if she's wrong?* Aya thought as she approached the cottage. What if the midwife's optimism was foolish hope? What if this and every pregnancy was doomed?

Funeral bells ringing up from the valley floor carried on the spring breeze. An infant had died of weakness. Aya had given balms, salves, and herbal tisanes to the parents for the past several weeks to no avail.

Mourners wailed grief in eerie harmony with songbirds chirping blissfully in the meadow's trees. Bells and drums of the funeral procession were muted by the high-pitched ringing that constantly whistled deep inside Aya's ears—a minor side-effect of the blight shared by all. Since that night when the blight fell like a thunderclap, everyone in Lisshardra Valley endured the same constant ringing in their ears, day and night, young or old. Now, four months later, she could hardly remember that it was not always this way.

At the crest of the grassy hill, Aya passed between square plots of sprouting onions, pea shoots, garlic flowers, beanstalks, turnips, and collard greens. Aya swallowed the lump in her throat as she dreaded approaching the door. *Be strong, be strong,* she encouraged herself, thinking in the language of the mountain people in her late mother's faraway land.

Aya kicked her sandals off at the doorstep but hesitated to move forward.

The midwife stepped backwards to maintain a space between them. "We've been waiting for you, Herbalist. The sun's well past mid-morning."

"I am sorry for taking so long. I had to venture deep into the forest. Some of the roots were hard to dig." Aya stepped barefoot onto the well-sanded boards that covered the dirt floor.

2

A few blinks adjusted her vision to the dim interior. In the stone hearth, dark orange embers glowed beneath a simmering cauldron of stew. A loaf of rising dough wrapped in cloth rested on the mantle.

The pregnant woman in labor reclined on a wooden frame cot. Her back lay to the fireplace. Her face was all in shadow.

Two children at the opposite wall kept their distance from the birthing bed. The five-year-old had to use a rag-wrapped wooden spoon to wipe the soiled buttocks of the two-year-old. The toddler fidgeted where he lay. Impatient at being cleaned, he raised his leg. The bare foot came close to touching the older child's forearm.

"No!" The five-year-old girl flinched away. "No touch! No touch!"

The toddler rolled onto his stomach and began to cry.

Aya's lower lip quivered in helplessly observing the child's distress. She recalled her own childhood when she had helped to care for her younger sisters. Now, because of the blight, she could not do such a simple thing as rocking a crying child on her shoulder. Not just her but no one in the room could risk cheek-to-cheek contact. *No touch. No touch.*

"Hush, hush." The midwife forced her strained voice into a soothing tone. "Why don't you both go outside? Find some good turnips and beans and onions to pay the herbalist. Go on. Go on."

The older girl put the soiled rag into a basin of water. "Come along," she ordered her little brother.

Still crying, the toddler bolted out the door first. His sister put on sandals before following him outside.

"I don't ask for payment today." Aya approached the cot's edge but kept a safe distance. "You need to feed your husband and your children, Goodwife Nuriasha, these two and the one yet to come."

"At least take an onion and some beans," said the farmer's wife.

"I couldn't," Aya began.

"There's plenty in the garden! You must take some." Nuriasha closed her eyes and breathed deeply. She lay on her side with a rolled-up blanket tucked between her knees. Sweat beads shined in small bright spots against her dark skin.

"Easy, easy." The midwife used wooden tongs to drape a cloth on Nuriasha's forehead.

Aya waited for the midwife to withdraw her hands, then carefully dripped herb-infused olive oil onto the cloth. "Inhale deeply. Let the scents soothe you."

"It's passing now," Nuriasha reported while stroking her belly.

The midwife said, "The waves of your labors are still few and far between. It may not be today."

"But no, I feel this is the day. This is the day the child will come. This is the day."

Aya kneeled on the floorboards to unpack the herbs, roots, and mushrooms from her basket. "I will mix a soothing tincture for the hours ahead."

"My thanks and gratitude, Aya," said the farmer's wife.

The inflection of the valley's language gave a peculiar sound to Aya's foreign name, emphasizing the second syllable and distorting the vowels, not at all the way her mother had pronounced it. Even after a lifetime of hearing her own name mispronounced with a rising lilt, she still noticed the difference. Now, with her mother's death a year ago, no one remained who could voice her name as it was meant to be said. Even her younger sisters spoke to her only in the valley's language. She had grown up since childhood with the farmer's wife as a neighbor but in this moment, Aya felt like a stranger just arrived from a faraway land.

"Your gratitude is received and appreciated, Goodwife Nuriasha," Aya said.

The midwife's large brown eyes observed her with a focused, sympathetic gaze. Aya shared the glance for a moment, hoping to draw strength from the hopefulness radiating from the other woman. Conversations of the past few weeks replayed in her memory. Aya had asked, *If no one can touch each other without pain, what is going to happen in the birth? How can the mother feed the child? Should we squeeze mother's milk into jugs as we do with the goats' milk? Will any babies survive if they cannot be held in loving hands? What will we do if the winter's blight drags on through spring into the summer? Into autumn? Into the next year and the next?*

"It won't be too much longer. The peaks of your labor pains are coming closer." The midwife spoke in a gentle, comforting tone.

"Yes, yes, here comes another."

Aya focused on her task of crushing sprigs of dried herbs with a mortar and pestle. By pinching, she measured the desiccated mushrooms flakes. Her fingertips felt the best of the freshly picked fungus petals. For this delicate work, she could not wear gloves.

Fresh waves of labor pains caused Nuriasha to grimace. Her chin tucked into her throat. Her shoulders curled. Her left arm flailed out as if trying to slap away the air itself that threatened to crush her.

Nuriasha's outstretched hand brushed Aya's wrist. Their skin touched. The blight flared up.

Burning pain engulfed Aya's forearm worse than falling into a patch of thorns. Hot needles pierced through to the bone. Pain raked down to her wrist. Her fingers went numb. She dropped the pestle but, with orange and purple sparkles filling her sight, she hardly saw it. The ever-present ringing in her ears crescendoed to an unbearably loud blast so that, for a moment, she was unaware of the pregnant woman screaming.

"Clumsy daughter of a mountain brute!" The midwife, wearing elbow-length knitted gloves, waved her wooden tongs like a weapon.

Aya hugged her own stinging forearm. The whistling ring in her ears lessened after a few deep breaths. Her vision cleared to ordinary dim colors. Yet spasms continued to jerk her fingers. Words failed to form in her throat.

The farmwife sat upright, thighs splayed wide, and groaned loudly at the space between her feet. Eyes squeezed shut in narrow slits between her furrowed brow and grimacing cheeks.

"Get out, you dim-witted bear-child." The midwife scooped up Aya's basket by the handle. She stomped a few steps across the room and threw it out of the open doorway. Mushrooms, herbs, and roots scattered in the sunlit dirt.

"I'm sorry," Aya mumbled as she staggered out the door. Blindly, she stepped into her sandals. She snatched up the wicker basket's handle but left behind its contents. Her feet carried her swiftly downhill and through the pathway of trampled grasses that were beginning to spring back.

Two

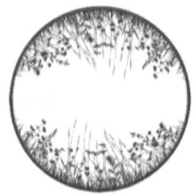

THAT EVENING AT SUNSET, Aya traveled the well-trodden wagon road that led to her younger sister's cottage. She wore a pale brown cloak over her wool tunic and belted skirt. Shadowy air chilled her cheeks.

To her right, the creek's waters gurgled loudly with springtime run-off of melting mountain snow. To her left, a field of wildflowers bloomed in vivid hues of yellow, orange, lavender, and pink. Sunset's gold-and-rosy hues spread over the broad expanse of farm fields where tall stalks of barley and wheat swayed in the cool breezes. Crickets chirped and cicadas hummed but the ever-present ringing in her ears drowned it all out.

Is there something I've forgotten to bring? she wondered. As her sandals sank with each step into the soft moist soil, her thoughts lingered on the events of earlier that day. She replayed her actions like a song in her memory. If only she had placed her mortar and pestle at the foot of the bed, out of reach of the laboring farmwife's arms. If only she had dared to go back and apologize. But then, she thought, what apology could atone for her carelessness? The pains of labor and the pains of the blight—was the farmwife strong enough to endure them both?

Her younger sister's wattle-and-daub cottage had a front door facing east. By the end of the day, the path to approach was all in shadow. Sunset's colors shined on the thatching and made it appear that the straw roof was on fire.

"Good of the evening!" Ioanoh, her brother-in-law, waggled a stick to herd a few straggling goats into the pen.

"Good evening, brother." Aya hurried up a pebbled pathway towards the stone threshold at the cottage's doorstep.

Dimylse slid aside the plank front door rattling in the grooves of the sill track. She stood filling the door frame and planted one fist against her hip. A wide leather belt cinched too tightly around her waist. Her chamomile yellow skirt, so pale that it was nearly white, contrasted with her sienna brown tunic. The wool's deep hues matched with her sister's skin tone so that, in the evening hour, Dimylse's face blended with the shadows of the cottage's interior at her back.

"There you are, Sister! I was starting to worry if you had a mishap on the way." As always, Dimylse frowned. Her broad squeezed her full-lipped mouth into a narrow slit.

"I was delayed, uh, helping the midwife with Nuriasha."

"Oh, is the baby born?"

"No, not yet," Aya said. "It won't be today."

Dimylse looked aside to where her husband Ioanoh was herding goats into the pen. A long silence hung between them until, at last, Dimylse returned her gaze to the basket hanging from Aya's hand.

"Did you bring the dried persimmons?"

Aya looked down at the blue cloth that covered an assortment of lemons, ginger root, finger-sized carrots, and toasted walnuts. "No. I forgot."

"But we talked about it yesterday and the day before. You promised!"

"Yes, Dimy, I know but—"

Dimylse stepped back and faded into the dim interior of her cottage. Aya took that as her invitation to enter. Ever since the blight struck four months before, no one hugged or kissed in greeting. No one touched. By now, it had become a habit to keep at least an arm's length distance from each other.

Baby Eathom sat upright. He splayed his legs on a blanket placed in between the firewood rack and a crate filled with dishes and pots. He held a chunk of river reed in both little hands and chewed on its tip. Saliva dribbled down his chin. Drool soaked the front of his shirt.

"I told you many times, Aya, that the baby is cutting a tooth. He's getting tired of chewing on these old sticks. I wanted to give him dry persimmons to chew. Can you try to remember when you come for supper tomorrow?"

"I will, Dimy, I promise." Aya set down her basket in the corner. In bending over, she felt herself slouch in weariness.

Dimylse stirred the contents of an iron cauldron simmering above the fire. The brew gave off a delightful scent of lentil-onion soup. A plump rabbit was roasting on a spit. A loaf of yeast bread had baked to the perfect shade of maple brown.

Her husband Ioanoh entered and whooped loudly. "Oh, that rabbit smells good! Are we ready to eat?"

"Almost, almost," Dimylse answered.

Quickly, Aya sat on a three-legged stool so as not to be taller than everyone else. Ioanoh was especially self-conscious of his stout stature and the need to raise his chin when looking Aya straight in the eye. Her longer legs and slender neck were a constant reminder that she alone had an unknown father in a faraway foreign land. Their late mother Aho was pregnant at the time she abandoned the mountain people and came down to live in Lisshardra Valley. Her lack of blood relations in the valley set her apart and hardly a day passed that something or someone failed to remind her of it. Both of Aya's sisters had a local barley farmer as their father who, in turn, was a head-and-shoulders shorter than his daughters.

Ioanoh tugged off his boots and hung his hooded cloak on a wall peg. "We worried about you arriving so late, Sister. I've seen a few vagabond tramps loitering on the outskirts of the village. You know what the fringes might do to a woman walking alone."

The rectangular table was the only furniture in the main room, apart from the dish shelves and a crate for the cooking pots. The table's knotty planks served as a barrier in between herself and the others. Aya got busy with pulling the leafy green stalks off the carrot tops.

Dimylse added, "I've heard those fringe tramps steal babies too. I don't feel safe with their kind coming in so close."

Briefly, Aya considered speaking up in defense of the wandering peddlers. If not for itinerant traders who traveled between the coast and the inland villages, there would be no sea salt, no pickled sardines or smoked whitefish, and no glassware in Lisshardra Valley. But her forearm still ached from the touch of the farmwife. She felt too weary to argue.

Ioanoh continued, "I'm going to complain to the elders again tomorrow. Someone has to do something about those fringes lurking about."

Aya felt tempted to ask, what exactly he would like the village elders to do? But her sister changed the subject.

"You know who came around to visit today? Wennylae, that's who. She pretended to be interested in how my baby's doing but, really, she stood over me while I planted a row of radishes. Then she nagged me and pestered me about how I'm doing it all wrong! Is there a wrong way to plant my radishes? She said that I was clustering the shoots too closely together. Well, I stood up, and looked her straight in the eye, and I said this is how I've always planted my radishes every year. She started to cry and claimed she was offended by my tone. That tricked me into apologizing. Now I regret it. She went home happy, and my stomach was in knots the whole rest of the day. Why should I apologize? It's my garden, not her garden, isn't it? She's the one being rude, not me, isn't she? What do you think, Sister?"

Aya used a clam shell to scrape the skin off a ginger root. "Well..."

The door slid open enough for Aya's youngest sister Feianthe to lean her face inside. "Hello? Good of the evening, is there space to come in?"

Dimylse grinned widely and opened her arms as if to invite a hug. Since the blight, no one could touch but the invitation itself was enough.

Feianthe entered with a bounce in her step. She removed her pale blue cloak to hang by the door. Gloves stayed on. Underneath she wore an indigo tunic and a calf-length gray skirt belted at the waist. Instead of a cap or a head kerchief, her wavy brown hair draped loosely off her shoulders. Bits of wildflower petals were snagged in her curls. Her sandals and her cloak's hemline were soiled with green grass and dark mud.

"We worried about you coming up the path so late," said Ioanoh. "I've seen a gang of those vagabond tramps lurking by the creek's bend. You know what those fringes might do to a woman walking alone."

Feianthe smiled and her cheeks flushed. "Don't worry so much, brother. I wasn't alone. I was with Ondrick, and he walked me almost up to your threshold."

Aya exhaled softly and focused on grating the moist ginger root against a textured stone. Her youngest sister was enjoying her seventeenth year of life. Despite the blight, she infused the name Ondrick with the musical lilt of infatuation.

Feianthe strolled a sort of blissful, aimless dance along the opposite wall. "Ondrick says that the Touch is going to fade any day now. He's sure of it. Now that the weather is warming up and the plum trees are blooming, the blight will go the way of winter's darkness."

"Let's hope he's right," Dimylse said.

Ioanoh wiggled the tip of his smallest finger into his ear. "Now that you mention it, the ringing is a bit less loud today."

Aya spooned the grated ginger paste onto a seashell as a serving dish. She said nothing, her thoughts turning inward, as the high-pitched ringing was as loud today as it ever was. *Did you not hear the funeral bells*, she wanted to ask but the words did not rise to her mouth. The family continued preparing supper as if this spring evening were no different from the evenings of the past year, as if the villagers had not buried a child that day, as if they had no worries for the risk of more infants doomed to perish.

Feianthe carefully danced around the baby sitting on the floor. She brought stoneware plates to set on the table. All the while, she continued to smile. Her eyes twinkled brightly in the firelight as her mind played thoughts of its own.

"I've been meaning to mention something." Aya spoke quickly to jump into that rare moment of silence. "Dimy? Feia? Soon, it's going to be a year since Mamma—"

"Mother always liked Ondrick," Feianthe said. "I'm sure she would be happy for me."

Dimylse pulled the roasted rabbit off the spit and served it on a cedar plank. "Mother never had a chance to see Eathom come into the world. I still remember the last time she touched my belly and said, 'I'm fighting this sickness as best I can. I want to see my grandson.'"

"Her memory is alive in our hearts," her brother-in-law said somberly. He paused for a beat, then inhaled loudly. "Let's eat! I'm hungry!"

"Yes but ..." Aya spoke up more loudly as the man took his seat at the opposite end of the table. "I had hoped that we could put on the ritual."

"What ritual?" Ioanoh asked.

Dimylse ladled soup into wooden bowls and served them at the table's four sides. Feianthe carried the loaf of bread wrapped in a towel. The two sisters maneuvered carefully to avoid touching each other.

"It's a ritual that my mother's people perform at the one-year mark of someone's death," Aya said. "Mamma described it to me. We would gather at the burial ground on the day. We would burn a bundle of particular herbs on her marker stone. We would sing a song that she taught to me."

Feianthe laughed softly. "I could never understand Mother's songs. The words sound like the bleating of goats."

"Mountain People songs. *Brrghh... blaagh...burr-blaaaa....*" Ioanoh's deep bass voice overpowered the girl's laughter. "Like the growling of bears."

Aya's cheeks flushed warmly. She glanced at Dimylse, hoping for support but her sister only looked down into her soup bowl.

"It was Mamma's dying wish, that we do not forget where she came from." Aya held back the rest of what she wished to say. Many times, she had suggested making a journey to visit the faraway snowy heights where the mountain people dwelled. Many times, her sisters had refused. *What would we say to them? They are strangers to us. Mother must have fled the mountains for a reason. She was happier here, and here we should stay.* On this evening, Aya felt too weary to launch into a repetition of the old arguments.

Dimylse said, "Well, she's gone. Mother won't know if we do her ritual or not. What does it matter, Aya? We all know where she came from. Isn't it more important that she finished her life here in a better place than where she began? Why should we draw attention to ourselves by standing on her grave marker, burning weeds, and singing a foreign song? What will the neighbors think if we start acting out a savage ritual over the buried bones of our mother?"

Aya blinked at the tears clouding her vision. In her memories, she saw her mother's emaciated cheeks attempting to smile one last time. She recalled the deathly stench in the blankets and the jaundiced tint of her mother's skin. The three sisters had gathered around for their mother's final moments. With tears glistening on all their cheeks, they had promised in chorus to honor Aho's last wish. Only a year had passed since their mother's eyes drooped shut, yet it felt as if an entire lifetime had passed.

Aya bent over to her basket on the floor, reaching for one of the lemons. The baby was there. He had crawled over and was also reaching for a lemon.

Their hands came so close that Aya pulled back sharply. "I'm sorry."

"Be careful! You almost touched him!" Dimylse hurriedly wadded up her long apron around her hands. At the same time, she rushed towards the baby on the floor.

His mother's sudden movement startled the baby into crying. He reached up, wordlessly asking to be picked up and cuddled. Dimylse grasped the child under the armpits but held him at a distance. Her arms stiff and straight, she began to cry herself as she dared not kiss the tears off his cheeks. As a mother, she could do nothing but cry in chorus with him.

"I'm sorry," Aya said.

"Careless, clumsy, mountain-head!" Her brother-in-law's deep voice boomed like thunder.

Feianthe asked, "But isn't the blight a little less strong than before? Isn't it? Isn't it? Would it have been so bad if she—"

"Don't defend her, Feia! She clings to the customs of wild, mountain brutes! She can't understand how to be careful around a fragile child."

In a long, noisy pause, Feianthe said nothing. Though her large brown eyes were moist with sympathy, her mouth stayed closed.

Dimylse sputtered and snorted to get control of her weeping. Soon, she would get her second wind. Soon, she would erupt in a tirade of repeating every insult or admonition she had ever said before. The wearisome phrases like a familiar song began to echo in Aya's memories.

Aya rose from her stool and turned away to the door. She left behind her sisters, the crying children, a warm supper, and her basket full of vegetables. Hunger gurgled in her belly. She ignored the sensation, like the drone of crickets chirping in the meadows, and kept walking. Twilight's gray turned to darkness by the time she returned home to her solitary cottage at the edge of the woods.

Three

AYA SPENT the next morning alone in the forest digging up herbal roots and foraging for various mushrooms. Because of her unusual height, she could reach farther up the tree trunks to harvest the unique mushrooms that sprouted like fish scales off the sides of the bark. A lizard scampered across the back of her hand. She smiled in brief pleasure at the touch of another living thing.

Near to midday, she emerged from the canopy of leafy boughs. Thick white clouds drifted across the blue sky, carried on the warm spring breeze. The floral-scented air hinted at light showers that had fallen while she sheltered under the broad leaves of sycamore, maple, oak, willow, and black walnut trees.

The midwife had not called for her to return. Perhaps the farmwife's labor pains had waned, and the baby had decided to remain in the womb for a few more days. Even so, as village herbalist she felt an obligation to venture back up the hill to inquire. Aya's long skirt pushed through the fronds of flowering buckwheat stalks that drooped over the footpath. The grain's white flowers brightened fertile fields to either side of her.

Brown ducks waddled across the path and briefly blocked her way. The ducks huddled closely together, wings touching. Aya turned her head to stare at such a common sight that she had known since child-hood. Now she felt as if she had never seen ducks before. Until recently, Aya had never taken much interest in puddle ducks, or vole-pigs, or goats that provided meat and wool for the people of the village. Ever since the blight began four months ago, she had a fascination for all the animals who could still touch each other. Why did it only affect the people? No one knew. No one could explain.

As she walked beneath the warm sunshine of spring, Aya recalled that late autumn evening when the Blight of Touch began. Early frost had dusted the village's thatched rooftops. Harvest time was done and the people made ready for the coming winter. Trees had dropped most of their leaves. Orchards had been picked bare. River waters flickered beneath the grist mill's wheel and continued a southwesterly course between the hills at the lower end of the valley. In the darkening sky, a faint sliver of waning moon had only a day or two before it shrank into the nothingness of a moonless night. Fathers came indoors from laboring in their fields; they removed their boots and hung up their socks to dry. Babies suckled on their mothers' laps while older children clapped out discs of flatbread to toast on the hearth stones.

On that fateful night, Aya was alone in her cottage. Despite her weariness and the late hour, she did not feel ready to lie down in the cold blankets. She counted and recounted her late mother's collection of seed pods, dried roots, and aromatic herbs stored in ceramic jars. In the privacy of her own home, she hummed to herself a foreign song that only rhymed if one chanted the words of the mountain people whom she had never seen.

The blight struck the valley without warning. Some villagers claimed that they saw a bolt of green lightning shoot from a drift of purple clouds. Others said that a funnel cloud appeared in the northern sky like a giant's fist that opened and quickly closed. Aya did not see the sky from being indoors with her windows shuttered.

Aya had felt what everyone in Lisshardra Valley experienced all at once. First came a thunderclap and a pressure in one's ears as if all the windows of the world had slammed shut. Then followed a sensation of one's skin being squeezed from all sides like a wave of the worst summer heat. Vertigo caused the standing people to stumble and fall to the ground. Mothers dropped their babies. Many of the villagers fainted only to awaken later and discover how everything had changed.

She never told anyone that the whirlwind inside her skull gave her a brief swirl of euphoria. So far as she knew, she was the only one to feel a rush of pleasure in that dreadful moment. Only she slept soundly that night and awakened in a happier mood. Hours passed before the first villager came to her doorstep sobbing for help. Even the hardiest of farmers, tradesmen, or the mothers of many children could not endure the burning agony of touch. No salves or ointments were strong enough to provide relief ever since that night.

Aya blinked out of her reverie.

Surprised, now she found herself at the edge of the village. How could this be, she wondered, that her feet had wandered in the opposite direction of where she had planned to go. Perhaps the humid sunshine had overheated her scalp.

The wagon road led between a pair of grain silos towards the village's market square. Aya shifted her grip on the basket's handle and braced herself for approaching the destination. She planned to cut a diagonal course and turn towards the farmwife's cottage after passing through.

Ever since she was a child, she had felt uneasiness upon entering the village. She preferred going into the woods to be surrounded by tree trunks and shaded by the canopy of walnut, oak, hemlock, birch, and sycamore leaves. The village was another type of forest all its own with an assorted collection of thatched cottages, weathered plank fences, and a few two-story wooden buildings. Movements were restricted to well-trodden paths. Neighbors and friends had barriers of fences and gates and walls between them. The rich scent of private vegetable gardens and penned livestock filled the air with the perfume of food and the earthy odor of manure. Barrels, idle hand carts, and plowshares cluttered the open spaces had turned barren underfoot.

Avoiding the possibility of uncomfortable questions, she side-stepped the workshops of the cobbler, the wainwright, the cooper, the brewer, and the blacksmith. A few children collected logs from the high stack of communal firewood. Aya passed the clack-clack of a weaver's loom and the swish-swish of a woodworker finishing the last few strokes of sandpaper on a new chair. In the air, she heard murmurings of their conversation in subdued tones. No one laughed. No one sang as they worked. Since that night when the chime struck, Aya could not recall the last time she heard the villagers be joyous.

Market Square was a circular space of well-trampled ground at the center of the village. A communal fountain was at the core. River stones formed a rim around the artesian well's waters that gurgled up from the depths of the earth.

A group of thirty or forty villagers assembled at the fountain. Curious as to what attracted the attention of so many people, Aya wandered closer.

One man—an outsider—stood upon a stack of hay bales next to the fountain. Unlike everyone else in the valley, the stranger smiled.

Everything about his appearance was foreign. He was slender but not skinny; youthful but not young. His nose was too large for his narrow face. The outsider wore drab clothing in varying hues of brown. Strands of wool fringe dangled from his tunic's yoke line and from the seams of his sleeves in the telltale fashion of an itinerant peddler. Village men all grew their beards as thick mossy bushes, but this peddler had shaved his jawline as cleanly as a young boy. Long straight hair flowed loosely to his beltline. Wayward locks hung as black fern fronds off his shoulders.

The stranger held a puppet the size of a toddling child. His figurine was exquisitely lifelike in every detail of its miniature costume, neatly coiffed hair, and a ceramic face. Jointed limbs moved gracefully to the rods manipulated by the peddler's other hand.

He recited the old, familiar rhyme that all children learned for remembering their measure of calendar months. *"Twenty-five, thirty, thirty-five, twenty-five, these are the days that keep Summer alive. Thirty-five, twenty-five, twenty-five, thirty, these are the days that make Harvesters dirty. Thirty, thirty, twenty-five, ten, in these days dark hours do the year end. In twenty-twenty-twenty, we start it over again."* His melody rang out alone, without instrumental accompaniment. He had a fine voice with a broad range, easily soaring to the upper registers in precise pitch then swooping to the deeper tones. His throat's lump bobbed up and down as each note formed with the accuracy of a wooden flute played by a masterful hand.

Aya joined the standing crowd but at a distance behind the outer rim of the circle. She looked between the heads and shoulders at the traveler performing with his puppets. Even though she stood among so many people, she felt utterly alone and unseen.

One figurine reclined sideways as if asleep. The puppeteer recited the verses, "*I am th' only man in th' forest, yet I am not alone. My friends are sparrows and crows. I lay in the embrace of the oak and aspen boughs. My riches are dewdrops and rainbows.*" He spoke in a chanting voice, a lyrical monotone somewhere between talking and singing, both and neither. His musical voice, like the purr of a hearth log, settled warmly into Aya's belly. She lost all interest in everything but the sound coming out of his mouth. The dismal and hopeless village blew out of her mind like snowflakes melting off her gloves. All that mattered was the bobbing of his throat's lump, the flexing of his lean jaw, and the bend of his lips forming words.

Hanging on strings from his fingers, a second puppet entered the scene. It represented a female dressed in an ankle-length gown belted at the waist. Her ginger-colored hair was braided into a single rope down her back. The peddler's voice changed to singing the verses in a feminine timbre. "*I have found you, the man who dwells in the forest. I have walked over mountains of ice. I walked through valley and woods, from the edges to the center of the world. Listening for the sound of your voice, your song, your breath, I have walked. Now, at last, I found you.*"

I know this story, Aya thought.

The puppets reenacted the legend of Eiyallandra and her faithful consort who had measured out the first calendar and taught the almanac to the farmers of the lowlands. As the storytellers taught the children, the pair of lovers counted the passing of each hour of each day. They reveled in the joy of each other's bodies at the passing of each night. Then afterward, they lay awake side by side to measure the movements of the moon and constellations.

The puppet representing the Man of the Forest awakened from his slumber and turned to face the woman. She extended her arms to invite his embrace. "*I am Eiyallandra, and I am your lover.*"

The Man of the Forest asked, *"How can this be if we have never met?"*

Eiyallandra sang, *"We are children of the light. The spirits of our ancestors haunt the silver clouds. We will always find each other. I have walked for a year of my life in search of you, to unite in body as we are already united in our hearts."*

The figurines embraced each other cautiously so as not to tangle their strings. His song flattened out to a monotone chant, *"You and I, one and one, two as one... we are one..."* Their ceramic faces came together to hold the impression of a kiss.

"Well, come on!" shouted one of the men in the standing audience. Aya recognized the voice of the Balancer-of-Scales and one of the Village Elders. By the slurring of his words, he had already imbibed a good amount of beer. "Is that all they're going to do? Where's the 'reveling in the joy of each other' and such?"

The peddler laid down the puppets on the fountain's stone rim with care. When his hands let them go, all the illusory life went out of them.

"They have ceramic faces, my good sir," he said. "They have ceramic hands. The rest is all fabric and straw and strings. What do you want me to do with them?"

"I want you to embellish a little, so we don't fall asleep! We dropped trade coins into your cup, here, thinking we'd get a good show."

A few of the men in the crowd grumbled in agreement.

"I don't do rutting shows," he said. "I'm an artisan bard. I perform epic stories."

"Stories?" The village's Keeper of Books stepped forward. Those standing on either side of the elder man backed away to maintain their distance. "If I wanted to hear boring stories, I shoulda stayed home and listened to my apprentice prattle."

The peddler waved his arm, and the fringes of his sleeve swayed like willow fronds. "My show is at an end! Go home! Ignorant, short-sighted clods..." His voice choked in his throat when he saw her.

Aya's gaze connected with his sparkling eyes through the crowd. For a moment, the villagers blurred into the distance. Only the two of them existed in all the world. The puppets' song still echoed in her mind. *Listening for the sound of your voice, your song, your breath, I have walked. Now, at last, I have found you.*

"Hello," he said hoarsely.

When he took a step towards her, Aya spun away and started running as hard as she could. She fled the village square and splashed through mud puddles to get away. Firewood stacks and hay bales passed in a blur. She ran between the grain silo and the threshing barn and kept going.

To her left, farm fields awaited the time to be plowed and planted. To her right-hand side, grassy mounds blistered the meadows that ended in a dark line of trees. Farther in the distance, the blue-gray cones of mountains cut into the cloudless sky. *Home... Home...* Her empty cottage promised safety in solitude. Aya kept running across the open meadows and did not slow down as her lungs turned to glass.

Four

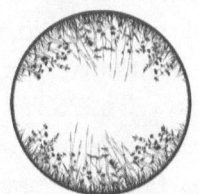

ONCE SHE REACHED HOME, Aya worked to brew a pot of chamomile tea in hopes of soothing her anxious mood. It was not appropriate to visit the farmwife in labor when her own heart drummed wildly, and her own hair was a sweaty, tangled mess.

Why did I run, she wondered. *Why did the traveler's eyes startle me? Why did his voice sound so clear?*

Aya sat at the small table where she had shared meals with her mother and younger sisters for most of her life. She nibbled on a crust of day-old bread dipped in her tea. Dried persimmons hung on twine from the crossbeams under the thatched roof. In looking up, Aya willed herself not to forget bringing some to her sister at suppertime.

"Hello?" The traveling peddler called from outside her door.

Mouth full of bread, Aya could not answer. She held her breath and waited for him to assume she was not at home.

He asked, "They say you're the daughter of a woman who came down from the mountains? Please don't be startled that I've followed you home. I need help. Will you help me?"

Aya guzzled her mug of tea to swallow the food. *Be strong, be strong,* she scolded herself in the language of the mountain people.

"Please? I have traveled a long way in search of her."

She rolled aside her narrow plank door to gaze at the slender man framed by sunshine. "My name is Aya and, yes, I am the daughter of she who came from the mountains."

He smiled broadly as if reuniting with an old friend. His relaxed demeanor put her at ease. Fears drained away as he approached the doorstep. "Hello, Aya, my name is Shadboyut."

Aya blinked, startled that he had pronounced her name perfectly with the tonal vowels and inflection. "Hello, we are well met this day, my good man Sha-... Shado-bo-... I'm sorry, your name is difficult."

"Thank you, Aya. You may call me 'Shad' if that's easier for you."

Aya nodded. "You are welcome in my home. Please come in. I don't have much on hand for a meal but I'm happy to share what I have."

Shadboyut stepped across the sliding door's sill track but hesitated to venture farther inside. He unburdened himself of the large wicker satchel that he had been carrying strapped to his back.

"You've no doubt walked a long way, Shad."

"Farther than you know," he said.

Shadboyut straddled one of a pair of stools at her wood block table. Aya collected an assortment of celery sticks, kale leaves, purple carrots, and walnuts to serve her guest. She observed that he did not express gratitude or thanks as she brought each item to the table. Perhaps, she thought, that is the way of traveling peddlers—to be rude.

She asked, "Why are you searching for my mother?"

"I believe my father knew her, as did I. We met her a long time ago in the mountains."

Aya felt a brief rush of excitement quicken her breaths. "You... You traveled to the mountains? You knew her?"

"We met briefly once," he said. "It's a long story. I recall her name was Aho, is that right?"

"Yes." Aya's lower lip quivered to hear this stranger pronounce her mother's name more elegantly than either of her sisters could.

"Where is she now?"

"She died," Aya said.

"Oh?"

"Last year, at this time, she breathed her last."

"I'm sorry for your grief."

His brown eyes sparkled in the firelight. Aya's heartbeat quickened at the gleaming color of wet charcoal. Such eyes! So quick and keen. So darkly bright. She avoided his direct stare and, instead, gazed down at her own hands. Blunt pliers cracked open a walnut. Chunks of shell and nut meats dropped onto the table.

"I'm thankful for your sympathy," she said. "It has been difficult since she passed from this life but on some days, I feel she was lucky to have never known the blight."

"What times we live in, eh? That we call the dead the lucky ones."

Aya chewed on the dry walnuts. "Do your people suffer from it too?"

"Yes." He took a swig of the tepid chamomile tea. "As far as anyone knows, the suffering extends through every farming valley from east to west, down to the seashore and probably as high as the mountain peaks."

"The mountains," she repeated thoughtfully.

"If I may ask, what caused your mother to pass from this world? Was it an accident or an illness?"

"Illness," she answered. "Mamma had suffered from a wasting disease for as long as I can remember. It got worse over the years."

"How peculiar," he said. "Did you ever name the ailment?"

"No but it never spread to anyone else in the village. Some days were better than others. Near the end, Mamma could not eat solid foods on most days and became very thin. Dream terrors kept her awake at night. Headaches kept her awake all day. I helped her to brew concoctions of powerful herbs that gave the appearance of health, but a time came when even those tisanes did not help. None of the villagers ever knew how deeply she suffered. When she finally passed, it was my sister Dimylse's idea to tell them a lie that Mamma was bitten by a snake in the forest. I went along with it."

"That was smart of your sister."

Aya looked down at a half-chewed celery stalk that she held. "I don't enjoy lying to people, but I was in such grief after losing Mamma. My sister worried that they would panic over a fatal sickness we could not name. I agreed that we didn't need to answer any of their questions."

"Villagers never ask the right questions." Shadboyut took out a carved bone pipe from a pouch on his belt. He put the pipe's stem between his teeth and thoughtfully flexed his jaw.

"You've said that you met her briefly, many years ago. Why are you searching for her now?"

His mouth broadened into a congenial smile even as his eyes remained solemn. "I was hoping she might have seen my lost papa."

"Your father is lost?" she asked.

"Yes, he wandered off in the last days of autumn and shortly before *that night.*"

Aya briefly lowered her eyes in recalling where she was, and what she was doing, on the night when a mysterious screech rattled the night sky.

Shadboyut shifted the unlit pipe's stem to the other corner of his mouth. "Which is why it's been hard to muster up a group to go searching for him. Folks are all consumed with being unable to touch. My father is a feeble old man who wears a stump boot for an amputated foot. He could have fallen into a ditch and been unable to climb out. I've been wandering for months, from one village to the next, asking if anyone has seen him. The first flicker of hope I've had is today when I met you."

"Me? Why?"

"Because the last thing my papa talked about, before he wandered off, was his fond memories of the woman that he and I met in the mountains. I regret that we argued. I called him a foolish old codger for hanging onto nostalgia for things that happened so long ago. Truth be told, my own memories of your mother are dim and faded. I was only eight years of age! I only know her name is Aho from the many times my papa re told the story of what happened to us."

"Can you be sure that Mamma is the woman you seek? Perhaps another woman with a similar name came down from the mountains to another village?"

"I've never heard of any other daughter of the mountain people immigrating to the lowlands. Think now, Aya, have you?"

Pausing briefly, she shook her head no.

Shadboyut's fingers tapped rapidly on the pipe's rim. "Listen to me, Aya, this woman I seek left the mountains exactly twenty-three years ago in mid-summer. How old are you?"

"I was born in the first moon phase of winter, about six months after Mamma came to live in the valley."

"How many winters past?"

"Twenty-four."

He said, "Then you are the right age."

She felt a ripple of cold realization go down her spine. "Shad, how closely did your father know my mamma?"

"Oh, no, Aya, I'm sorry if you're disappointed. We certainly are *not* brother and sister."

"Are you certain?"

"Very."

"You were only eight..."

"I'm sure," he insisted. "My papa knew her, but he didn't *know* her. He loved her but he didn't *love* her. I wasn't aware that Aho was carrying a child when she came down from the mountains, but I can assure you of this. My papa is not the man who fathered you."

Aya gripped her mug of hot tea. "I don't understand."

"That's the story I need to tell you." Shadboyut stood up and fidgeted on his feet. He flexed his lean hands as if hoping to catch over-ripened plums dropping out of trees.

"I'm listening," she said.

"I didn't expect that Aho would be gone. I'm not skilled at explaining things. You see, I'm a storyteller by trade and I don't know the ordinary way to tell you what happened between your mother, my papa, and me."

"How do you mean, 'the ordinary way?'" she asked.

He went to the door mat where he had set down his wicker satchel. "The way most other people tell each other stories, you surely know, by sitting around a fire and talking."

"Would you like me to build up the fire?"

"You may, if you wish." Shadboyut unpacked his satchel and carefully arranged kerchief bundles of assorted sizes on the stone floor. He laid out his puppet figurines as gently as someone putting their children to bed.

Aya went to her hearth and fed the flames with a few sticks and a small log. When threads of brightness reaching up for larger sticks propped around the log, the storyteller was ready to begin.

He used a dark scarf to bind his waist-length straight hair. An indigo shawl with dark fringe edges covered his clothing. His face and body became a living shadow. He kneeled on the floor in full sight but pretended not to exist.

Two puppets stood tall, facing Aya, under the animating power of the man's gentle hands. Miniature wooden feet stood on the floor's stones. His shadowy wrists raised and lowered in mirror image to their movements.

Aya watched his performance while sitting utterly still. His night-colored shawl obscured his body's silhouette but did not completely erase him. As the growing fire's flames illuminated the vivid colors of the puppets' costumes, their glazed faces took on an artificial vitality. He changed the tenor and cadence of his speech for each puppet's dialogue and used a third style of speaking or half-singing to narrate their actions. Listening only to the sound of the man's voice, Aya felt transported into the story of what happened twenty years ago on a mid-summer night.

Five

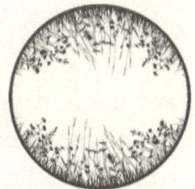

THE SMALLER FIGURE looked up to the taller one and asked, "Papa, why did those villagers throw clumps of sod to chase us away?"

The taller one rested his hand on the child's shoulder. "Do not harbor ill-feelings for them, Shad-baba. This is a difficult summer for the farmlands, as was the summer before that. You may not remember well, being such a young child. A poor harvest meant fewer seeds to be planted. In lean times the villagers worry about how many mouths they must feed. They have less to trade for the wares of neighboring valleys. They have even less to exchange for us to perform songs and stories."

"Where do we go now, Papa?"

The father turned his head to the left, to the right, and gazed farther back across his shoulder. Others in the troupe of travelers wished to venture westward to the coast and try their hand at trading with the fishermen.

"Shall we try the mountains?" the father asked.

A resounding hush, like the blast of a winter's wind, passed around the group. Mouth copied awestruck mouth. Face copied frowning face. They answered him, *no, no, no.*

"Why be afraid of them? Are the mountain people so different from the angry villagers in the lowlands, or the wary-eyed boatsmen on the coast? We are shunned as outsiders by everyone who walks the land, then why not try our hand in a new place?"

The child raised his hand. "I will go with you to the mountains, Papa. I am not afraid!"

So, it was the child's courage that inspired a handful of others to lace their boots and tighten their belts. *We shall go with you*, they said. *We shall accompany you to the highlands, Puppet-Maker, and seek to make trade with the mountain people.*

The group hiked for days upon days, higher and ever higher, following the sun's path by day and the stars by night. Northward, ever northward, they made their way on the footpaths worn by mountain goats. They ascended beyond the line of abundant trees to the sparse areas of hardy evergreens that survived in the cracks of granite. They came to the slanted lands, where snow never melted in the shadows.

They saw trail posts decorated with ominous yet beautiful crafts-manship: vulture skulls carved with strange geometric symbols, goat skulls with stone beads in the eye sockets, and bear skulls painted in stripes of yellow and red.

Those few who accompanied the puppet-maker and his son grew fearful. By day and by night, they watched the trees in anticipation of Mountain People springing forth to attack. *We should not be here*, they whispered between themselves. *We should not have come this far. We should go back and take our chances with the fishermen.*

On the fourth day after passing a trail post, the group encountered Mountain People for the first time. At first, they appeared to be cave bears as their clothing was entirely made of furry hides. Five of them had finished checking a contraption of traps. One held a dead snow rabbit by the ears.

"*Wug-dug-wa-doo!*" The loudest of the mountain people shouted angrily at the intruders in the language spoken only in the wild highlands.

"We offer trade," said the puppet-maker. "Do you understand? Trade?"

"'Trade?'" The mountain man repeated the word with an accent and then spat sideways into the snow. His companion tucked the dead rabbit into a leather sack.

"Before you say 'no' too quickly, my friend..."

The group of mountain people raised their stout walking staffs like clubs. The loudest, who appeared to be their leader, pulled a bear-skinning knife from his belt. In a chorus of roaring voices, they howled in fury.

The travelers screamed. They turned and ran downhill, as fast as wild rabbits themselves.

The child also ran away. But his feet were cold, and his legs were small. He did not run fast. He did not run far.

His father scooped up the child by the waist and carried him sideways.

A cleft in a rock offered shelter in the side of a granite cliff outcropping. They found shelter in the darkness and ventured deeper inside. The passageway grew narrow. He set down his son to walk on his own feet. The two of them walked deeper and deeper into the cave. They found safety in silence. They found safety in darkness. The puppetmaker hoped selfishly, with desperate shame, that the mountain marauders would chase his friends downhill and overlook the place where he sought to hide with his son.

"Let us wait for them to lose the trail and pass us by," the father said to his son.

"Are we turning back to the lowlands, Papa?"

"Yes, Shad-baba, as soon as it is safe."

Deeper in the cave, the darkness gave way to light. But it was not sunlight or moonlight. It was a color of green, like daylight filtered through mulberry leaves. Cold gave way to warmth. The air no longer scratched the boy's cheeks.

The sound of trickling water drew them towards an underground cavern. Logs of crystalline quartz lay fallen on the cavern's floor. Spikes of chartreuse crystal stood like trail markers in mirror image to spears of teal crystals that hung from the domed ceiling.

"What beautiful stones," said the puppet-maker. "Not precious jewels but lovely, nonetheless. If we gather a bag or two, we could take them to a stone polisher and sell them. Yes, we could sell them as charms... Infused with the healing spirits of the burned gods... Charms, yes, to place in the barren farm fields to attract the blessings. The lowlanders would pay handsomely for such a thing. By next year, the seed harvest may improve."

The boy smiled with enthusiasm at his father's great idea. His small hands eagerly went to work picking up gemstone pebbles.

He and his father did not see a pair of mountain people approach from behind. They did not see them until one struck, swept the father's legs from behind, with the stout staff. *Whack*! The staff smacked the man's left calf near the ankle.

The puppet-maker fell and rolled away. "Shad-baba, run!"

The boy froze in place. Fear held his feet to the ground.

"You... No... Here..." The man with the staff, who had struck the boy's father, loomed over him, making ready to strike once more.

"I'm sorry, I'm sorry! Please don't hurt us! Are the rocks precious to you? We will put them back. We mean no harm. Please." The puppet-maker gripped his calf with both hands. His face reddened and contorted against the pain.

The other pulled back their fur hood and revealed the face of a woman. She looked aside at the child and the fury in her eyes softened to motherly compassion. The words she spoke to her companion were foreign words, unfamiliar words, in phrases unknown to either the man or the child. Yet somehow, her meaning sounded clear. *Don't hurt them. Let them go. It's a child.*

The man grew even more enraged at hearing the woman speak. He yelled back at her face in a barrage of foreign words. His voice resounded and echoed powerfully in the cavern's chamber. Stones glowed all the brighter with their own eerie luminescence.

Neither the boy nor his father knew on that day, but they would later learn of the mountain people's lore. This cavern was not simply a bear's den or a shelter from the snow. He and his father had trespassed into a forbidden sacred cave where no outsiders were allowed to walk. This cavern of gemstones is the holiest of holy places. This abode is a remnant from ancient times known as the sanctuary for their god He Who Sleeps.

The woman argued that the outsiders did not understand their transgression. The man was unforgiving and elbowed her out of his way. He raised his staff poised for a final strike aiming to deliver a fatal blow to the fallen man's head.

Aho grabbed the man's upraised arm. She pushed him off and away from the fallen man. By accident, he stumbled and slipped on the slick icy stones. He fell backward off the edge and plunged into a ravine. His howls of rage turned to mortal terror. His screams echoed, fading for a long, long time before falling silent.

"Thank you," the puppet-maker said.

The woman bowed her head in shame. She crossed her arms over her belly.

"Can I ask for your help? I believe my leg is broken. I can't walk. Do you understand? Would you help me and my son to make it down off the mountain?"

The boy went to her and gently took hold of her hand. This woman was taller than most other women he had seen before in the lowlands. The top of his head barely reached the middle of her chest.

"Please help us?" the boy asked.

Tears fell from Aho's eyes. She nodded and then smiled sadly. She rested her hand atop the boy's head for a moment, then kneeled beside his father to tend to his broken leg.

All three of them sheltered overnight until the snowstorm outside and the darkness had passed. They drank the water trickling down the stone walls. They slept upon hard pillows of gemstones. Overnight, the boy dreamed of having wings and being nude in a cavern of ice crystals. He dreamed of rainbows frozen in gemstones, where ice did not feel cold, in a place that felt unlike any other place he had been. In the dream, the boy felt safe. He felt welcome. He felt at home.

In the morning, when the storm cleared, the woman guided the puppet-maker and his son down the mountain. She took them to a trading post where the merchants did their best to care for the man's broken leg. The boy never left his father's side. The mountain daughter stayed with the boy for a full week, or perhaps two, and made sure he was fed every day. She stayed long enough to learn a few words in the language of the valley dwellers—yes, no, thank you, and please. Aho sold her fur coat and buckskin leggings and bear-hide boots to the trading post in exchange for the tunic, skirt, cloak, and straw sandals of the lowlanders.

"Then, one morning," Shadboyut said with a lowering tone of finality. "She was simply gone."

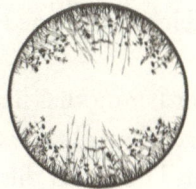

"IS that the end of the story?" Aya asked.

Shadboyut crossed the room to sit beside her at the hearth. Soft-soled suede boots hardly made any sound on the floorboards. He packed dry leaves into his pipe with the tip of his finger. Then he pinched a twinkling twig from the edge of the fire and puffed on the stem. Lavender scented smoke billowed out of his nostrils.

"We never saw Aho again after that day. My father's broken leg never recovered. After a few months, they had to saw off his rotted foot. He's been a cripple ever since."

"I'm sorry."

"She saved our lives, your mother did. That one rash act of compassion made her a criminal and an outcast of her own people. I'm glad that she found a new life in this village and, in the end, that she was happy. I'm sorry she's gone. If my father knew of her passing, he would surely lose any will to go living."

Aya looked away to the lifeless puppets laying on the floor: the man, the child, and a few other figurines that Shadboyut had artfully brought into the performance.

"Your father loved her?"

"Yes, of course, although their time together was brief. He never met another woman with such courage. He never loved another with the same passionate devotion. And, in my own childish way, neither have I."

He gazed off and away to the door and the gathering gloom of late afternoon. Aya shared his wistful mood. They sat in silence together with their own thoughts and memories of the tall, red-haired woman. At this hearth, Aya and her mother had cooked food and boiled water. At this table, Aya and her mother shared meals. It felt odd now, sitting beside a stranger, that she felt more aligned with someone who shared her mourning and grief.

It felt as if the funeral for her mother had taken place that morning and not a full year before. Sadness rushed back to pound on her heart as it had on that first day. She had never felt this kinship of grief with either of her two sisters who had been in such a hurry to move on with their happy lives.

Aya, the oldest sibling, had stayed in the cottage after their mother's death. She spent her days in solitary tending to their mother's garden of herbs or gathering wild mushrooms that would carry on the herbalist's service to the village. She rarely allowed herself the indulgence of fleeting companionship with farmers' sons. She visited the springtime festivals and the celebrations at harvest time but always returned home alone. She came when summoned to tend to the needs of the sick, of those in pain but had never afforded herself the leisure to tend to her own sorrows.

Aya blinked a couple times to get control of the urge to break down weeping. *Be strong, be strong. Not now. Not in front of a stranger.*

"When my father's ailment grew worse, his only wish was to see Aho again. I should have taken him seriously. I thought, he's a one-legged cripple. How far could he go? I underestimated his ability to charm passers-by into giving him a ride in their wagons. Crazy ol' coot! Then came the curse and nobody much cared to go searching for a wayward traveler. That's what we do, isn't it? We travel."

"Where is your last trace of him?"

"I've had no trace of Papa since the night he left. I spent a while traveling and asking, from village to village, to no avail. So, I changed my strategy and began searching for her."

The fire's heat at her back became too much. Aya stood up, brushed her long skirt straight, and strolled to the doorway. Outside, the afternoon cast long shadows from the flowering mulberry trees and the taller sycamores. On the warm breeze, Aya heard the wails of mourners and was briefly curious. She was unaware of anyone's funeral being held that day.

Shadboyut came to stand with her in the doorway. "How odd," he said while puffing on his pipe.

"What is odd?"

"That crying. It's coming from due south."

Aya stiffened and crossed her arms over her gut. "Are you sure?"

"Being a traveler, I know very well my cardinal directions and how sounds are distorted in the open air. Your village is a hair off east-by-southeast. Your cemetery is a straight line to the west. Who is crying due south of here?"

Nuriasha. No sooner did the name come to mind than a figure came into view. A man came running across the fields of wildflowers, kicking aside the thistles and tall grass with his knees.

"Herbalist!" The running man was Nuriasha's husband the barley farmer. He carried a bundle of rags in his arms.

Shadboyut gripped the rickety door frame. "A thin balsa plank is your door. You've nothing stronger to slam and lock?"

"My door...? What...?" Aya shook her head against the distraction. She focused on Nuriasha's husband running toward her. The bundle of rags became clear. It held the face of a newborn infant, eyes closed, mouth silent, and cheeks the color of gray granite.

"You failed! You failed!" the man bellowed as soon as he came within a stone's throw of the cottage. "For all your mushrooms and herbs and ointments, you failed! My wife perished in the birth and so did her child. When the baby emerged, both of them could not endure the pain of the touch. Look! Look at what your lies and empty promises have wrought!"

Aya's eyes welled full of tears. She moved forward as if to step outside toward the man.

Shadboyut grabbed her by the wrist to restrain her. "Don't go out there."

"But he's wracked with grief. I must..." Aya laid her hand over his to peel his fingers away.

Skin touched skin. All she felt was the warmth of his flesh.

Shadboyut's jaw opened in surprise. His pipe dropped to the floor. Yet he did not withdraw and did not convulse from a seizure of pain. Their touch was as ordinary as anyone's touch would have been before the night when the blight's screech had rattled the winter sky.

Aya pulled back at the same time he loosened his hold on her wrist. *It's over. It's over. The blight is over.* A rush of elation washed through her mind but like the splash of a rock in a pond, it soon passed drowned out by the approaching man's anguished wails.

Nuriasha's husband collapsed to his knees in the gravelly dirt. He laid the bundled infant on Aya's doorstep. Speaking in a choked voice, haltingly in-between sobs, he blathered a tirade of the most vicious expletives known to any farmer in the valley.

She stepped into the sunlight gingerly as if each step might break the fragility of the moment. Kneeling beside the infant's corpse, she tenderly stroked the cold forehead.

"May your heart be at peace, Urulshawn, for the memory of your wife and child. From this tragedy, may there also come—"

Aya laid her palm compassionately on the weeping man's cheek. Where their flesh connected came a burning chill. A rolling pin of sharp spikes coursed over her body. It started at the point of contact and raised each slightest hair on end, sharpening every bead of skin to a rash of pox, seizing and tightening beyond endurance. Prickles of pain seared up Aya's arm. The eyes had to close. The neck had to arch. The fists had to clench. Muscles tightened.

He pushed her away to break the touch. "Ah!"

She clutched her trembling hand to her belly. The pain throbbed in her flesh, strong at first but then lowering to a dull ache with each drawing of her breath. Ringing in her ears returned to its constant high-pitched whistle.

"Have ye no bounds to your heartlessness! Shit-eating daughter of a mountain she-bear!"

Farmer Urulshawn sprang to his feet and gathered up the bundled infant's corpse. He sprinted away backtracking from where he had come trampling through the weeds and wildflowers.

Aya rubbed her hands together slowly, palms sliding back and forth. Her own heartbeat pulsed at her inner ears. Words failed to arise in her mind.

"You felt it too?" Shadboyut stood casting a shadow over where she sat on the ground. "When we touched, you and I, you felt no pain?"

"It was a brief passing of hands," she said.

"No, it wasn't. You know it wasn't."

"Perhaps it was a moment of grief and sympathy," Aya said. "Our tender emotions transcended the pain as we listened to the man's cry."

"No," he said.

Aya let a sigh leak out of her nose. Weariness deflated her to the core. For a moment, she did not breathe, did not ever want to breathe again. The blight is not over... *Not over. All things end but not this. Not yet. He must be wrong. The chime still has its power over us. We are all doomed.*

When she saw the shadow of his arm extend forward, Aya jumped to her feet and moved out of reach.

"You're wrong, Shad. You must be wrong. Didn't you see what happened when I touched Urulshawn?"

Shadboyut looked at Aya from a dozen paces away but he may as well have been on the other side of a bottomless ravine. His eyes sparkled darkly with the sunshine behind his head. His expression of yearning and expectation were unlike any man who had ever looked at her before. That gaze invited her forward, tantalizing like an open doorway. Yet her sluggish feet did not move.

"Aya, please," he said. "Come to me. Try again. Touch me."

Afternoon breezes rustled the nearby trees. Songbirds chirped the same way as they had been chirping a few moments before. Aya crossed her arms and felt no different in her blood. She feared that if she were to touch him again, it might hurt as badly as when she had touched Nuri-asha's husband. Even now, her throbbing arm ached, as touching anyone always did for the past four long months. For the dread of erasing that precious memory of hope, she refrained.

"I'm sorry, Shad. If we touched for a brief moment, that moment is gone. We can hope that the Blight of Touch is not infallible, but we cannot allow hope to make us foolish."

"Please? No, please, let's try again?"

Aya turned aside and gazed up at the sky. A flock of honking geese flew in formation overhead. They flew this same path every evening at dusk in their daily cycle between the wetlands at River's Bend to their nightly roosting place by the grist mill's pond.

Nothing had changed.

She waited for him to give up staring at her and go away so that everything could go back to her routine. This traveling peddler and his lost father and his stories from the past—however intriguing—were a distraction.

Go, please, go, she chanted in her mind. *Go, please, go.*

Shadboyut stomped back into the cottage to collect his puppets off the floor. He packed up his wicker satchel and slung the strap over his shoulder. Long strands of fringe swung from his sleeves with every step. Slapping a wool cap atop his scalp, he walked away to the west.

Seven

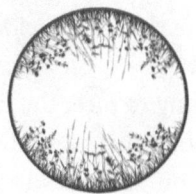

I SHOULD WEEP, she thought while sitting alone at her hearth. Aya watched the fire die inside smoldering log. *Why am I unable to weep?*

The constant ringing in her ears muted the last gasps of the dying fire. All else was silence. The slits in her window shutters darkened as twilight leeched all color from the world. In breathing slowly, she could barely feel her own heartbeat.

By this hour, surely her sister Dimylse had already fed supper to her family. Feianthe likely talked at length about her infatuation and her hopes for better days to come. Aya imagined Dimylse tucking the small children into their blankets for the night. Her husband would go outside to check on the livestock pens. One more day was coming to its routine end.

Aya looked up to the dried persimmons hanging from the crossbeams of the thatched roof. Her sister's loud voice replayed in her memory. *The baby's cutting a tooth! You promised to bring him something to chew. Can you remember to bring it when you come for supper tomorrow?*

She chose one of her large market baskets meant for carrying onions, carrots, turnips, and yams. Without needing a footstool, she reached up with a small knife and cut the twine of each persimmon. Tenderly she wrapped the fruits in a yellow kerchief and laid the bundle to rest at the bottom of the wicker weave.

Using the last of the dying fire, she lit the wick of a ceramic oil lamp. Then she stirred the ashes under the hearth log and scooped the cold gray dust to bury the smoldering embers. The wall of river stones that framed the fireplace were already turning cold.

She swirled her ankle-length hooded cloak about her shoulders and plucked her straw hat from a peg on the wall. Her thin plank door rattled on its sill track in sliding to meet the frame.

Lamp-jug in one hand, basket in the other, Aya headed in the direction of her sister's cottage on the outskirts of the village. Her straw sandals padded softly on the gravel of the footpath. Clouds obscured the stars. On this night, there was no moon to light the way. The faint glow of the flickering wick illuminated a narrow space ahead.

Overgrown grass obscured the path. Soon, she found herself knee-deep in dandelions and prickly milkweed. Her long skirt and cloak sprayed the fluffy white seeds on the breeze. Her lamp's tiny wick made them shine along with gnats and fireflies that swarmed in the field. Ground slanted upwards to the left, which meant she was heading southwest from the village, in the opposite direction of her sister's home. She turned and back-tracked over the ground she had covered.

By this hour, all the villagers had shuttered their windows. Aya could not see any lights from the artisans' shops or even the blacksmith's forge. She could not hear the creek's waters because of the constant ringing in her ears. Owls hooted in the distance, but they might be coming from either direction—the threshing barn or the dense woodlands.

How can I be lost? She marveled at her own confusion. Many times, she had traveled this path by night. Surely the soles of her feet knew the way if her eyes did not. She kept on groping blindly in the darkness in search of a landmark.

She walked for the better part of an hour or two. Or so it felt by the ache in her calves and the weariness in her arms from holding up the oil lamp jug. The wick burned low, but she had not thought ahead to bring tweezers to pull it higher. Nor did she dare to extinguish the tiny flame; she had left her tinderbox behind.

By the absence of floral scents and the odor of stone getting stronger, Aya knew that she approached the village's burial grounds. In the darkness, she could not see the ring of river stones that encircled the cemetery. She had to risk stubbing her toe on a rock if only to get her bearings by the landmark.

A small light flickered not far ahead like an evening star that had dropped out of the sky. It was the only spot of light in all the world. She cocked her head sideways at the peculiar sight. Who would build a fire in the middle of a cemetery?

She walked towards the firelight as a beacon. Her sandals felt the change in the soil from wildflowers to gritty pebbles. Aya picked her way respectfully between the square stoneware tiles that marked the remains of the dead.

"Hello?" she called out to a shadowy figure backlit by the campfire.

"Welcome fellow traveler," said Shadboyut.

Aya smiled in relief at the sound of his friendly voice. "How well it is to find you, Shad!"

"Is that you, Aya?"

"Yes."

She approached the place where he had created a cozy home without walls or a roof. He had unrolled a wicker mat and a blanket on the ground. A small fire lapped at an iron skillet containing some sausages and chunks of chopped cabbage.

"Shad, are you having supper here among the dead?"

"No one else in the village will welcome me into their home. I figured the ghosts wouldn't mind me." Shadboyut sat with crossed ankles. He puffed on his pipe while waiting for sausages to cook.

"You believe in ghosts?" she asked.

"You don't?" he countered.

Aya shrugged to avoid answering the question. She set down her basket of persimmons but remained standing. "My lamp is burning low. I've been trying to bring these dry fruits to my sister. I visit her home every evening at suppertime. It's so peculiar that I got lost in the dark. I walked and walked and, well, now I've found you."

He smiled in welcome with the pipe's stem still clamped in his teeth. "Come, sit. I have plenty of supper to share."

Aya wrapped her long cloak around herself before settling down to sit on the pebbly sand. "This feels wrong. Why did you set up camp here among the bones of the dead?"

"You truly are lost. Don't you realize where we are?"

On the edge of his campfire's glow lay a stoneware tile not yet weathered by the seasons. Phonetic lettering had been drawn in the clay before it went through the kiln. Even in the lettering of the village's script, they got her mother's name wrong. Aya's sisters had already paid the tile maker and did not wish to complain.

"Mamma," she whispered.

"I came to find Aho and find her I have," he said. "You said that she died about a year ago, now? Among my people, this is how we honor someone's passing. We cook a meal. We tell stories. Sometimes we even laugh in sharing fond memories of our departed loved ones."

Aya looked down at her lap. "Mamma's people have a ritual for marking one year of someone's death. She taught me a song, but my sisters did not agree to join me."

"I'll sing it with you," he offered. "I don't speak any of Mountain People language, but I can try to follow along."

"No," she said. "My sister is right. Mamma's gone. She won't care if we do the ritual or not."

Shadboyut chuckled briefly or perhaps he coughed from the campfire's smoke. "I know plenty of cautionary tales about ghosts who care very much for what their living relatives do."

"There are no ghosts," she said.

He glanced across his shoulder at the darkness. "Oh yes, I forgot the valley people are short-sighted in that way. 'The dead do not hear. The dead do not see.' Is that what they teach down here in the farmlands?"

Aya blinked at a tear forming in the corner of her eye. "You have strange ideas."

"Do I?"

Like Mamma, she wanted to say. The wick in her oil lamp jug fizzled out.

Shadboyut used a pewter fork to pluck the sausages out of the fry pan. He used a cabbage leaf for a plate and offered the serving to her. Aya hesitated, unsure of how to take hold of the food from his outstretched hand without touching his skin.

"Set it down, please," she said.

He placed the cabbage leaf on the ground. "Are you still afraid of touching me again?"

Aya pinched one of the hot sausages between her fingers. "I'm unsure of what to do. This day has been such an ordeal with the passing of Nuriasha and her child. I should go back and—"

"Don't go." He set his pipe aside before gnawing into a sausage.

"Why would you say such a thing?" Aya paused at the intensity of faraway spices that enhanced the juices of the meat.

"Stay the night here with me. Tell me stories of your mother. I will share what else I remember. Teach me the song of the mountain people and I will sing it with you."

Aya shook her head. "Someone might see us."

"Who will be strolling into the cemetery at this hour of night? You and I are alone here."

Aya wiped her mouth with a kerchief tucked in the cuff of her sleeve. Meat grease and spices stained the cloth. She gazed down at the soiled kerchief in her hand and, uncontrollably, tears dribbled out of her eyes.

"There will be another funeral tomorrow," she said in a choked voice. "For Goodwife Nuriasha and her baby—"

"I plan to be up at dawn and on the road well before the village elders organize the chorus of wailers." Shadboyut leaned over his knee to gaze at her intently. "You're welcome to travel with me."

"With you?" She sniffed up her tears in surprise. "Why?"

"That farmer was angry. He blamed you. I imagine you won't be welcome at the funeral."

"No, no, you're wrong. I need to apologize."

"Listen to me, Aya, I've seen angry villagers before in my life. They're suffering and they're looking to make someone else suffer so they can forget, even for a little while, about the pain of touching each other. They're weary of funerals and they're looking to blame someone. That someone might be you."

He passed her a ceramic jug. Aya pulled the cork and sipped his warm, flat beer.

"I understand that you've grown up in this village. You feel like these people are your neighbors, friends, and family. You can't imagine that they would hurt you. Believe me, they can. Didn't you hear that farmer's insults? 'Shit-eating daughter of a mountain she-boar,' is that what they call you?"

"Urulshawn was in grief," she said.

"Yes, and grieving people can do terrible things. I have been chased out of more villages in my life than I can count. You've heard the slurs they call people like me. You've seen how they treat us when market days are done. I know the mood. I can smell it like a rainstorm coming in the air."

Aya closed her eyes while resting the jug in her lap. She thought back on all the angry faces that had confronted her since the blight fell, or since her mother died, or even since she was a child who quickly grew taller than boys of the same age.. Only the traveler sitting beside her had spoken with kindness and sympathy. Only a stranger knew her heart better than her own hearth kin.

His warm hand rested upon hers. Aya flinched but did not pull away.

"Look," he said breathlessly.

Skin on skin, yet no convulsions of pain erupted. His sun-tanned fingers lay across her lighter brown hand. The ringing in her ears subsided and, for the first time in months, she clearly heard the chirping buzz of crickets.

Aya extended her free arm toward his face. Her fingertips lightly stroked his lean cheek, drawing down to his jawline. Warm skin met her skin. Serenity, not pain, soothed the months' long tension in her forearm.

"Oh," she gasped.

Shadboyut tilted his head to sink his cheek against her hand. His end-of-day whiskers lightly scratched her palm but even that discomfort caused shivers of pleasure.

"I forgot how good this simple thing feels." He breathed out a low tone somewhere between a sigh and a groan. "Four months... Four miserable, long months."

"So warm." She failed to remember when a simple caress had felt so remarkable. "So soft. Your skin is so soft for a man."

He laughed in a rapid, clucking patter that jiggled the lump in his throat. "Your hands are rough, for a woman but I don't mind. Your callouses are the most wonderful callouses I've ever felt."

Aya kept hold of his jaw and leaned forward into his face. Shad surrendered with eyes closed as if going underwater. Their mouths met in a tight, hesitant kiss. His lips tasted of beer and spices and the burned lavender of his pipe. Softly they blended and melted into each other as if their faces had never been two but always one. She inhaled that warmth of him and leaned into a deeper connection.

He pulled away first, breathing hard as if he had been running all the way from the foothills. "What is this, Aya? What's happening?"

"The blight is breaking at last," she said. "If not for everyone all at once but for the two of us as a start."

He looked around to the faint outlines of grave marker tiles. "Let's put out the fire and move to another place, where the ghosts aren't watching? There's a grove of flowering plum trees not far over the hill."

"I know the place." In summers long past, as children, she and her sisters used to sit in the shade of those trees to eat the sweet plums falling out of the trees. Blinking away the memory of happier times, Aya clamped her arms against her chest.

"Your mood changed," he said. "Do you not wish to lie down with me? Have I offended you?"

"We just met for the first time today," she said.

Shadboyut shrugged. "It is springtime, after all."

She did not return his inviting smile. "Why is it only the two of us? Why should we be free of pain and have the pleasure of each other's touch when no one else can?"

"Oh, I see." He picked up his pipe and sucked a deep puff off the stem. After holding his breath for a moment, he exhaled clouds of dull purple smoke into the campfire's dwindling flames.

"I'm sorry I kissed you," she said.

"Are you, now?"

"I'm exhausted. I'm not thinking clearly. This day has been such a—"

"...an ordeal," he finished. "So you've said."

"Thank you for the food."

"It's a traveler's sacred code of hospitality," he told her. "One cannot refuse to share food or shelter when encountering a fellow wanderer on the trail. It is the one thing that we can't fathom in the customs of the villagers, or the coastal fishermen, or the mountain people as well. You all reject and shun the outsiders, the wayward travelers seeking refuge, the cold and the hungry and the lost."

Aya gazed into the smoldering cinders of the dying fire as she listened to his melodic voice. Even when speaking, he was half-singing to a poetic cadence.

"It's why my father fell in love with your mother in the first hour they met. When she saved his life and tended to his injury, she showed hospitality where none of her kinsmen did."

Shadboyut finished his pipe and tapped out the ashes. The two of them sat in silence for a while.

She asked, "Do you think your father might have gone back there? To the mountain cave?"

He coughed. "That's a feverish level of foolhardiness beyond any man's wildest larks. A one-legged cripple making the journey up those heights, where the rocks reach higher than clouds? No, no, he couldn't make that trek even if he wished to return to a cold hole in the ground. Why would he go there if he knew that Aho made her life in the lowlands?"

"Yes, of course, you're making sense. You see? I'm not thinking clearly."

"To that, I agree. Even if you're not willing to lie down with me, yet, do you not wish to kiss some more?"

"I'm exhausted." Aya looked aside at his blanket that was only wide enough for one person. She felt the heat of a blush rise to her cheeks. "I'll sleep in my cloak."

"As you wish." Shadboyut unpacked a few of the shawls and stage cloths from his wicker basket. He spread the panels of fringed indigo on the gritty sand, on the opposite side of the campfire from where his blanket lay.

"I've never slept outdoors before," she said.

"My people say it's the best place to sleep." Shadboyut unbuckled his belt and put aside his pouches, flask, and knife. He reclined sideways on his blanket with knees curled up and facing where she lay.

"Aren't you afraid of wild animals?" she asked.

He pointed up to the sky. "The eyes of the hallowed are watching over us. Do you see them? Do you see the remnants of the ancient, burned gods, the architects of the world who perished in the flames of their own foolishness? Their spirits as embers carried up on the smoke to the sky. There the gods' ghosts dwell in the paradise of eternity."

"Mamma used to tell us a story like that."

Shadboyut smiled. "It's always a joy to meet someone who knows the same stories that I know. I'm sorry that your mother is gone but I'm glad to meet you."

Aya fell silent, too weary to talk with him anymore. Eyes closed, she licked her lips and could still taste the lingering flavor of his pipe's weed. Sleep came quickly and with sleep came a dream.

Eight

AYA'S SPIRIT rose swiftly out of Lisshardra Valley as a whisper on the night breeze. Even in the dark, her vision was bright. The landscape had an eerie hue of silvery cerulean. Every detail was as clear as a summer's day—every blade of grass, every flowering bud on every plum tree, every pebble in the trickling creek.

Her spirit soared alongside a white speckled owl. She passed over the treetops of the woods and to the foothills to where she had never walked before. Her sights merged with the current of cool winds blowing down off the mountain. She passed over the bluffs and waterfalls that marked the edge of the lowlands. She dashed by groups of peddlers' wagons parked for the night.

Beyond the lake, a range of mountains loomed higher than any mountain she ever imagined. She glided like an owl over herds of wild antelope, packs of wolves, and mountain goats. The massive pinnacle rose higher than half the world folded over and piled on top of itself. Aya's sights soared up vertical landscapes too high for mountain goats, almost too high for the eagles. Higher and higher she rose, to where icicles had formed in the first days of the calendar and had never known a spring's thaw.

Aya's spirit plunged into a crevasse that opened in the side in the highest mountain peak. A narrow tunnel led to a labyrinth of crystalline logs. The opalescent gemstone glowed from within as a lily pond in the summer—bright green.

She moved easily through and between the broken arches of green stone like a sparrow darting into the eaves of a roof. Without fear, she plunged over a cliff's edge and down into a ravine.

At the base of the cavern, in a pool of blue lava, there squatted a pair of inhuman eyes on a circular shell of clear jelly. From the sides of the gigantic shell, a set of jointed legs squatted in a lava pool. The creature was alive, semi-submerged in a puddle of blue heat, slowly being cooked but not yet dying.

And it screamed.

The creature screamed and wailed in its constant agony. Its cries echoed in the chamber and rang like chimes in the crystalline gemstones. Cords of tentacles emerged from the jelly crab, from time to time. Multi-colored threads of noxious filaments scraped helplessly against the walls of the ravine. Tentacles grew weary and fell back into the lava.

A man's skeleton painted in decayed, black flesh lay broken at the edge of the lava pool. Long ago, in the days of his life, the man had worn a heavy cloak of bear skins and carried a long walking stick.

Another man's corpse lay nearby. More recently deceased, he had been crippled long ago by the loss of one leg chopped off at the knee. He wore the garments of a traveling peddler adorned with fringe; his waist-length hair splayed loosely around his fallen body. One silver earring twinkled at his left earlobe.

Her spirit leaned over the second man's corpse. Her translucent fingers, like wisps of pipe smoke, reached out to touch his forehead. When they made contact, the hours and days spun on a wheel and walked backward into the time of days gone past.

Now the man was alive and lowered himself to the bottom of the ravine by a thick, hemp rope.

The jelly crab reclined in a pool of blue liquid, but it was not lava. It was not on fire. The crab's tentacles lapped and wiped over its bulbous eyes contentedly. From time to time, it stuck out its long tongue and sucked up the pearly white worms that wriggled among the fluorescent lichen growing out of the walls.

The man in the fringed jacket appeared to be terribly ill. His jaundiced face showed dark hollows underneath his eye sockets. *Just like Mamma in her last days,* Aya's spirit thought.

"Who is there?" The man's bloodshot eyes turned in search of her and, for a moment, their gaze connected. "You! Are you a wraith or a ghost?"

I am Aho's daughter.

He smiled and cackled wildly with glee. In the act of smiling, now, Aya saw the resemblance to his son.

"Tell her that I am coming to save her. Tell Aho that Zhardohut is coming to save her! I'm going to carve a bit of the flesh from the poisonous creature that stung us both. I'm bringing a drop of oil from the viper's venom sac!"

Aya's spirit was formless without substance and helpless to intervene. The man struck at the jelly crab with an ax. Its violet blood leaked into the pool and, once it contacted the liquid, the pool congealed into a fiery stew.

The creature screamed and. thrashed out with its tentacles. One whipped the man, throwing him against the cavern's wall. His head cracked as he fell. Dazed, eyes crossed, the last thing he saw in life was Aya's spirit drifting away.

The harder Aya tried to remain focused on the jelly crab, the harder it became to concentrate. An intense wave of vertigo seized her from within, spinning the cave until it blurred into an underwater memory. She reeled in mid-air as a dry leaf turned in the wind. Her spirit soared backward the way she came, tumbling through the snowy gusts blowing off the mountainside. Flurries of mist enveloped her like dandelion fluff. Her eyes squinted shut as she streaked face first southward to the lowlands, over the treetops, to the wheat fields and meadows of wildflowers, to the clearing of gray pebbles where the two travelers slept.

Aya plunged into her own sleeping body. Everything in her mind turned black.

* * *

Dawn's light shone through her eyelids. Morning dew moistened her cheeks. Aya drew in a deep inhale and immediately felt the painful throb of a headache at the center of her forehead. She licked her chapped lips and groaned before sitting up on one elbow.

"Shad?" Her throat felt dry, and her voice croaked as hoarsely as a frog.

Weeping on his knees, he curled his forehead to the ground near her shoulder. At the sound of her voice, he lurched upright in shock.

"Oh, no! Oh, no!"

"Shad?" she called again.

He collapsed back on his haunches. He pedaled his boots against the gravel to push himself away. He scooted dangerously close to the camp-fire that, apparently, he had time to rebuild by feeding it sticks and branches. Flames rose threateningly close to the fringe of his tunic and the edges of his waist-length hair.

Forehead still throbbing, and fighting the burning aches in every muscle in her limbs, Aya strained to sit upright. Her cloak fell off one shoulder and she had no strength to pull it back up.

"Shad, what is the matter? Did a wild animal attack us in her sleep?"

"You... You're dead!"

Aya raised her hands and flexed her fingers, palms out. "Obviously not."

"You were gray. You were stiff and cold!"

"I'm thirsty. May I have a drink, please?"

"A drink? Yeah, I can do that." With shaking arms, he offered the flask that was hooked to his belt.

She sipped the concoction of cinnamon barley tea. It took the edge off the scratchiness in her dry throat. "I'm not dead, Shad. Perhaps I got chilled sleeping out of doors."

"I have slept under the stars every day of my life. I've never seen..." Shadboyut reached for the beer jug but frowned as if wishing it contained a stronger liquor. "You were dead."

"I was asleep."

"You were dead, damnit!"

"In my dream, I became a ghost. I felt my soul took flight."

He snorted sarcastically. "Like the old legends of Eiyallandra and her Man of the Forest?"

"Perhaps," she said. "Yes, perhaps that's what happened."

Shadboyut loaded his pipe with lavender weed and used a twig from the campfire to light it. Aya sipped again from the flask and huffed up a lump of phlegm to clear her throat.

"You were dead," he said again. "I know what death looks like."

"As do I. " Aya put forth her bare arms straight out from her body. "Look at me... Look, I was never more alive! Shad, I think something wonderful and miraculous happened to me. The old stories are true!"

"Oh, gods have mercy." He took a deep puff off his pipe.

"This must be the explanation of why we're able to touch in spite of the blight. As I slept, my spirit took flight, and I traveled to the mountain peaks. I saw the cave, Shad, where my mother first met you and your father. I saw the corpse of the mountain man that she pushed into the ravine."

"Oh, did you now?"

Aya drank more of the barley tea and drained his flask dry. "I saw something else in the dream. I saw your father. He journeyed to the cave to attack a creature who dwells there. It's like an enormous sea crab the size of a wagon's tarp, made all of jelly. It floated in a pond of blue lava."

"Lava is not blue."

"Yes it was," she insisted. "As blue as shallow water."

He burst out laughing in high pitched twitters. Pipe smoke leaked out of his nostrils. "Oh, that's a magnificent nightmare! A pond of blue lava? A crab the size of a wagon, you say? My one-legged papa journeyed up to the mountains to attack it single-handedly?"

"Yes."

"Do tell, why would he embark on such a ridiculous quest?"

"He saw me, somehow. He said, 'Tell Aho that Zhardohut is coming to save her! I'm going to carve a bit of the flesh from the poisonous creature that stung us both. I'm bringing a drop of oil from the viper's venom sac.'"

Shadboyut slowly drew the pipe out of his mouth. "I don't recall telling you my papa's name. Did I?"

Aya shook her head. "No."

"I must have. You couldn't know."

She added, "He had a small scar across his eyebrow, a dark mole on his neck, and a chipped front tooth. He wears a small silver earring in his left ear... The same as you do, I see."

"Lucky guess," he said while fondling the hoop threaded into his earlobe. "Not hard to imagine. Many of us wear earrings."

"No, it's true! I saw it."

"How?" he whispered.

"I told you, Shad, I saw it when my spirit took flight. It's all so clear now. I've seen what happened. Your father attacked the cave crab because he thought it was the source of his ailment, and my mother's as well. He had the idea that perhaps a skilled herbalist could make a tincture from a sample of its flesh to cure what ailed them."

"Like a snakebite remedy."

"Yes," she said. "But something went wrong with his plan. When he attacked the creature, it screamed, and the scream reverberated in the crystals of the cave. I felt it rattle the air and echo into the mountain cliffs. It started an avalanche somewhere. Shad, I think the monster's scream caused the chime and the blight."

"Monstrous crab screaming in a mountain cave? *That* caused the curse of touch?" Shadboyut wagged his hand in the air as if to brush away her words. "Go back to telling me about my papa. Where does your dream think he is now?"

Aya lowered her eyes, unable to say the words.

"You imagine he's dead, don't you?"

"I'm sorry," she said. "I saw it."

Shadboyut sprang to his feet. "This has to be wrong. You're wrong! The old legends are stories, nothing more. People don't take flight in their dreams to see people they've never met or places they've never been or screaming monsters in mountain caves. I don't believe you. It can't be true."

"If there are such things as ghosts and chiming curses and burned gods watching us from the heavens, why can't I dream of your father, Shad?"

"No, no, no, it can't be." He paced back and forth on the opposite side of the campfire.

The crackling flames that wrapped the logs seemed more restless than before. Every spark had a life, a soul, and a mind. Every drifting ember held eyeless eyes watching. Perhaps the spirits of the burned gods watched over them after all but not as benevolent distant stars in the sky. *Why did you choose me for this gift?* She wanted to shriek at the eyeless embers staring at her. Aya restrained her thoughts out of fear that he would think her mind had gone feverishly mad.

Aya sat up straighter, her throbbing headache slowly fading. Strength returned to her aching muscles. She looked aside to the tiles of grave markers well-lit in the morning's glow. She focused on a certain one that was a smaller square than the others.

"Well, if you don't believe in my dream, may I ask you for another favor?"

"If it's a favor I'm able to do," he said. "My hands are yours."

"I want to take Mamma home."

Nine

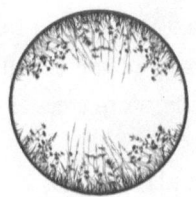

AYA USED Shadboyut's hand trowel to dig into her mother's grave. The gravelly soil was not difficult to excavate. The urn was buried no deeper than a garden jar for fermenting pickled cabbage. The ceramic jug filled with ashes and bone chips was capped with a balsawood disc and sealed with a layer of wax.

In the language of the mountain people she whispered, "Mamma, Mamma, I'm taking you home." Aya lifted the green-glazed urn out of the hole and held it reverently against her chest.

"You sound like one of them," he remarked. "Though you were born and raised in the valley, Aho taught you the words of her people?"

"Yes, inside the home, Mamma spoke to us that way. I was the only one to converse with her. My younger sisters could understand Mamma most of the time, but they always answered in the villagers' tongue."

"That's regrettable," he said. "It's useful to be able to speak to all sorts of people. What few words I may have picked up from Aho, as a child, I've forgotten it all. I don't know of many people who can speak Mountain... They keep so tightly unto themselves."

"I've always wanted to visit the high places," she said. "Perhaps I can meet someone who remembers Mamma or who knew my father."

Shadboyut used one of his linen shawls to rig a shoulder sling. Aya carried the funereal urn tucked into the sling as if it were a sleeping infant. One last glance over her shoulder, and she left behind the basket of dried persimmons in the cemetery.

* * *

The weather in spring was clear and cool but not cold, so they walked easily in the pleasant landscape of the countryside. They passed swiftly through the grove of flowering plum trees as white petals like snowflakes sprinkled on the green grass.

By midday, they chose a place to rest at a shallow creek meandering over slick green rocks. He did not build a fire or cook a meal. Instead, he shared with Aya a few cold sausages, shelled walnuts, and dried plums. Shadboyut refilled a couple of tin flasks with the flowing waters.

"We've drunk up all the beer, I'm sorry to say. If we keep up a good pace, we can make it to the lake by sunset."

"The lake?" she asked. "You mean, Twin Rams Lake? Is that too far to walk in one day?"

Shadboyut mouthed the stem of his unlit pipe as he smiled. "Have you ever walked away from the village?"

"Of course I have," she said defensively. "I've ventured into the woods to pick mushrooms."

"Ah, I see." He simply laughed and grinned so wide that his eyes narrowed in crinkles. Aya pinched his arm. He winced a little but kept laughing.

Shadboyut continued leading the way heading sure and straight to the northeast. Despite the lack of a wagon road or even a well-trampled foot path, the land was inviting to walk. Lush grass on the lightly rising slopes felt soft beneath her sandals. Aya kept up with his brisk pace for the next few hours.

Rocks became larger and the grass became thinner. Shadboyut turned his course left and right to make his way around successively larger piles of boulders. Tenacious weeds sprouted out of the crevasses in the granite. Lizards lay warming themselves in the open air. Aya marveled at the wildness of it all, as chaotic and unstructured as the gnarled roots and fallen logs of the woods she knew so well. This was farther than she had ever ventured away from the village. She felt ashamed at having lived her entire lifetime within the confines of a small circle. These rising hills were not so far—within a day's walk—and yet she had never dared to explore too far from home.

The afternoon shadows grew longer as the sun sank to their left. Aya looked ahead and saw a platter of blue water beyond the next cluster of rocks.

"The lake?" she asked.

Shadboyut glanced back over his shoulder. "Yes. How are you feeling?"

Her legs burned. Her calves ached. Her breathing felt dry and shallow. Even so, her heartbeat pounded with a sense of freedom and joy that she had never known before.

Aya paused at the cluster of boulders. Dark granite formed a rectangular block like an overturned wagon made of stone. She leaned her backside against the warm rock and gazed downslope at what she had left behind.

Lisshardra Valley spread as a grassy bowl inside a circle of green hills and blue mountain peaks. For a moment, she recalled her dream of becoming a spirit flying in the air. Her eyes saw for the first time what her sleeping mind had already experienced. The world was larger than she ever knew. The village where she had spent every day of her life seemed so small.

"We're almost there," he said. "See? I told you that we'd make it to the lake before sunset. I know a good place to make camp for the night."

She did not respond and did not move. Her sights remained fixed on the valley below. She caressed the funereal urn that she carried. "Mamma, is this what you saw when you first descended from the mountains? Is this where you wished to bear your children and spend your life?"

He laid his hand on the nape of her neck. Skin upon skin, the gentle pressure of his palm lured her out of her reverie. The touch quickened her heartbeat and brought up a rush of warmth like a roaring fireplace on a winter's night. She turned her shoulders to face him. He was so close that if she merely tilted her neck, their mouths again could connect. Aya licked her dry lips.

"Uhh..." His exhale was a mixture of sighing and groaning. "We aren't in a cemetery anymore."

Overhead, a brown hawk slowly glided in search of prey. Aya glanced upward and then expanded the roll of her eyes to take in the landscape.

"What if a hunter comes by?" she asked. "We're so out in the open here."

"To the lake, then." Shadboyut set off at a brisk walk.

Aya followed him over the last rise of rocks and downhill to the shores of the calm blue lake. He deposited his wicker basket beneath a cluster of massive willow trees. Their drooping fronds resembled the fringes of his coat. The traveler—the outsider—blended into the landscape all around him.

He jogged ahead to the water's edge. Though he had walked at a brisk pace from morning until late in the day, he barely seemed winded. Aya enjoyed watching him lightly running, springing off his feet, his arms at relaxed angles pumping him along. His long hair wagged left-and-right across his lean back. For that moment, she went breathless wanting to hold him in her arms.

Aya sat down on the grassy lawn beneath the shade of the willow tree. She watched Shadboyut dip his flask into the lake's lapping waters.

"Why has no one built a village here?" she asked. "It's so tranquil."

He returned to where she sat. "It's a bowl lake that's not connected to any river. There's no fish. The rocks make it hard to build a wagon road, in or out. There's a settlement halfway to becoming a village on the western shore but that's the long way around. If we're heading for the mountains, we follow the wild goats' trail around to the east."

He handed her the flask. Aya drank the cool, clear water that tasted unlike any water she had ever swallowed.

"How far have you traveled in this world?" she asked.

He hooked a thumb in his belt. "Oh, I figure I'm like most of my people. We travel around in circles, back and forth, from the ocean side to the eastern forest and everywhere in between. People in each place think they're different from everyone else but the more people I meet, the more I see that they're all the same at heart. We all want to sleep in safety, to fill our bellies with food, and to..."

Warmth rose to her cheeks at the sudden change in his tone. He never finished the sentence, but the meaning was clear—to sleep, to eat, to embrace. She licked the water on her lips and remembered how it had felt to kiss him the night before.

Shadboyut took a step backward. "Uh... I should look for some fallen branches to build a fire. I can snatch a lizard or a toad if you're not a finicky eater?"

"What does 'finicky' mean? I've never heard that."

He smiled. "Good."

Aya rose to her feet. "I can help dig up some bulbs of lilies."

"Wonderful! They're better than turnips, in my opinion. Oh yes, we shall have a fine supper tonight."

* * *

They ate a roasted lizard skewered on a stick and lily bulbs seared in his iron skillet. The small fire died down all too soon to a faint glow within a pile of ashes. Sunset turned the sky to a brilliant tapestry of orange, yellow, and pink that gave the lake's still waters the appearance of a pool of molten copper.

Aya used her thumbs to massage her bare feet as she had often seen a midwife do for a woman laboring to give birth. Shadboyut removed his soft-soled boots and, reclining alongside where she sat upright, he wriggled his toes against the grass.

"You'll need better shoes in the coming days. You can't journey up to the snowy mountains in straw sandals."

"Who will make me shoes?" she asked.

"No worries, I've no doubt we shall encounter some peddlers' wagons before the foothills. Spring is a good time to travel between villages and trade for all sorts of things. Shoes are a popular commodity."

He reached over to caress her foot. His thumb slid from her heel to her arch and raised shivers that rippled up her leg. Aya draped her arm across his shoulder to hold him nearer. Breezes stirred the fronds of the willow tree. Waters lapped a rhythmic *hush-hush* at the lake's edge. Although she felt weary from the days' walk, she was not exhausted. Never had she felt such contentment.

"May I ask again?" he said. "Would you like to—"

"Yes. Yes, oh yes." Aya bent forward and sank into kissing him. This time, neither one of them broke apart.

* * *

Hours later when the passion had passed, the two reclined face to face, legs entwined, forearms draped over each other. They could not stop smiling or melding their mouths repeatedly in leisurely, exhausted kisses. Darkness overtook the night sky. All the stars of the heavens twinkled in celebration.

Aya hesitated to speak at the risk of shattering such a perfect moment. For the past few hours, they had not needed to use words. Their hands, their lips, and their bodies had shared a story that no one else would ever be told. What she had felt in his embrace, Aya had never felt before in her life. On those spring festivals of years past, she had indulged in revelry and frolic with the villagers celebrating the season of planting seeds. Intoxicated by music and darkness, she had briefly known lovers but not love. On the mornings that followed the festivals, the villagers went about their business as if the wild cavorting of the night before had never happened. The men eventually chose other women for their farm wives. Each year, Aya only felt relief at her next moon cycle to know she was not burdened with a child.

"What are you thinking?" he asked. "I see your mood has soured."

"How long will this last?"

"Who can know? The chime struck so suddenly—"

"No, Shad, I mean this... Us... You and I..." She stroked a lock of his hair away from his face and exposed the small silver hoop that pierced his left earlobe.

"Oh, I see." He pecked another soft kiss on her lips. "I can't promise you a glorious love story like the ones I perform with my puppets. I can't promise you a contract of marriage and a home in one place. What I can promise is that I will not wander off unless you want me gone."

"Thank you," she whispered.

Aya's heartbeat settled into a slower rhythm. Her eyes closed. She breathed deeply, inhaling the man's exhale, and swiftly sank into sleep.

* * *

In the dream, Aya's spirit walked into her sister Dimylse's cottage. The baby Eathom was bigger and toddled about the hearth. Her sister pushed the child's hands away from the fire while barking, "No!" Their hands touched and appeared to feel no pain.

Her brother-in-law Ioanoh entered and went to his wife before removing his boots or cloak. He embraced her from behind with his hips pressed to the back of her skirts. "Ummm, that lamb stew smells good."

"Don't squeeze me so hard," Dimylse scolded. "My belly is tender."

"Will it be a girl this time?" His hands slipped upward to fondle her breasts.

"Don't! My bosom is sore, too." Dimylse pushed his wrists away.

Skin touched skin but neither of them reacted. *These are the days yet to come*, Aya's spirit thought with a surge of joy. *The blight is lifted. The villagers are free to touch each other. My sister is carrying her second child.*

"Heard any word from that sister of yours?" Ioanoh hung his damp cloak on a hook and pulled off his muddy boots.

"You know better than to ask me about that selfish, vagabond, fringe-fucker dung beetle. May she never show her bear-cub face around here again!" Dimylse made a repelling gesture with two fingers of her left hand.

Aya's spirit cringed to hear such venomous words spit out of her sister's mouth.

Ioanoh simply nodded along. "She always did have glacier water in her veins. If she's gone back to the mountains to live with the wild bears, then good riddance."

The toddler Eathom looked up at Aya's spirit and their eyes formed a connection. His tiny finger pointed in her direction. "Auntie," he said, slurring the word in a childish way.

"No, no, child," Dimylse said. "We won't talk about Auntie Aya ever again."

The scene blurred into a blinding white haze. Aya's spirit soared away, tumbling as she fell from the sky back into her own sleeping body.

Ten

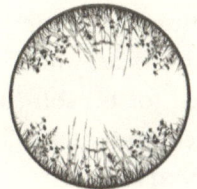

AYA AWAKENED to the sensation of Shadboyut's palm tapping her cheek. "Please wake up. Please wake up. Please be alive."

She inhaled deeply through her nose, held her breath for a moment, and exhaled a long sigh out of her mouth. As before, a headache throbbed in her forehead. With a scratchy dry throat, she strained to say, "It happened again."

"You looked dead. It's like before."

Aya opened her eyes. Morning sunlight shone bright green through the fronds of the willow tree. "My spirit few again."

He sat back cross-legged on the grass beside her. "Is this going to happen every night?"

"I can't say if it will or not. This has never happened to me before... before I met you."

"Oh, gods have mercy." Shadboyut offered her the flask. He eyed her intently while she rose up to one elbow and sipped the clear water.

"My sister hates me."

"How's that again?"

"I saw her in my dream. I saw her on a day in a springtime season yet to come."

"Oh, so now you're seeing things that haven't happened yet?"

Aya blinked at a tear dribbling out of her eye. "The blight will be lifted by this time next year. My sister and her husband will have another child. They should be happy. Why do they hate me? What have I done to earn their scorn? What have I not yet done?"

He caressed her cheek and used his thumb to gently wipe her tears. "You're still cold like death. Shall we rest here for the day? Shall I build a fire and see if I can snare a rabbit?"

Aya looked aside to the urn containing her mother's ashes. "No, I wish to continue. I don't want to delay in bringing Mamma home."

"As you say." He reached for his soft-soled boots. "With any luck, we'll encounter some peddlers and get you some good shoes. Yes, that's what you need. Shoes. You need shoes."

"Why are you babbling like a drunken man?"

"I'm anxious," he said. "It's not an easy thing to wake up in the arms of a dead woman who comes back to life."

"Do you believe me, Shad? Do you believe my dreams are true?"

He bowed his head. His long hair hung as a curtain to shield his face. "I'm not sure. Perhaps... It's not an easy thing to believe. If I do, then it means my papa is dead. All these past four months, I've searched for him thinking that he's injured and needs my help. If what your wandering spirit has seen is true, it means that he's been dead from the beginning, and I should have never had hope of finding him."

"I'm sorry." She fell silent and could not think of any better words to comfort him.

* * *

They followed the eastern shore of the lake for the better part of the day. Songbirds in the trees chirped unfamiliar patterns that defied her efforts to identify, yet the squawks of blue jays and the caws of black crows reminded her of home. A large patch of blackberry bushes held the promise of future delights, but the magenta buttons would not be ripening for another month. Aya spotted a couple of deer with fawns. The animals held frozen and waited in the bushes for her and Shadboyut to pass.

"I'm sorry to push you," Shadboyut said to her, more than once, as the hours plodded on. They ate whatever scraps of food they had left during short rest breaks but never stopped long enough to build a campfire and cook a meal.

"I can go on," she said. "Keep going. Keep going."

By the late afternoon, the wild goats' path turned northward and veered away from the lake. Willow trees and lush green grass fell behind. Evergreen pine and fir trees took their place. Different sorts of grass formed clumps of feathery bristles that spread sideways. Pinecones littered the path and Aya had to tread carefully. A blister developed on her left foot and felt like stepping on a pebble, but she did not complain.

The path narrowed to an uneven strip of trampled soil. Rocks and broken chunks of gray boulders formed a ridge on either side of the trail. They had no choice but to walk single file.

From time to time, Shadboyut looked back over his shoulder. "How are you feeling? Are you weary? Do you need to rest again?"

"I can go on, Shad." Her calves ached as the incline sharpened upward.

He raised his hand toward the west and, with an outstretched thumb, measured the course of the afternoon sun. "We have a little more daylight. I hope we encounter some travelers soon."

"How far is it to the trading post?" she asked.

"Two days, but your lowland sandals are not doing well. You need shoes."

"Perhaps I should remove my sandals and go barefoot?"

"Bad idea on these rocks." He paused to take a swig of water from the flask. "I don't suppose you can jump into one of your dreams and find the nearest caravan group?"

Aya received the flask he offered and drank the rest of the water. "I'm sorry, I don't know how to guide where my spirit flies or what I see in my dreams."

He laid his hand against her cheek for a moment. She rested her fingers on top of his and pressed his palm against her face, reveling in the warm touch of his skin.

"Oh, mercy upon me, Aya but we must be cautious when we meet up with my people. We shouldn't be seen touching each other."

"Why?"

"How can we explain that you and I can touch if no one else can? They will ask questions that we cannot answer. My people are kind-hearted, generous, and welcoming to fellow travelers but only to a point. Papa tested the boundaries of their goodwill all too often. I'd advise that we don't follow his example."

Aya let go of his hand still pressed against her cheek. "It won't be easy after what we shared last night."

"Yeah, that part was amazing before you—" His smile faded. "We need to be careful about where you sleep, too."

"Perhaps it's best if we avoid people altogether." Aya turned her head and slipped out of his touch. *It's how I have lived most of my life.* "It would be easier if we don't have to keep secrets or listen to questions that we can't answer."

In the eastern sky, a brown hawk dropped into a sharp dive. Shad-boyut pointed. "Look there!"

"Why? A hawk is catching a field mouse?"

"A mouse that is, perhaps, running away from a wagon." He sprinted to the top of the next ridge.

"Can you see anything?" she called.

"Yes!" He clapped his hands. "It's a caravan, all right. I can see four... no, five wagons."

"How far?"

He skidded on his heels to half-jog, half-slide back down the incline to reach her side. "It's not far but it's not close either. You may wait here, and I will run to them."

"No, Shad, I can walk."

"Your foot blister is bleeding," he said.

"I can put a salve on it when we reach the caravan." Aya stiffened her back and found the strength to move forward. *Be strong, be strong*, she chanted to herself.

"Truly a daughter of the mountains." He fell in line behind her and walked in her footsteps.

Eleven

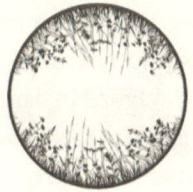

AYA'S BELLY fluttered nervously as they drew nearer to the caravan of wagons. She scolded herself and ignored the feeling, instead focusing on the discomfort of her blistered foot to give her courage to approach. She had seen traveling peddlers from time to time on seasonal market days but had never spent long in their company. Aside from bartering to exchange herbs for candles or rare forest mushrooms for iron cookware, she had never held a conversation with them. In her experience, the travelers in fringed clothing were sullen people of subdued temperament who kept to themselves. Once the market day's trading ended, they returned to their wagons and did not socialize among the villagers. If not for having Shadboyut at her side, she would not dare to approach the caravan alone.

As they drew closer, Shadboyut sprinted ahead on the wagon road to get within shouting distance. "Hello, good friends!"

"Welcome, fellow traveler," someone called in return.

Short-horned brown-and-white oxen in teams of two, side by side, pulled the wagons at a steady pace. The handful of people walking alongside each of the wagons carried wicker baskets or braided-rope satchels. They wore similar clothing as Shadboyut and, from afar, before she could identify faces, Aya could only discern their waist-length hair and the long strands of fringe that dangled from their shoulders.

She wondered if any of the wagons had come to the village before, if any of these peddlers had bartered with her in years past. From what little she knew of their customs each traveler's wagon had its own distinctive decoration. In basic design, the wagons all had the same shape of flat rectangular boxes made of wooden planks. Each box supported a framework of bent poles to form a cylindrical canopy made of animal hides. Unlike the drab hay wagons of the villagers, the traveling peddlers decorated their wagons in flamboyant colors.

Brightly colored paints marked each wagon's bed and canopy with unique designs in bold geometric patterns. Against the beige and gray landscape all around, the wagons' decorations were as vivid as a rolling bouquet of geraniums and marigolds. The leading wagon bore a pattern of blue and lavender checkered squares. The second boasted yellow and orange interlocking triangles. The third wagon diagonal lines in a hatch work pattern of scarlet, magenta, pink, and purple. The fourth wagon had overlapping circles of varying sizes, with softer hues of yellow and chartreuse outlined with indigo rings. At the rear, the last wagon had horizontal stripes of green, scarlet, and dandelion gold.

None of the five wagons' decorations brought up any memories from market days of years past. None of them had ever come to her village before. As many as thirty people—all strangers—filled the road and descended upon them.

Aya's strength finally gave out and she could walk no farther. She came to a halt standing on the road and waited for the wagons to reach her.

One fellow at the lead wagon waved a long stick in front of his oxen team's snouts. "Whoa, whoa!" At his command, the animals stopped walking. In turn, the drivers of the following wagons repeated the same action. Before long, all five wagons rolled to a stop.

"Shadbo-*yut*, is that you?"

"Thedgollas, you rascal, are you leading a caravan now?" The two came face to face but stopped short of shaking hands.

"For today, I am. Who knows what tomorrow will bring?"

The two shared a hearty laugh.

Aya scanned the faces of roughly two dozen people gathered on the roadside. While the adults walked alongside the wagons, the younger children rode inside the canopies. All the travelers wore similar clothing of long-sleeved coats with fringe hanging from the yoke line and sleeve seams. Men and women alike wore the same style of breeches tucked into flat-soled boots. Their dark hair hung loose, unrestrained, in straight long locks hanging past their belts. Men shaved their faces clean; Shadboyut was the only disheveled one with a few days' growth of stubble on his jaw.

"Clearly you've walked a long way, friend!" A person with a light-toned voice rushed to Aya's side to offer a flask. She croaked her thanks before taking a swig of ginger tea.

"Who is your companion?" Thedgollas rested a hand on his hip and shifted his weight to lean off-kilter on the opposite leg.

"Her name is Aya from the grist mill's village in Lisshardra Valley but as for *who* she is... Well, now, that's a longer story." Shadboyut pulled out his unlit pipe and set the stem in between his teeth.

"Always a story with you, eh?"

The person who had offered Aya the flask wore thick leather gloves and so was able to grasp her elbow and help her hobble over to the rear of the lead wagon. Looking more closely at the clean-shaven face, Aya noticed a feminine softness to the features. In those few shifting moments, she became unsure if the person was a man or woman leading her to rest on the tailgate of the wagon. *Shall I say thank you, goodfellow or thank you, goodwife?* Uncertain of how to politely address the peddler, she simply said, "Thank you for your kindness."

"Those blisters look terrible." An elderly person approached, their sun-weathered features likewise defying identification as either a grandfather or a grandmother. They brought a wicker basket full of waxy soap cakes and ceramic jars with corks.

"Do you have chamomile salve?" Aya asked.

"I prefer this." The elder with the basket uncorked a jar of honey. They used a wooden spoon to drizzle the liquid sweetness over the blisters.

How curious to pour honey on such a wound, Aya thought but deferred to the wisdom of an elder. *Not even two days' walk outside the village and already I feel that I've journeyed to the other side of the world.*

Thedgollas called out to the group, "What say you all that we park here for the night? Our newcomers can rest their feet with us."

Soon the oxen drivers unhooked the yokes and harnesses and tended to the needs of the animals. Others in the group raked a clear space to build a fire on the roadside. Everyone knew their task—even the children who collected sticks and bark chips for kindling. They set up a tall tripod and hung a cauldron. Large oaken barrels provided water. Sacks of dried lentils and bags of onions and cabbages came from a wagon painted with triangles. The scent of rosemary, sage, garlic, and parsley wafted on the warm air. Aya's stomach gurgled in anticipation.

"Story! Story! Story!" the children chanted as they gathered around Shadboyut and tugged at the fringe on his sleeves.

"Patience, little ones. My feet are weary and sore. Another time."

The children grumbled and whimpered in their disappointment. A few tried whining, "please, please," but Shadboyut firmly shook his head. They drifted away in twos and threes to return to their chores. Older ones tenderly guided the smaller toddlers.

Bandages done, Aya tried to get off the wagon's tailgate. The person who had tended to her blisters held up their gloved hand as a block.

"I wish to help prepare supper," she said.

"Rest your feet," the elder ordered.

Shadboyut strolled over to the tailgate. "Listen to the advice, Aya. You'll offend us all if you don't accept kindness and hospitality."

The nearness of him quickened her heartbeat and brought a flush of heat to her cheeks. Her lips parted. Her tongue felt dry, thirsting for the taste of him.

He backed away and cleared his throat. "I'm, uh, going to the head of the caravan and talk with Thed for a bit. He may have supplies to share that will help us in our journey to the mountains."

Aya looked away from him to quell the quickening of her blood. "Good idea."

Though she did not watch him leave, and did not hear the footfalls of his soft-soled boots on the dirt, she felt him move away. As surely as stepping out of a warm home's door and venturing into a frosty night, she felt the distance grow cold between them.

The elder person who had bandaged her foot asked, "You're going to the mountains?"

"Yes, we are."

"Why? You're a villager, aren't you?"

Aya shook her head. "I may have spent every day of my life there, but I've never felt like one of them. My parents were Mountain People though I never knew my father. My mother came down from the mountains alone to live in the village shortly before I was born."

"The overseeing gods must have guided Shad's feet to find you," they said. "He and his papa went to the mountain heights years ago. None of the rest of us know the trail."

"So he told me."

The sympathetic expression dimmed into sincere concern. "The people of the high lands meet us at the trading post to barter and exchange, but they don't like us going any farther than the tree line. They never come down to the lower lands, either."

"I know." Aya peeled back the edges of the shoulder sling to reveal the urn of her mother's ashes and bones. "This is my Mamma's remains. I'm taking her home."

"May the spirits of the soil guide your feet. May the ghost of your mother protect you on the journey. May the mountain people welcome you as one of their own."

Aya paused, unsure of how to answer someone who spoke of spirits, gods, and ghosts. "Thank you for your kindness."

Their expression turned into puzzlement and curiosity. "Indeed, you're unlike any villager I've ever met. So modest. So quiet. How could you endure a lifetime among those thistle-headed farmers? Do you truly see simple hospitality as a remarkable act of kindness?"

Aya blinked in struggling for the words to answer. "I had nowhere else to go."

The elder smiled and pointed to the caravan of wagons. "There is always somewhere else to go."

* * *

71

One by one, each person strolled up to the gurgling cauldron. They received a ladle's serving of lentil porridge topped with a hearty buckwheat dumpling. Each person, young and old, carried their own implements for mealtimes as a collection of trinkets tied to their belts: a tin tankard, a small knife, and a soup spoon carved of oxen horn. Aya did not carry anything of her own, but a bowl, spoon and a cup passed into her hands.

She voiced her thanks repeatedly until someone laughingly told her to stop repeating herself. "Say one thanks at the end of the meal, if you must," they scolded with a grin. "You're embarrassing us all."

Aya followed the elderly person who had spread honey on her blister. From behind, she watched the posture of how this person walked in the hopes of determining whether to address them as goodfellow or goodwife. However, their age and the hardships of a life on the road caused this elder to hobble stiffly. Too many layers of fringed clothing obscured the contours of their torso. Man or woman—at the age well past their prime, it was impossible to tell.

Thirty or more people sat like a string of beads at the edge of the wagon road. Legs crossed or feet outstretched, they all faced southward in the same direction. Of course they did not touch. They left gaps so that their elbows did not risk bumping. Even through gloves or sleeves, as Aya well knew, sometimes the Touch could still burn skin.

"How's the foot?" The elder settled down to the roadside and left a space open. The next person gestured to invite Aya into sitting down between them.

"I'm much better already." Aya tugged her long skirt straight in draping over her knees and shins. She kicked off her straw sandals. Wriggling her toes felt warm and refreshing.

"You need shoes," the elder said.

"Yes, I'm aware."

Aya looked to the side, down the long row of legs and faces, at the two men chatting and laughing together. Shadboyut sat close to his friend Thedgollas, the leader and driver of the ox team at the first wagon of the caravan.

"Have you anything to trade for shoes?" the elder asked.

Aya swallowed some of her porridge while thinking about the inventory of her meager belongings. Everything she owned had been left behind in the cottage. It had only been a few days, but she could hardly remember the myriads of dried herbs and wild mushrooms that stocked her shelves. The only thing that mattered was the urn of her mother's remains.

"Well, I suppose I have a bit of willow bark that I collected by the lakeside."

The elder nodded approval. "That's good for headaches."

"Yes, it is."

"Tell you what, I offer a trade. I have an extra pair of shoes, if you'll part with the willow bark in your pouch and..."

"And?" She braced herself for what the next demand might be, for she had nothing else but the clothes she wore.

"Tell me a story."

Aya looked down into the residue of lentils and parsley in the bottom of her gourd bowl. "I'm not good at telling stories."

The person to her right-hand side smiled widely. "Don't be shy. Come now, let's have a story."

Children farther down the line clapped their hands. "Story! Story!"

Even Shadboyut and his friend turned their heads to see the commotion. His friend murmured words that Aya could not hear. Her companion laughed heartily before he called out to her, "Thed wants to know the worst-tasting food that you've ever eaten."

"Oh." Aya's mouth broke into a smile. "Oh yes, when I was small—I believe my sister Dimylse was toddling about and not yet weaned. My youngest sister Feianthe was not yet born. It was early in the season. I remember helping collect the ripened plums in the orchards. That was a happy time when the villagers and Mamma worked together at the same task. We filled baskets upon baskets with the little golden plums. I wanted to eat the fruit, but Mamma told me, 'No.' I had to wait. I had to be patient."

One of the children blurted out, "I don't like waiting!"

Aya nodded in the child's direction. "Neither do I but I obeyed Mamma because I was a good little girl. I helped her pack the crock jars with salt, water, and plums. I waited and waited and waited some more.

We added purple parsley and kept on waiting as the weeks of summer rolled on."

Aya paused to swallow. She gazed down at her lap, becoming less aware of the thirty-odd faces turned in her direction. Memories swelled in her mind, the colors and the sound of her mother's voice speaking in the language of the mountains.

"'*Bah'greth, bah'greth,*' my Mamma said to me every day. In the words of the mountain people, it means patience... No, it means looking to the horizon in the hour before first light with the hope of another sunrise soon to come."

Aya rested her hand across the urn containing her mother's remains. The memory rose fresh in her mind as if it had happened the day before.

"On the day Mamma opened the first crock jar, I was so tired of waiting! I plunged my little fingers into the salt water. I pulled out a pickled plum and shoved it into my mouth. Oh... Oh, such a taste it had! Sour and bitter... My face puckered. I spit it out."

"Why do they taste so sour?" asked another one of the children.

"Mamma said they're meant to be used in beet soup, or eaten with cucumbers, or simply brewed in boiling water for a tisane. They aren't meant to be eaten the same way as raspberries or cherries."

The elder prompted, "And what was the lesson you learned?"

Aya cocked her head to the side, for she had never considered the question. "I suppose I've learned that the bounty of the earth has different flavors. We can find a way to enjoy even the most bitter of foods... *if* we're patient."

Hands all up and down the line erupted in applause. Aya startled at the sudden burst of clapping palms. Even the children hooted, "Good story! Good story!"

Shadboyut sneaked her a wink. He raised his tankard to offer a tavern-style salute. Aya blushed at the mischievous sparkle of his dark eyes. Even with a dozen people sitting between them, she felt as if he had just kissed her.

* * *

"We'll make a storyteller out of you yet." Shadboyut showed her by example how to fashion a bed on the ground. Up and down the length of the caravan, the group of traveling peddlers performed the same actions for sleeping beneath the open sky. He unrolled a straw mat, a wool blanket, and a pillow bag stuffed with buckwheat husks.

Aya lay down with her mother's urn to one side and her companion on the other. She gazed up at the darkening sky and felt no fear of wild animals in the night. Surrounded by strangers who had met her only that day, she had never felt more at home.

"You'll have to help me remember your friends' names," she said quietly. "I'm sorry I can't keep them in my head."

"They understand. Villagers never remember our names. We stopped expecting it a long time ago." He puffed on the last few embers in his pipe. The small bowl in his hand flared up bright orange with his every inhale. Lavender smoke floated like a cloud above his head.

She whispered more quietly, "I'm also sorry that I can't tell who is a man or who is a woman. I think it would be rude to ask."

"Very true. It would be rude."

"Could you help me, Shad? Tell me?"

"Why?" He tapped out the spent ashes in the gravel of the road.

"So that I can properly address people."

He pulled aside his waist-length hair before lying down on the mat. The southern constellations cast a gentle silvery light on his stubble jawline.

"Listen to me, Aya. You don't need to 'properly address people' here. No one is a goodwife or a goodfellow if we all ride the same wagons. The rain falls and the sun shines on each of us the same. We don't have prestigious occupational titles. We don't own land. We have no surnames and no rules for preserving a family bloodline. We have no etiquette except the one—to share what we have and to help each other in need."

"I don't understand," she said. "Who bears the children and who sows their seed?"

Shadboyut chuckled softly in huffs snorting out his large nose. "Whoever wishes to."

"That's a poor answer." Aya crossed her arms over her belly. "I feel you're mocking me for asking such an ordinary thing."

"I'm not mocking you." He raised his hand towards her, then caught himself and withdrew. "It's true, I call the man Papa who fathered me. I have fond memories of Maman the woman who bore me. Then again, I've had a dozen more parents in every adult in the caravan who cared for me and taught me how to behave decently in my life. Everyone my age in the caravan is my sibling. Every child is like a child of my own. We aren't neighbors, we're a family. Do you see?"

"It's a strange idea but I can't deny you all seem happy in each other's company."

"We are. We are." He closed his eyes and breathed deeply on his way to sleep.

Aya pulled the wool blanket up to her throat. She clamped the fuzzy fabric close to her chest. The man lay so close that, if she were to reach out her left arm, she could touch his face. Warmth from his body radiated to the length of her body that faced him. Her back felt cold. She tightened her grip on the blanket as her guts ached with the longing to jump into his embrace once more. She closed her eyes and forced herself to try to forget the nearness of him. All around, she listened to the sounds of the night's crickets and the hooting of distant owls. Children lying down in nests of pillows within the wagons softly wept. Adults spoke murmuring words of comfort. No one touched. No one could ever touch but it did not poison their temperaments with bitterness.

The fog of slumber settled over her thoughts. Aya inhaled the man's breath that carried the scent of burned flowers. The rumble of his soft snorting prickled her skin.

Twelve

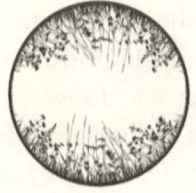

IN THE DREAM, Aya stood solitary in the village's burial ground. A group of four burly farmers carried a funeral bier. The good wife Nuriasha's husband and her brother carried the front end. Two men from neighboring farms carried the rear. The woman's corpse was shrouded in rust-colored linen gauze. Two stalks of purple lilies lay across her legs. One smaller bundle of ruddy linen nestled against the corpse's chest. Aya knew it by the size and shape. The infant's swaddling covered its face. Together in death as they never could be in life, the mother and child were being carried solemnly to the funeral pyre.

A few goat herders walked behind the bier. They wailed the funeral dirge in unison. The men's voices screeched like barn owls.

In spirit form, Aya trailed behind the small procession. They tread respectfully between the grave markers to reach the ustrinum at the center. The blacksmith had already stoked and fanned a roaring bonfire inside the tower of charred stones.

The Keeper of Books raised a hand-held copper bell and shook it four times. Then he sang the recitation of verse, "Do not weep for the end of suffering. As autumn follows summer, and winter turns to spring, so shall we all come to the same end. Here we stand together to say good-bye to our neighbor."

Nuriasha's husband and her brother took turns laying their hands on the corpse's gray feet for the last time. Her brother dropped to his knees and succumbed to convulsions of sobbing. Her husband was left standing, with tears dribbling into his beard.

The goat herders carried the funeral bier the rest of the way. They rolled the pair of shrouded corpses into the center of the ustrinum's brick cylinder. Incense-scented smoke and embers, like butterflies with fiery wings, billowed out of the bonfire pit.

Aya's spirit stood quietly in sorrow to watch the small group expressing their grief. *I wish that I could have done more. I wish that mushrooms and herbs and salves were enough. The midwife was wrong to have hope. This blight is beyond the natural way of things.*

Then, from behind, she heard the rustle of more sandals in the grass. A second funeral procession approached, with another group of mourners wailing in unison.

Aya rotated in place with her spirit's feet floating slightly above the ground. Another corpse shrouded in gauze was being carried forth. The poles of the bier were carried by the midwife's husband, the midwife's two sisters, and the midwife's former lover who remained her lifelong friend.

No, no, no, her spirit cried out. Yet no one else could hear her voice. No one else could see her formless being like a human-shaped wisp of smoke.

They carried the midwife's corpse on the same path that the farmwife's procession had followed. Nuriasha's brother and husband had to step aside to make room for their arrival at the ustrinum.

The Keeper of Books rang his hand-held copper bell once again. "Do not weep for the end of suffering. As autumn follows summer, and winter turns to spring, so shall we all—"

"No!" screamed the midwife's husband.

The mourners carried the bier to the edge of the funeral pyre. One of the corpse's arms shook loose of its shroud. A dark line marred the gray skin of the midwife's forearm from her wrist to the pit of her elbow.

* * *

Aya jolted into awakening. She lurched upright from the ground and trembled from the shock of returning to her flesh as if she had dropped from a great height. Her hands were cold and numb. A headache, as always, throbbed at the center of her forehead. Dark fabric covering her head dimmed the morning's light. Aya's arms felt too weak to pull the shawl away.

"Good of the morning." Shadboyut brought her a cup of warm water containing a few shavings of ginger root. He held it to her chapped lips. Carefully, he tilted the cup enough for her to take a sip.

Why did you cover me with a shawl? Her throat felt too raw to speak.

The caravan's leader Thedgollas squatted on his heels at Aya's feet. "How's she feeling?"

"It'll be a bit of a bit, Thed," Shadboyut said to his friend. "She's a villager, y'know, not familiar with sleeping under the stars. The morning dew gets her hair wet. She often awakens with headaches."

"Careful with that cup, Shad," his friend warned. "You don't want to risk a touch."

"Yeah, yeah, of course." He placed the cup on the ground next to her hand.

"Do you need to borrow gloves?"

"I have some, Thed, I'm being careless. Silly me."

Aya bowed her head forward, thankful for the indigo shawl that veiled her head and shoulders so that the rest of the group could not see her weep. The sight of the midwife's corpse and her self-inflicted mortal injury haunted her thoughts. Tears dribbled uncontrollably out of her stinging eyes.

"Looks like it's going to rain hard," Thedgollas said. "We can wait a couple of hours for the showers to pass, and then, Shad, I'm sorry to say we have to keep moving on. We are bound for Tall Pine Village for their springtime market days."

"I understand, Thed."

Her hands gained enough strength to lift the cup and drink from it. Turning her attention to the happy people enjoying their morning repast by the roadside, Aya's bout of weeping subsided.

A wheel of cheese got passed from hand to hand—cautiously, so as not to touch—and each person used the knife at their belt to hack off a chunk. Others dangled their legs off the tailgate of the wagon decorated with triangles. They worked to crack walnuts from a wicker basket in between them. The people had crammed their entire existence into boxed cottages on wheels. Aya marveled at how they could enjoy a life with no land, no farm, no permanent place to call home except what belongings they packed into those wagons.

"Can you stand yet?" Shadboyut asked. "Or shall I get you something?"

"I'm not hungry," Aya whispered, straining against her sore throat.

Thedgollas, with hands inside of thick gloves, patted his friend's shoulder. "You're welcome to travel with us, Shad."

"My thanks to you but we're heading north to the mountains, y'know."

"As you say, friend. May the gods watch over you and guide your feet."

"Yours as well."

Aya reached aside for the urn of her mother's remains still nestled at the edge of the blanket. She took small comfort from the cold, smooth surface of the glazed ceramic. *Perhaps I'm seeing these dreams because Mamma's spirit was never given a proper funeral. I dreamed for the first time in the cemetery. Perhaps if I bring her bones to rest and sing the song that she taught me, I won't be tormented every night in my sleep with visions of pain and death.*

Shadboyut gently pulled the shawl off her hair and let it fall to drape across her shoulders. "How are you feeling? Better?"

Drawing in a deep inhale, Aya caught the stony-metallic scent of a coming rain shower. "I saw the funeral of the farmwife and her infant," she whispered.

"Oh, gods have mercy."

"There's more, Shad. I saw the midwife of the village at the funeral, too. She's dead. She... She chose to end her own life."

He bowed his head forward. "What a tragedy."

"People are suffering under this blight and not just the people who cannot touch. The sorrow is spreading and spreading. Soon it will overtake us all and be the end of everything."

"It has to end soon," he said.

The gray sky filled with mists that rapidly turned to a light drizzle. The travelers brought out their buckets to catch the rain. Droplets of water dripped off the fringes of their clothing and, at last, Aya realized the purpose of the decoration. Like thatching on a cottage's roof, or the layered feathers of a duck's wings, the fringes helped to keep their underclothing from getting soaked.

Aya turned again to the children poking sticks at the gravelly roadside looking for worms or lizards.

"Why are there no babies?"

"How's that again?"

"Shad, there are no babies in this group. None of the women are carrying a pregnancy. Why?"

"Oh, I hadn't noticed." He frowned as the rain pattered more steadily around them.

"Is anyone missing? Has anyone perished in childbirth? Have any infants been lost to starvation?"

He put the unlit pipe stem into his mouth and chewed on it. "I don't dare to ask."

"They seem so happy," she said. "But perhaps it's an illusion, like a story. No one can be happy in these days of the blight."

Showers fell more steadily. Rain turned the dirt of the road into a slick sheet of wet clay. People called the children and gathered to take shelter beneath the wagon beds. Shadboyut and Aya, still wrapped in her wool blanket, squeezed together beneath the open tailgate of the last wagon. He rested a hand against her back. Even though he wore gloves, someone spoke up to caution him, "Be careful of touching, Shad."

Aya stared southward at the valley from where she had come, at the beaded sheets of rain pouring out of the slate-colored sky. It should have been a joyous morning of celebration for the life-giving waters that filled the creeks and nourished the farm fields. Instead, she felt only gloom and despair; of a journey on pause, of wheels that should be turning are bogged down in the mud. *We must do something to end this*, she thought, while cradling the urn in her lap. *We must find the path to the cave of the screaming monstrous crab and find a way, somehow, to end this. Mamma, help me be strong. Mamma, show me the way.*

While waiting for the showers to let up, some folks took out small fifes and played high-pitched melodies. Others clapped along in rhythm. Aya thought it odd that there were no drums as the villagers played at festivals. The novelty of whistling melodies felt fresh and wonderful. Once again, she felt amazed that, even in the gloom of a spring rain shower, these people managed to find joy in the moment. A renewed sense of purpose and resolve straightened her back and squared her shoulders. These people deserved to experience true joy—not the fleeting moments of making the best of hours spent hiding from the rain. They deserved to dance in the open sunshine, to laugh uninhibitedly, and to touch each other without fear of pain.

I'm going to fix this. I won't give up. I won't stop trying until I find a way to end this blight.

Thirteen

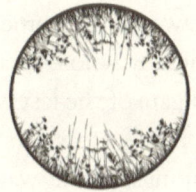

"OH LOOK, HERE COMES GERRIE!" Shadboyut stepped away from the tailgate of the last wagon.

Aya looked up from her feet. Borrowed boots with soft padded soles had a crisscrossing of lacing strings through tabbed holes punched in the leather. For a while now, she had been working to thread the lacings and draw the flapped sections tightly around her shins. The tubes of softened cowhide fit snugly reaching as high as her knees. Fringe dangled from the turned-down cuff in the same style worn by Shadboyut and everyone else in the caravan.

One solitary man approached from the southeast. He walked pulling a two-wheeled goat cart that was over-stuffed with a large cedar chest and numerous wicker baskets with balsawood lids. Shadboyut trotted away to meet this person called Gerrie, back down the road from where the caravan had come the day before.

The others were busy packing up their wagons after the rain had stopped. Soon they would continue their journey to attend springtime market days at Tall Pine Village farther to the west.

Even from a distance, Aya could see that Gerrie was a large fellow— taller and broader in body than any man she had ever seen. Fringe on his clothing only widened his shadow's imprint on the ground. Shadboyut approached him to offer jovial greetings at a body's length distance. Although they appeared to be about the same age, the stark difference in height and girth made Shadboyut seem like a juvenile next to a burly, full-grown man.

Oxen drivers at the front of each wagon paused from their tasks of hooking the yokes and harnesses around the necks of the golden-brown horned animals. They waved their arms high. They called out in staggered voices, "Yo there, Gerrawgon! Welcome, friend!"

Aya spoke to someone nearby who—wearing thick gloves—boosted a small child into the rear tailgate of the last wagon. "Who is that?"

" Gerrawgon? Oh, now there's a travelers' traveler..."

Someone else strolled alongside the wagon. "Doesn't stick to one group. Hops from caravan to caravan, alone but never alone. Gerrie always has the best wares to trade."

"And the best stories!" One of the older children, perhaps about ten or twelve years old, grinned widely and waved their hand.

Shadboyut trotted alongside him and spoke a welcome at a close distance. They extended their hands towards each other but stopped short of clasping to greet.

"How are you all now!" Gerrie's voice was as large as his body and carried easily across the air.

Gerrie's booming voice briefly quelled the constant ringing inside of Aya's ears. She furrowed her brows in study of the stranger approaching.

"Doing well, friend," said the oxen driver of the last wagon. "And yourself?"

Gerrie brought his goat-cart up close to the rear. He set down the handles and his cart tilted forward in coming to rest. "I've come from the glassmakers to the east. I bring a basket load of carafes, flasks, bottles, and colorful beads. Where are you headed?"

The oxen driver said, "We are westward bound for the springtime market days at Tall Pine Village."

"May I join and walk along with you, friend?" Gerrie asked.

"Of course, Gerrawgon, of course! You are always welcome to walk with us."

Shadboyut returned to the spot on the roadside where Aya sat lacing up her boots. "Gerrie says that he saw our campfires last night from a distance. How well met that he caught up to us, won't you say?"

"Yes, Shad." Sitting on the ground, Aya strained her neck to look upward at the taller man approaching. "Hello."

"Hello." Gerrie's eyes widened in curiosity, rolling side to side to assess her clothing. "You're a villager?"

"I am." She lowered her gaze to return her concentration to the lacings of her boots. "I *was*. I've left my home behind."

"There's a story in that, I'm sure. I look forward to hearing it on the road."

Gerrie nodded with hand on heart to politely excuse himself—a gesture that Aya had only seen the elders of the village perform to each other. A traveler's traveler, she reflected; welcomed by them but not exactly one of them. He walked up the length of the caravan to engage in greetings and conversation with the leader at the head of the group.

Shadboyut squatted down to his heels beside her. "Y'know the story I perform of Eiyallandra and her faithful Man of the Forest? I learned it from him but adapted it for my puppets. Gerrawgon does it better. I've heard him recite over four hundred stanzas of metered verse! Every word the same, every time."

"I never heard anyone tell stories like that," Aya said. "There's something odd about him, don't you think so?"

"Odd, yes, of course... and amazing! Gerrie sets up a proper stage for his performances with poles and curtains. But he also does drinking songs and children's rhymes. Oh, you never can predict what will come out of his mouth. What a singing voice he's got!" Shadboyut reached out to help Aya finish tightening and tying her laces. His lean dexterous fingers worked rapidly on the strings until he tied off the square knot under her knee.

Gerrie strolled back to the rear of the caravan to where she sat on the ground. "Hello, Goodwife Villager. They tell me your name is Aya? That's not a typical name of valley dwellers. I'd be pleased if you'd walk alongside me. Would you tell me your tale?"

"I'm not much of a storyteller," she said.

"Oh, don't be shy. You told a great tale yesterday about eating a pickled plum." Shadboyut laughed as he brushed his hand affectionately across her shoulder. He wore gloves. She wore a cloak over her wool tunic. Even so, a few heads in the caravan turned to cast concerned frowns in their direction.

Gerrie hoisted up the poles of his goat cart. "I see you're carrying a funeral urn?"

Aya rose to stand alongside her companion. Boots felt odd swaddling her feet and calves, yet the sheepskin fleece lining and the quilted padded soles gave her the sensation of standing on a tightly woven rug on a solid stone floor. She felt balanced, steady, and confident of being able to walk the rugged trails leading up to the foothills of the mountains that loomed in the distance.

"It's my mother's remains." Aya picked up the urn with the gentle touch of handling a child. She set it in the cradle of the fabric sling and adjusted its position to rest across her left shoulder.

"Why isn't your mother still buried in the meadow of ashes, Aya?"

"She doesn't belong there. I'm taking her home."

"Where is home?"

Aya and Shadboyut made the same gesture, in unison, pointing to the upward sloping ground and beyond to the looming blue-gray pyramids of frost-streaked heights.

Gerrie turned to face northward. He held that position for a long quiet moment, lost in his own thoughts. When the oxen drivers called out, "Yo, ho, away we go!" he did not move. The drivers waved their long sticks and tapped their oxen. The large, docile beasts lurched forward.

Shadboyut approached the man. "Ho there, Gerrie? Let's be off?"

After a long pause, when the last wagon was rolling ahead, Gerrie blinked out of his reverie. He cleared his throat.

"Yes, yes, let's be off." He started walking with a pole in each hand. The cart's large wheels rolled smoothly behind him.

The two walked on either side of the man. Shadboyut chose the right-hand side of the cart's handlebars. She strolled at Gerrie's left elbow.

Shadboyut extended his arm to Aya invitingly. "Tell him! Tell him your story."

"I'm not sure where to begin," she said.

"Think of what is most important," Gerrie suggested. "Think of your mother. What do you wish to say about her? What do you want a stranger to know about her? Don't look at me as your audience. Listen to the words in your own thoughts and let the words come out."

Aya looked ahead to the caravan of wagons rolling forward on the road. She paused for a moment to collect her memories. While walking forward, stroking the urn of ashes through the sling's fabric, she began to speak.

"My mother was born on the mountains in the high-facing lands where the villagers never go. I think she was shunned by the mountain clans, but she would never tell me why. I don't know why Mamma came downhill to make a new life in the villages of the valley. We only knew enough—my sisters and I... We knew better than to ask. She would often say, '*Dh'ggn th'molrk*'..."

Gerrie nodded with an expression of familiarity and understanding when Aya spoke those words in the language of her mother's people. It was not a response that she was used to seeing. Her skin prickled. Her heart quickened. *A traveler's traveler; perhaps he has heard their speech before?*

"...which means, 'no need to complain.' Mamma never complained."

Aya waited for him to make a comment. When he stayed silent, she continued. "Mamma was carrying me in her belly when she left the mountains. She gave birth to me a few months later in the orchards by the creek. By then, she had befriended a village midwife and in turn shared the mountain people's knowledge of soothing the pains of birth. She taught the midwife about wild forest mushrooms and herbs. That old midwife spoke on her behalf to the village elders. They welcomed her to stay in the village. For the rest of her life, she stayed there. She had two more children—my sisters—fathered by villagers in chance encounters at spring festival time."

"As so many are," Gerrie remarked thoughtfully.

"Mamma never signed her name in the Book of Families as anyone's wife. The men later settled into other homes with other wives. We lived in a cottage set between the village and the forest and, for most days, kept to ourselves. Mamma taught me the craft of herbal salves, ointments, and tinctures that I have carried on after she passed."

Aya fell silent for a moment thinking of the villagers who could never pronounce Aho's or her own name correctly though she had lived among them for her entire life. She recalled the angry faces screaming at her. *Dim-witted bear-child. Shit-eating daughter of a mountain she-bear!*

Gerrie asked, "So, you're saying that you were not fathered by one of the villagers? Aho was already a'gotten with child before she came down from the mountains? You're certain of this?"

"Yes," Aya said. "My father is a man of the mountain people, but Mamma never spoke of him. She always got so sad. I never understood why. My sisters and I felt she carried unhappy memories. We never pushed the question. Well... No, I should say that my younger sisters were never curious about Mamma's past life. They have different fathers than I do and are friendly with their households. They feel strongly that they belong in the village."

"You don't feel the same?" Gerrie asked.

Aya shook her head. "I love my sisters, of course. Yet I feel there is a difference in how we look at so many things. I wanted to perform the one-year ceremony after Mamma died but they don't want to sing the song. They don't want their neighbors to look at them as if they are anything but village born."

"That's an attitude we've seen all too well, eh," Shadboyut commented.

"Indeed," Gerrie said softly while staring straight ahead. "Indeed, we have."

"Until I met Shad a few days ago, I never heard the story of how he and his papa met her in the mountain cave. I never knew that she saved a man's life and helped to bring the injured man down to the trading post."

Gerrie nodded along. "Oh yes, Zhardohut has been telling that same story for years. By the stars, has it been twenty years or more? Mercy, I've heard that tale so many times... But I've never heard the detail that Aho was carrying a child when she pushed her brother into the ravine."

"What's that you say? Her brother?" Shadboyut skipped forward and walked slightly ahead of Gerrie to gaze back at the man from across his shoulder.

"Her brother?" Aya gripped the pleats of the sling bearing the urn.

Gerrie kept his attention focused on the tailgate of the wagon rolling in front of himself. "Oh, I'm sure ol' Zhard must have mentioned it at some point over the years."

Shadboyut emphatically shook his head. "No, no, Papa never knew that man's role in her life. We assumed it was her husband."

"Oh yes, well... Husband, brother, I could be mistaken." Gerrie changed his mood with a large wide grin that exposed his white teeth. "The gods must have guided your feet, Shad, for the two of you to find each other."

"I was searching for Aho, in searching for my papa." Shadboyut pulled out his pipe from his belt, stuck the stem in his mouth but without a fire he could not light it up.

"Yes, how sad that he's gone wandering off. This curse of the skin has driven everyone to madness. Any news of Zhardohut?"

"No."

"How sad. How very sad. Is Aya helping you search for him? Does she have any ideas of where to go next? Or, any dreams of where he could be?"

Aya caught her breath at his tone of voice in saying that simple word: dreams. *He can't know. He couldn't know. No one could ever guess what happens to me in my sleep.*

"I've given up hope of finding him alive," Shadboyut said.

"I'm sorry," Gerrie responded. "My sincere condolences."

"Thanks."

"By the way, friend, with all this talk of ol' Zhard in search of his unrequited love, I don't recall ever hearing stories about your birth. I'm curious. Do you know your mother? Can you tell me about her?"

"Maman is a honey gatherer. She's a traveler's traveler, much like you are, Gerrie."

"Oh, is she now?"

"She meanders solitary to wherever her feet will take her. There's many well-established honeybee hives in the forests of the foothills and the woods around the villages. Maman knows them all. Every burned-out hollow tree. Every fallen log. Every crevasse and overhanging shelf of granite rock that could shelter a good beehive, she knows where they are and how to harvest the honey or wax."

"When is the last time you walked with her?" Gerrie asked.

Shadboyut fiddled his fingertips around the bowl of his unlit pipe. "Let me think, oh, it's been a span of ten or twelve years since we spoke. Yes, yes... Hold the thought... It was around the spring festival's market days in the valley of the Fuller's Mill to the east. I must have been in my nineteenth year, I remember now. I took to wandering off on my own for a while. Funny, isn't it, how the years pass by so quickly as we get older?"

"Yes."

"I heard news of Maman's whereabouts for several years after we parted ways but not lately, now that I think about it. Hmmm... It's been two or three winters since I've heard someone speak her name. Could it be, as she advanced in age, Maman settled into a village to ply her trade with beekeeping in a box?"

"What is the name she goes by?" Gerrie asked.

"Flessandra is her full name." Shadboyut flexed his jaw to mouth the stem of his pipe. "But to her friends and family, she is called—"

"Fless," Gerrie repeated. The tone of his voice drained of any sensitivity or welcome.

Shadboyut tilted his head in curiosity. "You're acquainted with my mother?"

"Oh indeed, I have known Fless for a very long, long time." He loudly sighed in weariness. "Let me just say that we are not friends."

"You're not?"

"Whenever our paths have crossed over the years, we tend to argue. We disagree over the simplest of ideas. It's come to the point that we avoid each other."

"These are some odd things that I'm hearing from you today, Gerrie. All my life, no one has ever said a sideways word about my mother."

"I meant no offense, friend." Gerrie cleared his throat. "Say, I've been working on a new story. Would you like to hear it?"

Shadboyut frowned deeply in a way that she had never seen before. Aya raised her eyebrows, noncommittally. Once more, a feeling nagged at her gut that this fellow was peculiar and secretive.

Children looked out eagerly from the rear of the wagon's tailgate. Side by side, they were shielded from each other's touch by fringed shawls and wool blankets. They shouted out, "Story! Story! We want a story!"

Gerrie's smile brightened and refocused on the children's faces. "A story? Yes, I have a story for you! Settle down, children, and listen well."

"We're listening!" the children responded in a high-pitched chorus.

Gerrie cleared his throat. "Once upon a world, much like this world but again a world of its own, there was a child who was not a child."

"'A child who is not a child'?" Shadboyut repeated critically.

"Yes, a child who was not a child, not a human, not an animal, not a bird or lizard or fish or bug. The child was spawned and hatched from a golden eggshell..."

"Wait," Shadboyut interrupted. "You just said it wasn't a bird, but it hatched from an egg?"

Gerrie raised the volume of his voice and continued speaking without losing a beat of his rhythm. "...a golden eggshell in a nest made of precious jewels. The child hatched into a sea of rainbows. Its emergence was celebrated with a chorus of song. The nest—or perhaps it's a hive—floats high about us in the sky."

He spared one hand briefly from gripping the cart's poles. He pointed straight up at the drifting clouds in the afternoon sky.

"Do you see? Look there! When night falls, you may see it as the brightest speck of light in the southern sky. Look next to the South Star's three tails and you may see where the hive made of jewels still floats above our heads. The child's kindred are still incubating in their shells, snuggled up safe, waiting for their time to hatch."

Aya asked, "Don't all ducklings in a nest hatch about the same time?"

"It is not a duckling," Gerrie said. "The child was very much not a bird, for the child had no feathers on its wings."

"But it had wings?" Shadboyut asked.

"Yes, it had wings. Like a dragonfly or a bat."

"Those two things are very different," Aya commented.

"Would you be so kind as to stop interrupting?" Gerrie gave them both in turn a stern, scolding stare. When he was sure of their obedience, he continued. "The hive of jewels was perfect in form or so its builders believed. They did not see its one tiny flaw. There is a crack! Yes, a crack in the crystal walls. Every so often, after a hatchling emerges from an egg, it falls through. So many have fallen over the eons of time...

"And so, this child fell from the heavens and into the poisonous vapors of this flawed, imperfect world that the feet of our ancestors have tread upon. The child's delicate wings crumbled into ashes. Then its limbs turned to dust. Then its body flaked away like sand being washed out by the ocean's tides."

Aya, who had never seen the seashore or the ocean's rides, squinted to try to imagine it but did not interrupt again.

"The child screamed as it plummeted. More of its body crumbled away until the last thing left was its voice...and its cry. Before it dissolved into nothingness to be scattered on the autumn winds, it saw a man! A man tending to his olive orchard heard the child's cry from above. He looked up. And in hearing it, the man's ears filled with the echo of the child's scream. His filled with the ringing of the child's voice. His soul turned color as when red beets are dropped into boiling water to make dye. Until the man was no longer a man, and the child was no longer a child."

Aya inhaled a faint scent of mint and jasmine flowers wafting from his breath. Something about his story gave her an unsettled feeling. She sensed a tremor of emotion in the undertones of his voice that was more than a passionate oration.

"The two blended into each other, becoming one face and one voice. Neither and none, together and both."

Gerrie stopped talking and seemed strangely sullen, as if this fantastical legend felt particularly important. Sunlight twinkled off the corner of his eyes, catching a tear that welled up on his lashes. For a moment, Aya saw a flash of rainbow light. Until he blinked and the tears fell away.

She felt her tongue go dry and realized that she had been walking with her mouth open for some time. She wanted to ask but hesitated to give voice to such fantastic questions. Is this a true story? Is this what happened to you? Are you a creature of legend—of a fable that no one has ever told before? Are you not a man as you appear to be? A man who is not a man? A child who is not a child?

Shadboyut gestured to the faces of the children who remained unmoved and wide-eyed as if expecting more. "That story is a bucket of wet clay. I'd say it needs some work before you try it on an audience again."

"Yeah."

"It's not one of your best. Not even close."

Gerrie pouted childishly. "You've made that clear, Shad, thanks. I'll work on fixing the problems and write a new version."

"How about one of the classics?" Shadboyut asked.

One of the older children called out, "The Folly of Gromm the Giant!" The other children squealed in delight and clapped their hands.

"Very well but I can't use my hands to gesture while pulling this cart. It will have to be the short version." Gerrie cleared his throat, and the tone of his words took on a lyrical lilt in between speaking and singing.

"Once upon a world, much like this world but again a world of its own, there lived a giant named Gromm. He was a fearsome, ugly fellow taller than a pomegranate tree. He was bald and buck-toothed and had floppy ears like a goat. His hands had only four fingers. His feet had only four toes. Basically, not a desirable husband."

Aya's mouth crept into a thin smile, amused at the idea of any woman—even a giantess—choosing such an ugly brute for a husband.

"Now, Gromm the Giant was going about terrorizing villages, swallowing sheep and calves in one gulp as he went, and drinking up whole ponds dry. He plowed a trail of weeping farmers from one valley to the next. Well, as Gromm came closer to one village, the people panicked. 'What'll we do? What'll we do?' they said." Gerrie imitated the villagers' voices in an exaggerated, high falsetto.

"And a hero came forth, a brave and strong man who could split a log with one chop, chase off a pack of wolves with one shout, all that sort of thing. He set off into the countryside to find the giant. Now, there's a long tale-within-a-tale of his battle against Gromm. Forgive me, children, if my mouth is too dry to give that part a good telling today. Let me say, he got his nose promptly kicked straight back to town."

The children in the wagon giggled.

"Another hero comes forth, this time not a physically strong man but a clever fellow. They say he could trick a nursing baby off its mother's breast, and so on. So, he set off into the countryside to confront Gromm the Giant. The tale gets quite long at this point with all the games and trickeries that he attempts to confound and enrage the giant. Forgive me, children, if I say he also got his nose kicked in and fled back to town."

Gerrie paused for dramatic effect. He cleared his throat by swallowing a few times.

"Meanwhile, there was fellow named Binjarr who was ignorant of all these goings-on. He was not a strong man. He was not a clever man. He should have been at work like the other villagers but instead he was sitting by the river, getting blissfully drunk on a wagon-load of apricot mead."

"Was he a traveler?" asked one of the older children at the wagon's tailgate.

"Perhaps he was," said Gerrie. "We could say he was, if you wish it to be so."

"Yes, yes!" the children called out in chorus.

"Very well. So along comes Gromm the Giant, and he says to Binjarr, 'I'm going to eat you up.'" Gerrie lowered the pitch of his voice to the deepest bass rumble that Aya had ever heard a person manage to growl. Then, just as quickly, his voice switched back to a man's normal range of speech.

"And Binjarr says, 'Why?' And the giant says, 'I'm a giant, that's what I do all day.' And Binjarr says, 'I'm a drunkard, and this is what I do all day. Join me.' So Gromm the Giant plucked a barrel from the wagon and slammed it down in one gulp, *hauwmp*. It was so tasty that he slammed down another, and another, and one more. By then, the giant was feeling a bit more pleasant company. Gromm sat down by the river next to Binjarr. The man had no skills besides being able to talk, so he told the giant every bawdy story he knew."

"Every *what* story?" the smallest girl asked.

Gerrie answered, "Husbandry things you're all too young to know."

"I'm not!" exclaimed the eldest child, who was grinning.

Shadboyut pointed at the child's face. "Lying little scamp, yes, you are. Hush, now. You're interrupting."

"And in these bawdy stories, Binjarr exaggerated his own personal accomplishments, and then gossiped about his neighbors, and then started inventing fanciful tales that strained the limits of one's imagination. So it was that Gromm the Giant got so drunk, and got to laughing so hard at these bawdy stories, that he fell into the river—*whoomp!* and was washed out to the deep waters of the Deep Sea, and never set foot on the land of men again."

"Whoomp! Whoomp! Whoomp!" the children chanted. "Into the river he fell!"

Even Shadboyut chuckled and joined them in chanting, "Whoomp, whoomp."

"So, children," Gerrie asked, casting his gaze wide to include Shadboyut and Aya as well. "What did we learn from that story?"

The oldest child in the wagon called out eagerly, "Be careful at the riverbank and don't fall in the water!"

"That's a good answer, child." Gerrie turned his attention to Aya. His eyes felt as if he gazed deeply into the hollows of her heart. "What did you learn?"

She said, "A foolish, ignorant drunkard saved the villagers when men full of pride had failed the job."

Gerrie grinned broadly. "That's another good answer, child."

Aya exhaled a hesitant laugh from her nostrils. How peculiar it felt to be called a child by a man who appeared to be not much older than herself.

Children hanging their arms out the tailgate called, "Tell us another story, Friend Gerrie!"

He shook his head but only slightly, as his torso and shoulders worked to pull the goat cart. "No, no, children, I'm all tapped out of stories for now. Do your tasks! Get the little ones to take a nap. Off you go!"

The man's fatherly tone of voice was not scolding or threatening. Yet his firm authority left no room for disobedience. The children ducked behind the curtain that dangled off the rear of the wagon's canopy.

Fourteen

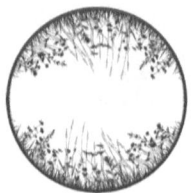

SHADBOYUT RAISED a hand as if to clap him on the shoulder but stopped short of making the connection. "Story well told, Gerrie but if you don't mind, I should like to walk at the head of the caravan with Thedgollas for a while."

"Go on ahead, Shad, don't hold back for my sake."

Shadboyut trotted ahead and left the two of them walking alone behind the wagons. Aya's gaze tracked him speeding up the entire length of the caravan to reach the lead oxen driver. The warm springtime sunshine brought up a blush in her cheeks. Briefly she felt ashamed for being rude, even in the privacy of her own thoughts. For all the other thirty-odd people walking alongside the rolling wagons, her attention was captured wholly in the figure of a single man.

"Not yet, not yet." Gerrie spoke sideways to the eagerness in Aya's posture.

At his comment, she realized that her back had straightened with curiosity. Her eyes brightened to fixate on the profile of the taller man walking alongside her. How odd it felt needing to tilt up her face to gaze into his eyes; for her entire adult life in the village, Aya had always been the tallest person in any group.

Gerrie slowed his pace. Aya's legs surged with the energy to walk faster and felt strained to to slow down alongside him. A somber mood like a foul odor settled over the two of them. She sensed he withheld speaking in front of the others.

"I hope you won't be offended if I say there's something odd about you," Aya said.

"Odd, you say? Me?"

"That story you told," she said. "You spoke with such sorrow and passion. Please don't laugh if I sound foolish, but I must ask."

Gerrie licked his lips as if tasting the flavor of her words.

"Is it true? About golden eggs, bejeweled clouds, and falling... Did that truly happen to you?"

"Yes."

Yes! Aya huffed through a rush of satisfaction as if she had raked aside a large pile of dry leaves to discover a cluster of rare medicinal mushrooms underneath.

"Why do you keep it a secret? Why not tell your friends that you are a...? What *are* you?"

He glanced sideways in her direction. Sunlight flashed off the corner of his eye. "I have told a select few from time to time, over the years. More often than not, they have given me cause to regret my decision. Don't make me regret this, Aya."

"You sound very selfish," she scolded.

"Do I?"

"The people of this world need your help!"

"Clearly you've misunderstood the lesson in my story. When I fell into this man's skin, I am now merely flesh and blood." His jaw flexed into a frown that dragged down the lower half of his face. "I can smell the brightness of colors. I can see the floating waves of sound. What else can I do to 'help' people? I walk on two feet. If I am injured, I bleed. I sleep, eat, breathe, and shit in a hole like any man. Except for the memories of what I was before, I am no different from anyone."

She insisted, "You must know of the curse! You dropped out of a jeweled cloud under the watchful eyes of the all-seeing gods."

"You surprise me, child, to use that word. A 'curse' implies a malevolent action by an intangible spirit. I thought villagers did not believe in anything they can't see or touch."

"Stop evading the question," Aya said. "How did it happen? Do you know? How can we end it? Tell me!"

"I have no answers for you, child. I'm suffering the same as everyone else. I haven't touched another person's skin in more than four months, same as you."

Aya's throat tightened and snagged on her next breath. Briefly her eyes rolled to the side. She gazed all the way up the length of the caravan, past the wagons and the people dressed in fringe. From behind, Shadboyut and his friend were indistinguishable in their clothing and physique. They both had straight black hair grown long past their belt-lines. They both walked in synchronized step, left and right, left and right. Yet to think of him brought a cold tingle to her lips that Aya licked away in thirsting for his kiss.

Shadboyut from a distance rotated his head briefly and glanced back across his shoulder at her direction. His dark eyes twinkled in the sunlight.

"Oh, by the stars." Gerrie's tone of voice lowered to nearly a growl. "Are you both immune to it?"

"No, I've suffered it too, until a few days ago when I met Shad. He and I..." Aya cleared her throat as a blush rose to her cheeks. "But we can only touch each other. We don't know why. Could it be that we are creatures like you?"

Gerrie snorted a discouraging huff. "Do you remember being hatched out of a golden egg, falling out of a crystal nest, your body crumbling into embers before plummeting into the heart of someone on the ground?"

"No," she said. "But I see things in my dreams. I've seen places where I have never been, people I have never met, in the time of days long gone and in the time of here and now."

"Only since you've met Shad, of course."

"Yes." Aya stroked the urn of her mother's ashes. "I think it's because we met in the cemetery. Perhaps I am haunted by my mother's ghost."

"No, you're not."

"Are you certain of that?"

"Very certain." Gerrie furrowed his brows. "Haven't you already puzzled out the answer, child? Surely you know what sort of mystical creature you are."

"I am?"

"You've heard the legends of Eiyallandra the Matron of the Calendar and her faithful companion Man of the Forest. Remember how the stories say they were always together? Two wheels of a cart, or two wings of a bird... However the comparison is made, you should keep that rule in mind. It's only when you are in each other's company that two halves are made whole and your abilities are manifested."

"It's true, it's true." She spoke as much to herself as to the man walking beside her. "I felt a sense of kinship for him in the hour we first met. At the end of each dream, I feel drawn to return to him. It's true, then. It's all true. Everything that I see in my dreams is real."

"Well, actually, you are not seeing dreams. What are dreams but a sleeping mind telling stories to yourself? No, what you've experienced is your inner spirit separating from the shell of your flesh. You've gone flying into the realm of the unseen. Your spirit travels to the places where your feet may or may not be able to go. Tell me, when you return to yourself, your body had lain in the appearance of death?"

"Yes," she said. "I am a creature of legends and so is Shad?"

"Only when you are near enough to inhale each other's breath. You must be together in each other's company for it to work." Gerrie raised the tilt of his chin and used his nose to point toward the lead wagon of the caravan. "Do you see how far away Shad is? Do you feel colder to be beyond shouting distance from him?"

Aya walked for a short while in silence. Indeed, the afternoon's breeze cast a chill over her cheeks.

"It was the same for Mullind'groth," Gerrie said.

"Who?"

"Mullind'groth the faithful Man of the Forest, don't you know his name? Has that part of the story been lost? Mullin was like you, child. His spirit took flight, not hers. His eyeless eyes saw the visions of things yet to happen or that happened elsewhere. He charted the patterns of days, years, decades, and centuries from soaring across the waves of time. Eiyal spoke to the earthly winds that lifted birds' wings and she—being a competitive, jealous sort of woman—used her skill of mathematics to construct her own calendar of days. Oh, oh... To hear them argue and bicker! My version of the epic poem devotes over ninety-nine stanzas to their most pointed disagreements. Well, as best as I can recall..."

"You speak familiarly as if you knew them in life," Aya said.

"Yes, of course I knew them."

"How? They lived so long ago!"

"Oh, did I neglect to mention that I age very slowly?"

Aya beheld his smooth face with a fresh look. The assumptions that clouded her gaze fell away. Clearly, he did not appear to be close to Shadboyut's age in his early thirties. If she had met him alone, judging by the smoothness of his cheeks and the lightness of his shaved stubble, she would have assumed him to have barely reached his twentieth year. He looked to be a farmer's son coming into maturity but not ready to pledge himself to a wife or sign his name in the Book of Families.

"How slowly do you age?" she asked.

"For every one hundred years, this flesh ages a single day."

Aya's thoughts whirled to try to imagine such a long span of time. "When did you fall? How old are you?"

"Nine hundred seventy-four years have passed," he said. "Yet my skin has aged a little over a week. I can feel the passing time in every sinew of my flesh, every follicle of every hair. Every day, I sense the subtle changes."

"How does it feel to be nine hundred years old?"

"The days and the seasons wash over me in cycles. Spring follows winter and summer turns into autumn again and again. Every century feels more the same as the last. As I wander from seashore to seashore and valley to mountain, it feels more and more that I've seen everything before. I've seen the same trees grow from saplings into lofty branches. But the people... People's lives bloom and wither more quickly than plum blossoms. Everyone that I—that this man—ever knew in his life has aged and died a dozen of lifetimes ago."

"That must be lonely," Aya said.

"It can be if I dwell on the thought." Gerrie drew in a deep inhale. "Which I prefer not to do. Tell me your stories, child. Tell me what your spirit has seen in your sleep."

Aya described in detail the series of visions she'd witnessed thus far:

the funeral of the farmwife and the midwife; her sister and her husband speaking unkindly after the blight had been lifted; Shadboyut's father attacking a monstrous crab in a mountain cave; and that same mountain cave where Aho had pushed her brother into a ravine.

"Do you think the cave is the source of the blight?" she asked. "What if, when Mamma threw that man—her brother—into the ravine, it aroused and offended the monster?"

"No, I doubt it," Gerrie said. "Why would the ol' pest wait twenty-four years to be so offended as to curse everyone with the blight on touch? No, no, it's more likely that Zhardohut did something when he went back there a few months ago. The timing fits."

"He attacked the crab with an axe," she said.

"And it screamed, yes, that's certainly worth looking into."

She brightened and quickened her pace, pulling ahead of him and looking back over her shoulder. "Come with us!"

"No."

"Please? We need your help!"

"I would be more of a burden than a help," he said. "Have I not been clear? I smell colors. I see sounds. I don't age quickly. Otherwise, I'm not useful in hiking up the mountainside and confronting monstrous cave beasts. No, no, such adventures are better suited to kids like you."

Aya smiled, undaunted. She said no more but felt determined she would later try again to convince him to come. Of course, he felt weary of the world and had lost all hope, but she was sure that with persistence she could change his mind.

Up ahead on the road, she could see the blotch of evergreen fir trees that darkened a bend. Where the hillside slanted and folded like a roll of dough, a thin silvery line of water sparkled.

"We're approaching the crossroads," he said. "We should speak no more of these things."

She nodded to show she understood but could hardly wait to get Shadboyut alone to tell him all the wonderful secrets she had learned. Her hands stroked the urn of ashes in the sling, and in the secrecy of her thoughts she vowed, *I'm going to bring you home, Mamma, and I'm going to fix everything.*

Fifteen

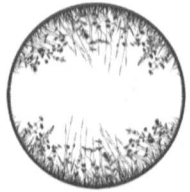

AYA KEPT TRYING—AND failing—to find a chance to speak with Shadboyut alone but there were always people nearby. The travelers settled into the campsite at the side of the crossroads where a well-trodden clearing of ground was encircled by a grove of old-growth, white pine trees. She helped to feed kindling sticks into the growing fire at a well-established pit of stones as he shared the pipe's weed with the leader of the caravan. She waved her hands to invite him behind the circle of wagons, presumably to gather walnuts and wild berries but he shook his head to decline the offer. As the evening grew dim more quickly under the canopy of trees, Aya helped to unroll the straw mats upon which the people would sleep that night.

Gerrie produced a lidded bucket from his two-wheeled cart. When he removed the lid and revealed the contents, several people exclaimed their joy. "Olives! Pickled olives!"

Aya ducked aside from the rapidly forming line of children and others, making her way sideways to where her companion and his friend loitered by the firepit. As she approached, Thedgollas excused himself to go check on securing the oxen teams for the night.

Shadboyut strolled away toward the olive bucket but winked at Aya to follow. She balled her hands into fists; how could she get him alone? *I have so many things to tell you!*

He strolled up behind the larger man and, while puffing his pipe, remarked, "I need to say that I've been feeling disappointed in you, Gerrie, all afternoon."

"Is that so, Shad?"

"You spoke so unkindly of Maman, y'know, I felt it was rude. Not like you at all. But now, well, I can't be annoyed with you for very long. We're friends, yeah?"

"Yeah, of course we are. Have some olives?"

"Thanks!" Shadboyut looked back over his shoulder at her. "Aya, come closer and have some of his olives. He knows some secrets of flavoring the brine that are—"

"No, thank you," she said.

"Oh, you can't say no."

Aya touched his fringed sleeve at the elbow. "Come with me. I have things to tell you."

"Things? What things?"

He drew a deep inhale from his pipe. Fire glowed deep in the dry weed. Bright specks floated upwards on the smoke. Each tiny ember flickered and lingered above his hand. They hovered like fireflies and, the longer Aya looked at them, she saw little eyes on each one. *Play with us! Play with us!* Small voices whispered in her thoughts.

Shadboyut yanked the pipe out of his mouth. "Mercy! What is that!"

"You saw them too?" Aya whispered.

He waved his hands as if to brush away gnats, but the embers remained floating near his face. They lingered, drifting in obedience to the shifting angle of his wrists.

Gerrie tilted his head, frowning in such a way that warned her to be cautious.

She pulled at Shadboyut's sleeve fringe, leading him away from the group that had gathered to partake of the bucket of olives. She led him back to the center of the clearing, to the firepit where a hearty bloom of flames crackled high in constant motion like a maiden's hair blowing in the wind. The hiss of the brightness called to her in words that were not words, an alluring song that tempted her to issue a command. Fire was restless. It craved release from its confinement in the fuel; it wanted to dance and play.

"Do you still see them?" she asked.

Shadboyut opened his palm, flattened and facing upward. "Since I was a child, I've heard the legends of fire sprites, but no one has ever seen them. I never believed they were real."

At his invitation, a sparkling cluster of embers drifted off the tips of the highest flames. The cluster came to him, answering his unspoken call. Like a dandelion's fluff floating backward, the embers hovered above his outstretched palm. In that moment, the constant ringing fell silent deep within Aya's inner ears. Instead, her skull echoed the tone of the flame's droning hum.

"How can this be?" he whispered.

A warmth like being deeply kissed spread over her and through her core. She closed her eyes and drank in the heat. Voices in the flames whispered, *Yes! Let's play!*

Gerrie clapped Shadboyut on the back. "Hey!"

The cluster scattered into a spray of yellow-orange specks that glittered off in all directions. The droning hum within Aya's inner ears dissipated. The incessant chiming of the blight returned.

Shadboyut grinned and breathlessly blinked. "Did you see that, too? I think they were fire sprites like in the old legends."

"Hush, hush," Gerrie said. "Keep your voice down. Don't let the others hear."

"Why? Why not? This is incredible!"

Aya added, "I need to speak with you alone, Shad. There is so much to tell you."

Gerrie clamped both of his hands to each of their shoulders. "Not now, child. Not yet. Not here."

Shadboyut backed out of the man's grip. "Why so dour? Aren't you excited to see it?"

"I've seen them before." The blunt sharpness of Gerrie's tone stifled whatever the man was about to say.

"You have? When? You never told me."

People began to gather around the fire, bringing their little tin pots and circles of flatbread to roast on rocks and skewers of sausage to toast.

Always keeping an arm's length of distance, they politely took turns in cooking their servings of food.

Gerrie drew the two aside, past the edge of the fire's glow. Leading them away from the group, he said nothing until they reached the gnarled roots of a large tree.

"Listen to me, Shad, the fire sprites are full of mischief. They are not to be played with! They might be useful if you can coax them into behaving. They may serve you in a time of need. Be careful what you ask them to do. Remember, they are capricious and jealous. Now that you've invited the embers to play, I strongly advise you to give no attention to the elemental sprites that dwell in waters or stone or wood. Now that they've taken a liking to you, it's the fire sprites who will dog your heels for the rest of your days."

"Thank you," Aya said. "It's sage advice. We will honor your wisdom."

Shadboyut's eyes darted rapidly from Gerrie's face to hers, back and forth. "Mercy! What stories have the two of you been sharing all afternoon?"

"Hush, hush," he said again. "Not now. Not here."

A small child toddled up to Gerrie's side. "I swallowed an olive pit! Is a tree going to grow in my belly?"

Gerrie sank down to one knee and looked the child straight in the eye. "No, it won't. Have no fear, child."

"I love you, Friend Gerrie." The child puckered up to kiss the air and then, happily, ran off to join the others at the fireside.

Aya reflected on what he had said earlier about being over nine hundred years old. She wondered how it must feel to watch the cycles of generations pass by. She imagined watching babies grow into adults who aged and died. This small act of kindness to the child must have been repeated countless times. She saw in the weary slump of his shoulders the hopelessness and loneliness of a solitary man.

Gerrie walked back in the direction of the firepit where more people gathered in the light. "I'm going to have some supper."

"Is that you're going to tell me?" Shadboyut called out to the man's back as Gerrie walked away. "Tease half a story and then close the curtains?"

"Please, let him go," she said. "We should find a quiet place to ourselves where I can tell you everything. I've been trying to catch you alone all day!"

"I need a smoke." Shadboyut tightened his fist around the bowl of his pipe. "I need to be alone. I'll find you later."

She turned her back to the fire and watched him walk into the darkness. Air turned cold as the distance between them increased. Fighting the temptation to sprint into the moonlit shadows, Aya closed her eyes and focused on her own rapid heartbeat. Gradually, she calmed the tempo of her breathing. She knew that if she ventured blindly into the darkness, she could easily find him. She sensed how far he had walked before sitting by himself on a log. She caught the faint odor of his pipe's lavender weed burning.

A few twinkling embers flew out of the group's campfire. Traveling on the night air, they swirled above Aya's head. She waved them off like gnats. "Let him have his peace," she scolded the floating sparkles.

* * *

The two chose a place to lay out their straw mats at a spot far away from the others who encircled the campsite's firepit. A pair of large trees with roots entwined blocked them from view. Even so, they were careful to leave a gap between their mats and left an arm's length distance. They lay down facing each other. In the moonlit darkness, underneath the canopy of trees, Shadboyut's face appeared gray.

Aya told him what she had been burning to share, that the story Gerrawgon had told was actually true. She explained how he carried the shining soul of a hatchling creature inside the marrow of his bones, that he had walked the earth for over nine hundred years, and that he was very lonely.

"Lonely, you say?" Shadboyut responded. "I'm feeling more annoyed with him, the selfish clod, than I was before."

"Why?"

"He shared these secrets with you on the first day you met! I've known him for over twelve years..." His voice trailed off and he fell silent.

Aya saw the flicker of his eyes and assumed he was thinking, at that moment, of how many years he had known the man. *He's beginning to understand and believe it now. After a decade or more, the man he knew as a friend has not aged a day. He appears younger than he should be to anyone with an unbiased eye.*

"He wasn't eager to share his secret, Shad. It's only because I told him about my dreams. He knows all about the mysteries of ancient days! He knew the Matron of the Calendar and her faithful companion the Man of the Forest during their lifetimes, as he is speaking to us now. Can you imagine? Isn't it wonderful? He taught me about my spirit soaring into dreams, that it was the same with Mullind'groth."

"Who?"

"The Man of the Forest! That was his name, but it's been lost in the retelling of the stories over the centuries."

"Oh, mercy be on us." Shadboyut rolled onto his back and gazed up at the starry sky through the pine branches.

"I believe he must feel some of the loneliness I felt in the village," she said. "Although I had friends and felt at home, I was like a black goat in a herd of white sheep. Your people are wonderful, Shad, so welcoming and accepting. Even so, I wonder how they would feel if they knew the truth of who he is."

"He never gave us the chance." Shadboyut yawned. "Lying, selfish clod."

"You're tired." She stretched out her arm and brushed her fingertips along his cheek. Despite his end-of-day prickly stubble, his skin was buttery soft. "Don't be angry at him. We're keeping secrets from them, too."

"Mmm," he grunted. "Yeah but... but... Oh, mercy on us."

She pulled the edge of the upper blanket over her head, like the hood of a cloak, and settled in to sleep.

* * *

In the dream, her spirit flew westward to the seashore and continued across the endless deep waters. She arrived at a distant land and plummeted into a wild meadow of dry, pale weeds. In daylight, the sun shined harshly on the land. No clouds broke the smooth serenity of blue sky above.

Aya turned toward the sound of honeybees buzzing. She saw a row of small storage boxes set on stilts. Beyond, up a gravel footpath, there stood a cottage built of round blue-and-yellow river stones and a roof of blue clay tiles. The style of the cottage was unlike anything Aya had ever seen before. Wooden planks, not terra cotta flagstones, formed a porch.

A woman sat in the shade underneath an awning made of animal hides stretched across a framework of poles, much like the canopies of the traveling peddlers' wagons. The woman held a swaddled infant to her bosom. One tiny fist broke free and patted the woman's throat. The infant's jaw flexed to suckle the milk from its mother's breast.

Slowly, reverently, Aya approached the scene that a few months earlier would have been overlooked as utterly ordinary.

The woman raised her gaze for a moment, away from admiring the infant at her breast. "Hush, hush, he's almost asleep."

Who are you? Aya's spirit asked.

"My name is Flessandra. Who are you?"

You're Shad's mother.

When the woman smiled, Aya saw the family resemblance in the shape of her wide mouth and the twinkle in her eye.

"What a mercy, I'm so glad my lil' Shadboyut's found his one pure love."

Love? But I've only known him for less than a week. Aya's spirit withdrew a step.

Flessandra cuddled the infant more closely to her breast and, rocking slightly, began to sing. "I am your mother, and you are my child. Through a hundred summers, and through a hundred winters, I will always know you as mine." The melody line was simple enough with a few notes that rose and fell in a repetitive pattern.

Where are you now? Aya wished to know.

The woman made a shoo-shoo gesture with her hand as if swatting away a fly. Aya's spirit soared backward and away. All the while, as she streaked across the sky and the sea, the melody of the woman's song echoed in her memories.

Sixteen

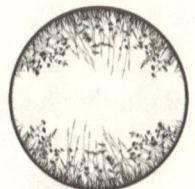

DAMP LINEN COVERED HER FACE. The scent of grass and soil and tree bark seeped through the coarse fibers. When she drew the first inhale of the morning, Aya's chest ached to re-inflate after not being able to move in her sleep. How long did a dream last, she wondered. How long was her spirit floating outside of her body? The now-familiar sensations rushed in—the crushing headache, the dry cake of soreness in the back of her throat, and the tingling prickles in her toes. Again, she took a breath; again, her ribs seemed to creak like old wooden boards within her chest.

"Ah, there she is." Shadboyut rested his gloved hand across her belly. Two layers of skirts, a wool tunic, and a leather belt muffled his touch. The weight of his palm gave some comfort as she labored to breathe in a more regular rhythm.

"I've heard that valley dwellers do not fare well sleeping under the stars," said a man's voice that Aya recognized as Thedgollas. "But I've never seen such a frail traveler."

"She's not frail, Thed. She just, uh, sleeps very deeply." He removed his hand from her belly.

Aya rolled onto her side to face away from him. Using her elbow, she pushed herself off the ground. Head bowed, her cloak's hood and the shawl still shrouded her head and shoulders. Being halfway sitting up helped her breathe easier but the throbbing headache gave her waves of nausea that rose and fell. She gulped on bile that burned that back of her throat.

Another person approached and kneeled by her side. They set down a tin cup and a half walnut shell on the edge of the straw mat. "I ground up some of the willow bark into a powder. Take a pinch under your tongue."

Aya followed the directions and washed it down with the honey-ginger infusion. The throbbing in her forehead began to ease. She sat more upright and let the shawl drop away from her face.

"My thanks." Warm water had a spoonful of honey and some grated ginger root swirling at the bottom of the cup. The first swallow hurt. The next gulp hurt less.

Aya squinted at light shining through the fringe-like pine trees and realized the height of the sun's angle in the sky. Dawn had come at least an hour ago. Already, the peddlers had eaten a morning repast, rolled up their sleeping mats, and wiped and shaved their faces. Now they worked hooking up the oxen to the harnesses. Not long, they would be rolling out of the clearing to resume their journey following the wagon road to the next village.

Thedgollas leaned in nearer to Shadboyut's side. The fringes of their garments touched even if they could not.

Y'know, Shad, you don't have to go trekking up the mountainside. I wish you'd stay with me."

"I would like that too, Thed, but I made a commitment to Aya."

"I've missed you, Shad."

"Me too."

A long pause lingered between the two men. They breathed softly and slowly while staring into each other's' eyes.

"Our trails will cross again, Thed," Shadboyut said in a gentle tone. "Look, we'll go uphill as far as the trading post and hopefully meet some mountain people to make arrangements for receiving the remains of their kinfolk. That's all she wants to do is give her mother's bones a proper burial in the place of her birth. A couple of weeks, at most."

"A couple weeks... You promise?"

"I promise, Thed."

Thedgollas stood up smoothly by rising off his crossed ankles. Shadboyut watched him stroll away to rejoin the others preparing the wagons for the road.

Once they were alone, he said, "You're still pale in the cheeks, Aya. This... These visions are taking a toll on you."

"Life takes a toll," she whispered. "It serves no use to complain. I can endure a few headaches. My dreams are too important."

He leaned closer to her shoulder. "What did you see?"

One last gulp and the gritty pulp of ginger tingled in her throat. "I saw your mother."

"Where?"

"I figure it must have been a vision of days gone past. She was young... Well, not exactly young but younger than she would be now. I'm not sure of the place. It was far away and not familiar, across a large body of water."

"Has to be the Twin Sisters Lakes to the east," he said while gazing thoughtfully across Aya's shoulder. "Clearly that puts her in Blue Heron Valley where I was born. Yes, she and my papa's wagon often traveled in the east."

"Perhaps I lost my sense of direction." In her dream, Aya recalled soaring westward and across the Endless Sea but that made no sense. A wagon-riding, traveling peddler woman could not have traversed the deep, uncharted waters that spanned to the horizon of the sky. Even the coastal fishermen did not venture their boats too far from shore.

Aya looked straight into his eyes. "She was so happy, unaffected by the blight. On her lap, she suckled an infant."

"Me?"

"It must have been. She sang a song, 'I am your mother, and you are my child. Through a hundred summers, and through a hundred winters, I will always know you as mine.'"

Shadboyut smiled. "Oh yes, Maman used to sing that to help soothe me into sleep. I used to be afraid of being in the dark or getting lost. Her song always made me feel brave."

Their faces were so close that Aya could smell the lingering scent of porridge and raisins and barley tea on his breath. Though he had the cheekbones of a man, and a fuzz of unshaved stubble along his jawline, his smile brightened the youthful twinkle of his eyes. It was not hard to imagine him as a small boy afraid of the darkness.

"You understand, don't you? I know that what I see in my dreams is true. Everything that I've seen is true."

"Yes." He fingered the pipe stuck in his belt. "I believe you."

"I'm sorry about your father."

"Thanks."

Aya looked beyond the tree trunks at the rising grassy slope. "The answers are up there, in the heights, in that crystal cave. No matter the hardship, we must try to find the source of this blight. We can do it—you and me. We can fix the pains of the world. When you meet your.... your, uh, friend next time, you will be able to embrace him once more."

He looked aside wistfully. "I look forward to that."

* * *

Aya hurried around the outskirts of the wagon circle and sliced useful mushrooms that grew on the sides of trees. She stretched her arms up as high as she could reach to gather as much and as many as she could while the travelers made ready to roll out of the campsite. She rushed from one lofty tree trunk to the next.

"Wait, wait!" she cried out. Aya brought what she had collected, holding up the hem of her outer skirt with one hand. She delivered the pile of orange, purple, and yellow buttons to the tailgate of the wagon. "They're called wood-gizzards, child's cap, and sun butter. Delicious in soup or fold them into toasted flatbreads. It's my gift to you... My thanks."

"May our trails cross again soon," said the elder who had tended to her blister on the first day they met.

"Yes, I hope so." Aya smiled warmly.

Gerrawgon tapped her elbow from behind. She startled, unaware he had strolled so closely. The ground was well trampled in that spot where the wagons had parked. His flat-soled boots made no sound on the moist soil.

"Come walk with me, child."

Aya said her last goodbyes to the group of peddlers before she turned away and followed the man. He walked at a brisk pace, effortlessly, with long legs and broad strides. Soon they left behind the circle of wagons and the grove of old-growth trees. They emerged onto the open road.

From that point, the wagon trail forked into three directions. Avenues of possibilities lay at her feet. To the east, the road extended back to the valley from where she had come. To the opposite direction, the wagon road extended through low-lying hills and would eventually end at the seashore. A third path rose sharply uphill to the north and, by the oxen-sized boulders and lack of wheel ruts, that was the path less traveled.

Gerrawgon's two-wheeled cart was already packed and ready to roll. Ropes secured the lid of the cedar chest. Baskets dangled from knotted cords at the sides.

Aya asked, "Are you coming with us to the mountains?"

"No," Gerrie said.

"Why? Why not? We need you—"

"No. Stop. I'm walking with the caravan and there's no argument you can make to change my mind."

"But—"

Gerrie held up his hand, palm forward. "Shush."

Aya bit the corner of her lip.

"I have some things to give you, though." From one of his wicker baskets, he brought forth a blue kerchief tied into a knot. He held it forth and Aya received the bundle from beneath, being careful not to brush his fingers with her own.

She kneeled on the ground to work the knots loose. Then, spreading the kerchief open, she beheld the assortment of tools. Two items were familiar. A steel knife with a thick blade was packed tightly into a leather sheath. A tinder box was well stocked with dry moss and charred rags. The other two items perplexed her. A flat-bottomed wooden cup contained a tarnished silver spoon with a small bowl and a long handle. As she held the cup in her palm, the spoon's handle rotated.

"The tip of the spoon's handle will always point south," he said.

"Is it enchanted with the spirits of the earth?" she asked.

"No, it's called a lodestone. It won't speak to you. It won't do tricks for you. It simply functions as reliably as the grindstone of a mill."

Aya picked up the last item in the kerchief, a silver fork with two long prongs. "What is this? It's too short and blunt for a cooking tong."

He sank down to one knee at her side. "Allow me to show you."

She withdrew her hands to a safe distance for him to reach over and pick it up. Gerrie tapped the prongs against his kneecap. Then he held the blunt end of the fork's handle against a flat rock on the ground. A single tone hummed out of the prongs. The purity of the note prickled her skin and quickened her heart. The metal sang more clearly than any human voice could ever achieve.

He grasped the prongs and the tone fell silent. "I've crafted a few dozen of these over the years. To my surprise, there are not many who appreciate the value. Balladeers are too often offended at the suggestion they need a clear tone to start."

"It's beautiful," she said. "Thank you."

Footsteps padded up the grassy slope from behind. Even before he spoke, Aya knew that it was her companion drawing near. The cadence of his steps and the tapping of his sleeve's long fringes against the wicker basket he carried on his back belonged to no other man.

"Beautiful tool but useless," Shadboyut said. "I'm still carrying one of your singing forks that you gave me years ago, remember?"

"Oh, did I give one to you?" Gerrie stood up to face the approaching man.

"Of course I don't expect you to remember. It must be hard to keep it all straight in your head, who you've met, what items you've gifted or traded, after nine hundred gods-accursed years!"

Gerrie looked down at Aya with a frown of deep disappointment. "You told him."

"We have no secrets between us." Still kneeling on the ground, she worked to tie up the kerchief bundle.

"Yes, she told me!" Shadboyut craned back his neck to look up at the taller man. "The woman I met less than a week ago tells me things that you, my friend, have concealed. After all the years we've walked together, all the meals we've shared, all the stories we've exchanged, and what a shock to discover that you're treating me like a stranger."

"You *are* all strangers." His eyes darted side to side to be sure that no one else was within earshot. Nonetheless, he lowered the volume of his voice to a whisper. "Think of it, Shad, if I had revealed my true origin story on the first day we met, you might have felt awe or curiosity or fear. Would you have worshipped me as a star-god fallen out of the sky? Would you have shunned me or hunted me as an abomination of the netherworld? Would you have sliced my skin to see if I bleed the color red?"

"I don't know." Shadboyut practically growled through gritted teeth. "But you never gave me a chance."

"I've given too many chances to too many people. It has never gone well. So, I've settled on a routine. I count the years on the calendar very carefully. I wait for anyone who knows my face to finish their lifetime before I wander back to the same roads again. All too often, I have pretended to be my own son or my own grandson. And the cycle continues again and again. When I've stayed with any group more than fifteen summers at the most, I depart and move elsewhere."

"Eleven or twelve years," Shadboyut said thoughtfully. "That's about how long we've known each other."

"Just about." He hooked a thumb in his belt. "Mercy be on us both, Shad but you're clearly starting to look older than I appear to be."

Shadboyut scratched the stubble at his own chin. "So, my friend, this means you're leaving and won't return?"

"Yes."

Aya stood up. "I asked him to join our journey to the mountain and he said no."

"Selfish lying cod," Shadboyut said. "Immortal or not, we don't need him. C'mon, Aya, let's be off."

She hesitated, feet unwilling to move, heartbeat unwilling to withdraw from this man's presence. How lonely it must be, she thought, to live for so many centuries as a vagabond without a home.

On impulse, she reached out to Gerrie's hand that hung by the thumb hooked in his belt. She laid her palm across his knuckles in a gesture that, before the blight, would have been a welcome act of compassion.

Sharp hot spikes of pain raked up her forearm, penetrating up through her bicep and turning her shoulder numb. Gerrie jumped backward a few steps. Crying out in the agony, he hunched forward letting his affected arm dangle loosely.

"By th' fires, child, why did you do that?" Gerrie growled.

"So reckless and careless," Shadboyut agreed. "How could you?"

Aya blinked away the tears of pain dribbling out of her eyes. Yet she drew her spine up, tall and forthright, frowning to work at the puzzle. "I hoped that...you being what you are..."

"I told you, child, I'm suffering with it the same as you." Gerrie flexed his gray fingertips that were beginning to return to their normal brown color.

"Forgive me but I had hope it wasn't only the two of us."

"Clearly it is," Gerrie grumbled with his eyes still closed. "It will always be just the two of you, in everything."

Aya brushed her knuckles to the back of Shadboyut's hand and felt only the warmth of his skin. "Now I am certain that the answers lie in the crystal cave in the mountainside. Only Shad and I have explored deep into that cavern—he as a child and I in my mother's womb. We drank the waters that trickled off the glistening walls. We breathed the air that glowed bright green in the shadows. Something in that cave infused us both, as children, with an anti-venom to the chime that afflicts everyone else."

"Interesting." Gerrie opened his eyes. "Yes, that's a good chain of thought. But remember that the cave poisoned both of your parents."

Shadboyut bowed his head forward.

Gerrie added, "The mountain people have forbidden anyone to enter that cave. It's been so many centuries they've forgotten the real reason why. They tell legends that grow more ridiculous with each generation but at the core of those myths is a tiny seed of truth. It's certain death to go there, for anyone..."

The caravan of wagons was rolling out of the campsite and taking to the road. The oxen drivers called out, "Ho! Ho!"

"...anyone but the two of you, children." Gerrie picked up the poles of his two-wheeled cart. "If there are star-gods watching over us, may their light guide your feet."

"And yours as well," Aya said. "We're going to fix it all, you'll see! Don't give up hope. Be strong."

Shadboyut said, "Our paths may yet cross again."

"Perhaps." Gerrie started walking, pulling his two-wheeled cart behind. "If you survive this foolish quest, you may track me down in your dreams."

Seventeen

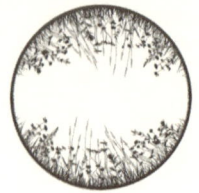

TO MAKE WALKING EASIER, Aya pulled up the rear hemline of her long skirt between her legs. She tucked a handful of russet and blue linen into the front of her belt. Now the ankle-length hooded cloak was her longest free-swinging garment. The sling carrying her mother's funeral urn hung comfortably at her left hip.

They walked followed a well-worn road that had not been used for some time. Two parallel rows of wagon ruts had a row of green grass sprouted up the center. Aya kept up Shadboyut's steady pace. Her new soft-soled boots felt like a second layer of her own feet. Her heels sprang easily off the soft ground.

Springtime weather was clear and cool. Humidity of the previous day's rain lingered in the air. The two walked easily up the gentle slope of the wagon road leading first to the northwest. Higher up on the hillside, Aya could see where the road turned a switchback and turned northeast.

"Must we follow the wagon road?" she asked. "We could save time by going straight up the hill like goats."

"I feared you might get weary too soon if we climb over rocks and hop gullies. You've never been so far outside the village."

Aya turned off the wagon road into the tall grass and challenged him to follow. "I have walked, Shad! I've walked from my cottage to the village to the woods and from one farmhouse to the next in a day. Just because I've walked in circles, instead of a straight line, doesn't mean that I'm a caged hen with no strength in her legs."

"My apologies." He hoisted the shoulder straps of the large wicker basket on his back. Pumping his knees, he plunged into the waist-high fronds of wild lettuce, cheesecloth lace, yellow and white mustard, and blooming dandelions.

"I wish Gerrie had come with us," Aya said. "I'm sure there's so much more he could teach us. Think of it! What wisdom he must have gained in nine hundred years of walking the earth."

"I'm glad he's not with us. Lying, selfish clod. Whatever wisdom he's got, well, he's keeping it locked up in his head. He's a storyteller so he won't be rushed to reveal the conclusion too soon. Oh no, no, you've got to listen to the whole gods-forsaken narrative that he morsels out piece by piece, word by word, and waits for his audience to respond before he goes on to the next scene."

They climbed up a bank of sandstone boulders that were like the steppingstones of a staircase from the crumbled remains of a giant's house.

"Or he skips over the best parts of a story entirely, like he did in that telling of the Folly of Gromm the Giant. He did a shoddy job of that one, by the by. I've heard him perform that tale many a time before. The telling could have lasted for several hours and fill up the time walking on the road but no.... Oh no, he only tells what he feels like telling and not what the listener needs to hear."

"Please don't waste your breath being angry," she said. "There's no good to come of railing at a man who isn't here. As my Mamma used to say, '*Dh'ggn th'molrk*'... There's no need to complain."

"Damn it all to the garbage fires of eternity," Shadboyut said.

"Let's not talk about him anymore. What's behind us is behind us."

"Agreed."

They topped the stack of boulders and came to a shallow creek that trickled over flat black rocks. Shadboyut bent over to fill his water jug.

"The last time I came up here was before..." His words trailed off into wistful silence and paused.

Aya nodded to show that she understood. *Before the chime struck.*

"After last year's autumn harvest, a few of us including Papa transported a collection of wares from the village at Fuller's Mill up to the trading post. We made some good exchanges with another group of wagons that came from the seashore. I remember trading skeins of dyed wool for sacks of dried seaweed."

"Seaweed?" she repeated.

"Yes, they had five or six different kinds of dried weeds that were harvested from the ocean's shallows. Very good in soups."

They carefully picked their steps to cross the ankle-deep rushing waters. Aya managed to avoid trampling on a flurry of tadpoles in the hollow between two larger rocks. Sunlight glistened off the flowing creek and, in the sparkles, she glimpsed tiny eyes that floated freely, unattached to natural bodies. *Be careful,* she remembered Gerrie's warning. *Fire sprites are capricious and jealous. Now that you've invited the embers to play, I strongly advise that you give no attention to spirits that dwell in the waters or stone or wood.*

Shadboyut continued talking. "It's not even a full cycle of seasons but it feels like half a lifetime has passed."

They continued up the hillside and crossed the switchback of the wagon road. Aya glanced back across her shoulder and judged that they had, indeed, saved considerable time. From this height, gazing down the slopes to the broad vista of the valleys and the distant horizons broken by other mountains to the south, it felt as familiar as the village where she had spent her entire life.

"Shad, this is the path where my soul flew. This is the place I have seen without ever having walked here before."

"Then you must know, at the crest after the next switchback is a fallen oak tree. It's a good shady place to rest and have a midday meal."

Aya raised her chin to the course ahead. "I'm not sure. It all flew by so quickly. My spirit was adrift like a plum blossom on the wind."

"Can't you control where you go or what you see?"

"No."

"Perhaps you need practice. Let's see where you go tonight?"

Aya kept walking, kept putting one foot in front of the other but lagged behind his pace as her mind filled with thoughts and questions. They walked single file, now, with him leading the way.

She wondered but had no answers for why her spirit had taken her to the scene of Flessandra nursing her infant son. The dream of a day thirty years in the past seemed to have no purpose, no meaning, no relevance to their urgent goal of saving the world. What did the dream show her that Shad did not already know? His mother was a honey gatherer, so it was no revelation that farmed a hive of honeybees in boxes. His mother was warm-hearted and loving, who sang lullabies to her child so he would not fear getting lost in the dark. Nothing was a surprise. Nothing was new.

Perhaps it was meant to inspire her to recall the happier days of long ago and what people had lost from suffering under the blight. She told herself, *we can have those happier days again, if we find the source and put an end to the pain of touch.* The constant background ringing in her ears muted the chirping of songbirds and the buzzing of insects. She held out hope that, once they reached the crystal cave in the mountains, they would find a way to fix all the world's problems.

At a fallen oak tree, they sat down together in the shade. Aya had not realized her legs were throbbing with the hours of walking until she stopped to rest. They ate a mixture of walnuts, raisins, dried figs, purple carrots, and cold sausages.

Shadboyut fingered his un-lit pipe. "Do you think if I built a fire, the sprites would come?"

"Not now," she said. "We don't have time to play with them. How far is it to the trading post?"

"We can make it by sunset if we keep going at the pace we've been going." He laid his hand on her knee. "We have a little bit of time to... to rest?"

The nearness of his body aroused a rush of warmth. She hugged the urn of her mother's ashes and reminded herself of the important mission ahead. Be strong. Be strong.

"We should keep walking," she said hoarsely.

"Hmm, yeah." He leaned in closer to breathe deeply the scent of her hair and skin. "I can't be sure if I'm feeling admiration or frustration at your restraint. If I listen to my urges and draw you into my arms here, I would not want to continue walking for next several hours. I would wish to revel in your skin until the sun drops below the hills, until the moon rises, and until the stars gaze down at the two of us entangled in the joy of each other's touch. It's just been so long... So long..."

Words formed in her mind. *It has only been a few months since winter turned into spring.* Aya held back from speaking her sensible thoughts. Her heart, her bones, and her soul ached in a timeless quagmire that knew nothing of how to count the days on the calendar. One day felt like one hundred days under the suffering of the blight.

Aya hooked her hand behind the nape of his neck. "We can spare a little time for a kiss?"

"Yeah." He grinned as he brought his face closer. "Just a quick kiss, eh."

Their mouths joined and their arms coiled around each other. A quick kiss turned longer and deeper, impossible to separate. Time melted away in surrendering to the moment. All that mattered was the touch and the taste of each other's skin.

* * *

Sunset passed and faded into twilight by the time they finally arrived at the trading post. A rocky plateau was the first step in a series of ascending levels that textured the foothills of the higher mountains. From this point, the earth sloped upwards to the sparse timber line and granite boulders rocks beyond. In the background, slanted pyramids of blue mountains cut off half the sky. Streaks of never-melting snow marbled the tips of conical peaks. This was the edge of the civilized lands. Only renegades and the most adventurous of traveling peddlers came to this point.

On either side, a wagon road leading up to the trading post had a retaining wall of gray blocks long ago buried and covered with silty mud and overgrown with thickly rooted rosemary bushes.

Shadboyut explained, "The legends say that in ancient times, another group of people once lived in these foothills. They built a circle of colossal obelisks and worshipped the burned gods. They sang hymns to the stars of the night. They had some among them they called..."

Aya waited for him to finish the thought until she had to prompt, "Called what?"

"Prophets," he said, practically choking on the word. "They called them prophets. They claimed to see dreams of things. Oh, mercy on us. Can the stories be true? Have there been more like you?"

"Like Eiyallandra and her Man of the Forest," she said. "Gerrie told me."

"The lying selfish clod, he's the one who taught me those legends. He knew! He might have known the ancient stone circle people as well as he knows you and me. The accursed sod knew all of this, all the time, and he never—"

"Hush, we're getting close." Aya quickened her pace to cover the remaining ground leading up to the doorstep of the trading post.

The shingled old wooden building was painted bright green. Weathering had peeled the cracked paint to reveal older layers of yellow paint beneath. Round river rocks encircled the foundation. Moss grew thick on the north side's shingles. Behind the eastern side of the building, a pine tree soared at least three times higher than the roof. The tree's thick roots warped the joists of the lopsided porch.

Storage sheds were guarded by a pair of burly men in broad-brimmed hats. They carried whips coiled on their shoulders as they sauntered back and forth in front of the porch.

"Ignore them," Shadboyut advised. "Keep walking. Don't want them to think we're thieves giving eyes to the layout."

"Do we look like thieves?" she asked.

He shrugged. "Anybody can be a thief. Be careful, Aya, for you aren't in your village anymore."

Together, they ascended the broad flagstones of the doorstep. Shadboyut turned the door's iron latch and pushed the oaken planks inward on well-oiled hinges. Narrow windows held honeycomb panes of glass disks, darkened to a deep shade of purple by the passing of years. The glass windows let in the orange colors of sunset but not enough light to illuminate the floor.

Aya blinked a few times for her eyes to adjust to the dim interior.

Ceiling beams resembled thick branches of old-growth trees overhead. Smells and sounds told her more of the room's contents than her eyes could see. Bitter spices—anise, cinnamon, pepper, cardamom—clashed with garlands of savory herbs and garlic bulbs hanging from the rafters. Smoked pork, smoked venison, and smoked fish were on hooks near barrels full of dried barley, spelt, millet, buckwheat, and pink lentils. Olives and shredded cabbage floated in jugs of brine. Wool blankets, folded on a bench, still reeked of animal musk. Lamp oil, iron tools, and leather belts cluttered the shelves that jutted out from the wall. All the material riches of a village marketplace were contained here, minus the singsong of hawkers in the streets.

Shadboyut led the way to the center of the broad room. A hub of tables arranged in a semi-circle was the throne of the trading post's master. She was a matronly woman with long, curly hair turned gray. She wore a thin knitted shawl of delicate threads that formed designs of flower blossoms and birds' wings in a monochrome tapestry that spread across her broad back. Aya marveled at the craftsmanship; she had never seen such intricate patterns in a garment. Short fringe tipped with white beads dangled past her hips.

A candle flickered near her elbow. Left-handed, she wrote neatly in a ledger book a record of inventory and the latest trade. By the sag of her shoulders and the forward thrust of her neck, she had not moved from her stool for hours, if not all day.

"Hello," said Aya as the matron did not look up from her ledger book. "We'd like to—"

Shad interrupted, "Lace, my dear friend, it's so good to see you again! How goes the exchange today?"

"Shad, you bog-dweller, I haven't forgotten what you owe."

With a broad smile widening his mouth, he set down his wicker. "Yes, yes, Lace, of course, I haven't forgotten either. Your hospitality is much appreciated."

"I don't offer hospitality." Lace grumbled, still not looking up from whatever she was writing in her ledger book.

"Of course, of course." Shadboyut produced an oxen's horn capped with a cork. "I bring you a horn full of pink salt granules. The best salt in the—"

"I have too many sacks of salt. What else do you have?"

"Uh..." He rummaged deeper into his basket. "An abalone shell? It's pretty."

Lace extended her right palm to receive the shell. Silvery rainbow colors shined from the inside of the bowl-shaped crust. "Perhaps but it's not quite enough. What else do you have?"

Shadboyut glanced sideways at Aya for a moment, as if asking permission but then forged ahead. He pulled out the silver prongs of a singing fork, a twin of the tool that Gerrie had given to her.

"Watch this." He tapped the prongs on the table and flipped them over to press the tip of the handle into the boards. A clear tone hummed into the wood. Aya shivered at the purity of it and glimpsed little eyes awakening in the crevasses of the wood grain.

"Oh," Lace said. "You must have crossed trails with Gerrawgon, the ol' slog. He's traded three or four of these tools to me over the years. They don't sell very well. Most balladeers don't like using them."

Aya briefly wondered how many years it had been since Gerrie had traveled as far north as the trading post. Perhaps that was one reason why he had not wished to accompany them on this trek.

"Yes, it's one of Gerrie's all right." He smiled even more broadly. "Will you accept it, Lace? Are we square?"

"For both the shell and the singing fork, we are."

"Great! You're the best."

"Uh-huh," she grunted.

"May I ask if you've seen my papa? He's wandered off a few months back—"

"Yeah, ol' Zhard came through here sometime before winter fell. He paid me with a sack of fennel seeds and nutmeg kernels. My boys fashioned him a leg brace. I told him it was suicide to hike up the mountain with the frost of winter coming on, but he didn't listen."

Shadboyut asked, "Did he ever come back down?"

"Nope, unless he came back some other way." Lace paused and added more kindly, "May your trails cross again."

"Thanks. Now, my companion and I need a spot in your stone bed for the night."

Lace looked up from her ledger at last. Her eyes were large, broadly spaced, with irises a soft color of mottled hazel green. *She resembles my mother's complexion*, Aya thought as her heart quickened its pace. *She could be blood kin of the mountain people.*

"No more stone bed," Lace said.

"What's that you say?" he asked. "I can see it, right there!"

Aya looked to the far side of the broad room. Her eyes had adjusted to the dim light. A platform of terra-cotta tiles covered a sizable portion of the floor.

He explained rapidly, "You see, Aya, there's a crawl space underneath the floorboards and they slide in smoldering fire logs that make the tiles warm. It's the best night's sleep you'll ever have in these gods-forsaken chilly heights."

"Can't do it," Lace said.

"Why not? There's plenty of space for the two of us. You've got no other visitors!"

"It's only sunset. I might get some stragglers looking for a place to sleep before the first star rises. I'll tell you the same as I tell any traveler, as I've told you all since that night."

Aya lowered her gaze. *That night... when the chime struck.*

"I've got extra tarps," Lace said. "I've got poles and stakes. Go outside and make a leaning shelter on the trees. My sentinels keep watch all night. You won't be bothered by scavenging animals or thieves, I promise."

"But the night's winds will be cold!" he said.

"You can borrow blankets if you give 'em back by morning. Guaranteed free of ticks or fleas."

"Damn it, Lace! Must I beg for kindness?"

"Beg all you like, Shad. This is non-negotiable. My answer is still no."

He gritted his teeth and grunted frustration.

In response, sparkles spewed forth from the tip of the candle's flame. The spray of orange embers danced across the ledger book's page. Lace cried out and slapped them.

"We're sorry!" Aya cried out.

The sparkling embers danced mischievously, avoiding the matron's slapping hands.

"Oh yes, mercy on us, we're sorry to be difficult." Shadboyut gestured with his hand to call the fire sprites away. "We promise to behave. We won't make any more trouble."

Embers swirled beneath the table, out of Lace's line of sight, in a trail like a murmuration of starlings. Aya could still hear the sprites giggling, *let's play again*, as they dispersed into the darkness of the floor.

Eighteen

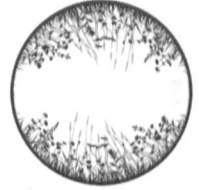

THE TWO OF them crawled together into the tent of canvas tarps. Even with a pair of straw mats, the ground felt cold. Aya worked at housekeeping, spreading out the wool blankets and the pillows stuffed with buckwheat husks. Shadboyut slipped his arm around her waist as he pressed his hips against her skirts.

"Did you hear them, Aya? Did you hear the fire sprites singing and calling us to play?"

"Yes, they nearly set her ledger on fire."

"But we didn't! I called them away! They obeyed me like sheep being herded by a shepherd's stick. Why aren't you excited about what we can do?"

"It's dangerous," she said. "He warned us."

"Oh hush, where would my life's path have taken me if I listened to warnings? I never would have experienced half the pleasures I've found in traveling from one valley to the next. If I didn't follow the group exploring the mountain heights, I never would have known your mother's kindness in saving Papa's life and mine. I never would have met you..."

He squeezed her closer. Despite the coldness of the earth beneath her knees, Aya felt the warmth of her blood rise. She rotated within the circle of his arms and aligned her face with his. From the corner of her eye, she briefly checked to be sure the tent flap was securely staked to the ground. She did not wish for the sentinels of the trading post to know what they were doing inside.

* * *

Hours later, after they had exhausted the urgent callings of their passions, they lay facing each other. Half-dressed and half-undressed, Aya's arms felt numb as she pulled a wool blanket over them both. Shadboyut smiled, although she could not see his face clearly in the darkness; she could hear the change in his tone, the slant of his words spoken with his lips spread wide.

"How can the world survive without this?" he asked.

"It can't," she said. "We must fix it."

"Are you going to sleep now? Are you going to dream?"

"Don't be afraid." She snuggled closer and used his arm as a pillow.

"I'll try not to be. You give me courage." He kissed her one last time in a long, deep, lingering connection as his mouth drank in the warmth of her lips.

Aya sank into sleep while he was still kissing her, and her mind slumbered in the contentment of darkness and ordinary dreams. Her sleeping mind imagined walking on white stone steps that descended downhill to the village from where she had come.

Sleep passed the hours until the morning's light shined outside the canvas tarp. The oiled fabric turned from black to a deep shade of burned gold. Aya drew in her first breath of the morning and smelled the scent of pine trees, wet hair, and the man lying at her side.

He lay with his face and body turned away. As soon as she drew in a breath, though, he asked, "Are you back?"

"I'm awake," she said. "I don't think I had a dream. Well, I mean, I did but it was an ordinary dream."

He rolled onto his back and cast a studious gaze sideways. "No, you still look very much alive. How do you feel?"

"As I usually feel on most any other morning. I don't have a headache. My throat is not so dry."

They sat up together and looked at each other's faces for answers.

"Well," he said. "Perhaps it doesn't happen every night? I'm going to have to try harder to remember the legends of Eiyallandra and her Man o' the Forest. The old stories are not specific on useful details, y'know."

Aya clenched her fists in the blankets. "I need to know where to go, what to do, what happens next. I wish Gerrie had come with us."

"Well, he didn't and here we are. The immortal clod has left us alone to figure out this puzzle by ourselves and, by the burned gods' eyes, we will."

He crawled outside of the tent and stayed away for a short while. When he returned, he brought a lidded flagon of hot apple cider and a kerchief with a couple of hard-boiled chicken eggs. "We're in debt to Lace again."

"Thank you." Aya shared sips of the hot apple cider.

"Her sentinels fell down on the job, by the way. I saw the pair of them sleeping by the stack of firewood. Critters and thieves could've had their run of the place. Things have gotten sloppy since I was last here."

"It's how things are now," she said. "Why should sentinels guard the well-being of others when they feel only pain themselves?"

"Hmm," he grunted thoughtfully while peeling the brown shell off one of the hard-boiled eggs.

"Let's pack up and start walking. The sooner we embark on the mountain trail, the sooner we can find that crystal cave."

"The *forbidden* cave," he reminded her. "Let's hope we don't encounter any mountain people."

Aya rolled up the blankets. "Don't be afraid of them. I can speak their language. I can ask for their hospitality as a kinsman, as you did with your people."

"What do you know of them, from what your mother told you?"

"Very little," she admitted. "Mamma did not speak of her past and she was always so sad if we mentioned the mountains. I know they pride themselves on being strong. They inhabit a harsh environment and hold in contempt the lowland villagers for being weak."

"That's about the limit of what I know, as well. Those are people who cohabitate with big brown bears and wean their babies on the icicles of highland cliffs. Y'know, I've heard stories. All I remember from being a child is how... how... how damned large they were! Tall, brawny, and fierce, they had vicious eyes like no one I had ever seen before. Aho's mate—"

"Her brother," Aya corrected.

"Yeah, that's right, Aho's brother was so full of rage at us trespassing in that cave. I had never been so afraid for my life before that moment. When she saved us by pushing him into the ravine—"

Her thoughts came too quickly to speak aloud. *It all began in that cave and we must journey there to end it. We are the only hope for the world. Help me end it, Shad. Don't be afraid to help me end it.*

Morning sunlight gained strength shining through the canvas. The varying tones of his black hair and brown skin took on new hues of color. A kaleidoscope of orange, red, magenta, pink, purple, and blue swirled in a halo around him that spread between them both. All her senses came alive. Everything on her half of the tent rang in tones of bluish silver. Everything on his side had the scent of greenish gold. The contrasting jewel-like hues merged into a cyclone of glossy filaments, sparkling as if lightning bolts were being spun upon a threader's wheel. At the core where their chests mirrored each other, brightness in a warm wind rushed up from between their knees. A surge of light exhaled from the earth itself. Neither one of them moved, yet Aya felt her flesh lose its solidity. Warmth passed through her as if her skin were a sieve of cheesecloth.

Aya's sense of herself blurred. His dark irises mirrored her own. Whatever existed beyond the rims of their eyelashes no longer mattered. In that instant, he was not a man, and she was not a woman—they simply existed. In a blink, her awareness sank into his eyes, turned about, and looked back at her own narrow face.

* * *

Aya's spirit floated effortlessly above a wagon road made of black marble. She approached a cube-shaped structure that was taller and larger than any building she had ever seen. The honeycomb framework of silver beams was a metallic net that stretched around the mirror-like glass interior.

Her spirit seeped through the glass windows of the sixth floor. Inside, dozens of people in clusters of small groups strolled about in various directions. Some carried brightly colored flasks and sipped chilled beverages. Others chatted, excitedly describing the delights of their last meal, or the meals they looked forward to enjoying that night. Children ran about chasing each other. Parents scolded them to behave.

All the people wore well-cut clothing of a type of thin fabric that Aya could not identify. Men and women donned the same style of loose-fitting trousers and sleeveless shirts. No one bore hooded cloaks or leather belts or walking boots. They wore strange jewelry on their wrists that appeared to be onyx stones but within the gemstones shimmered lettering in an unfamiliar script.

One tall person with flaxen-colored hair called out to a group. "If you'll assemble here on this marked line, the tour is about to begin! Where is everyone from? Don't be shy. Call it out. You, good friend, where have you come from today?"

"Heron Valley," said someone in the crowd.

"I'm from Xol Harbor."

"The peninsula."

"Kakiachak, the Isle of Giants!"

Heads turned. Mouths smiled. A few murmured amongst themselves.

The tour guide exclaimed, "Really? What are you doing on vacation here? This time of year, sipping a spiced cocktail on the beaches of the Isle of Giants is where I'd rather be. But I digress! You're all here today to follow the journey of Aycha and Shedbou and the Crystal Cave of Doom!"

Those aren't our names. Why can't they remember our names? Where am I? How far have I traveled into the realm of days yet to come?

Aya floated along with the group into a corridor. The walls on either side brightened with illumination as they passed each of the panels. One depicted a realistic illustration of her home village as seen from above, as if drawn by the hand of a bird. One showed a diorama of the peddlers' wagons. Other panels showed the village cemetery, the willow tree by the lake, the trading post, and a trail up the mountainside illuminated in fuchsia pink.

Their story was told without poetry or sentiment as a series of facts and bland details. According to the tour guide, the pair of heroes discovered they could touch. They embarked on a journey up the mountainside with the goal of finding the source of the blight. The guide called it "the ancient plague" and gestured briefly in passing to a large diagram of a crab-like creature. A schematic of innumerable lines and symbols overlaid the creature's image. *That is what I saw.* Aya's vaporous hand reached out to the diagram illuminated on the wall panel.

"Thank you for your participation in this tour. You've been great! Now, if any of you bought the premium tickets, you can continue with your choice of immersive experiences. To my left is the virtual reality booth. Through this door to my right is the docking pad of the monorail that will actually take you there! However, as I'm sure it was made clear to you at the time of purchase, for the price of a basic admission ticket, you may only select one."

Someone in the crowd asked, "What if I want to hike up the mountain on foot?"

The tour guide laughed and infected the crowd into chuckling along. "On foot? Oh no, no, my friend, you'd have to purchase a hiking permit and accept the additional cost of renting hazardous environment protective gear. Plus, you'll be required to sign a legal waiver absolving us of any responsibility in case of injury or worse."

"I'll sign it," the fellow insisted. "I'm an experienced outdoorsman."

Aya turned to look at the tall, lanky fellow with high cheekbones and vivid blue eyes. He had shaved his scalp bald and grew out a full bushy beard, as if all the hair had slid off the top of his head to collect at his jaw. He carried a tablet the size of a flatbread made from a single sheet of gold on one side and mirrored glass on the other.

The tour guide waved their hands to herd the crowd through the doorways ahead. "Very well, go talk to my boss in the gift shop."

"Gratitude." The lanky fellow ducked into a branch corridor. Aya followed and then felt someone else walking behind her.

"You're being an idiot, Johel," said the man strolling at Aya's back.

"Why are you always so negative? Why don't you offer more

encouragement as I'm so close to submitting my doctoral dissertation to the academic committee? You are the absolute worst research assistant!"

"You can do your research from the comfort of the monorail car."

"Everyone else does research from their armchairs without ever leaving home. I need to distinguish myself from all the other run-of-the-mines doctoral candidates. I wish to experience how my ancestors lived by putting on my shoes and getting out there!"

"Minus the fleas and head lice, one hopes," his companion quipped.

The so-called gift shop was a reconstruction of the trading post complete with artificial wooden floors, fabricated stone walls, and an assortment of figurines and trademarked keepsakes. Aya floated a short distance away from the two men. She marveled at miniature figurines for sale, figurines of herself in villagers' clothing, of Shadboyut in his fringed jacket, of brightly-colored peddlers' wagons with accessories sold separately, and a gigantic crab molded in a strange sort of unbreakable transparent resin.

"Hello, good morning, excuse me but I heard that you might sell me a trail map for hiking up the mountain to the Crystal Cave of Doom?"

"Sure," said a person wearing an apron. "It's three hundred... Uh, wait, three hundred and fifty, plus the rental of personal protective gear."

"Of course." Johel tapped his onyx wrist pendant on a silver cube on the desk. A green light briefly glimmered.

Aya drifted nearer to peer over the lanky man's shoulder. She saw lines of script scroll by on the tablet in his hand. He was reading it all quickly but thoroughly. At the bottom, when the script ceased rolling, the fellow tapped his thumbprint on the glass.

The screen cleared of script to be replaced by an ink drawing on a sepia tone background. One hiking trail in bright green shined up the center of the image. The contours of the mountain and notable landmarks were clearly marked in purple lines.

"I still say you're being an idiot," said Johel's companion. "Why waste a whole day-and-a-half trudging up the rocky hillside when you can be there by monorail in sixteen seconds?"

"It's the only way to experience real history, Gerrie."

If Aya were not a specter formed of vapor and smoke, she would have gasped. Floating off the floor, she rotated and faced the other man.

Gerrawgon looked to be the same age as when she had left him by the wagon road, or perhaps he was older by a week. He still had wavy brown hair but had trimmed it short above the collarbone. Unlike the other people in the crowd, his close-fitting shirt had short sleeves that reached his elbows. His hands tucked loosely in the side pockets of his pleated trousers with an air of confident strength.

"You can go back to the hotel room by yourself." Johel studied the map on his own mirrored golden tablet. "Order a meal. Watch a few shows. It's all on me, pal."

"Is your tell-it fully charged with battery?" Gerrie asked.

"Yes, of course."

"If you get into any trouble, you won't hesitate to call for a park ranger?"

"Yes, yes, I will." Johel looked up from his tablet. "I wish you'd come with me."

"No."

"Please? I'm sorry for my earlier outburst. You are not the 'absolute worst' research assistant. Truthfully, you take good notes."

"No." Gerrie turned his head to look straight into Aya's eyes. "There is no argument you can make that will convince me to change my mind."

We must have succeeded, Aya said without speaking. *If they are telling our story, then we must have won. But how? Show me, how?*

"You have all the tools you need in your own hands," Gerrie said to her softly. "Trust yourself. You can write your own history. You can make the future true."

Johel's eyes darted back and forth. "Who are you talking to? Are you getting a call on your tell-it?"

"No," Gerrie said. "I'm talking to a ghost."

The lanky fellow broke out laughing. "Oh, you are such a crap-slinger! What stories you tell. I can never stay mad at you."

The immortal chuckled along with his friend even as he snuck one more wink in Aya's direction. The edges of the scene blurred and began to fade into whiteness. Aya's spirit withdrew floating backward out through the glass windows. She dissolved into the winds blowing off the mountainside.

* * *

Tears filled her eyes and clogged her throat. Aya kept her face buried in her naked arms even after she awoke. It took a moment to realize she was still inside the tent, reclined on the straw mat where they had slept the night. Restraining an urge to vomit under the pounding pulse of a headache, she struggled to contain the storm of emotions raging within her.

"Oh, you're back!" Shadboyut slid his arm beneath her shoulders to help her sit up.

The sunlight shined more brightly through the canvas. Apparently, he had been awake long enough to comb out the tangles in his waist-length hair and wipe his face clean. He had used a razor to shave away the overnight growth of stubble from his jawline.

"How... long?" It hurt to croak out even those words.

"I held my hand against the sky and the sun rose four fingers' worth. Lace and her boys are calling you a lazy villager. She wants her tent back. I've been stalling the best I can. By the burned gods, Aya, I was starting to fear that you wouldn't revive this time!"

He offered a flask of tepid beer. Aya swallowed a mouthful and winced against the pain in her sore throat.

"I saw a dream," she said hoarsely.

"You weren't already asleep this time. You fell over and went out! Mercy on us, what if this had happened in front of other people?"

"Can we say that I have a fever in my brain?"

He shook his head vigorously. "You don't swoon like a farmer on a hot summer day. You die. Hear me? You look dead... very, very dead. Slack jaw. Flat chest. Eyes rolled up. You're a gray corpse without a heartbeat for a good part of an hour. We can't explain that away."

Aya breathed slowly and deeply while listening to him speak. Gradually, the ache lessened in her throat.

"Then let's hope this was the only time," she said. "The dream I saw in this place felt more important than the others."

"Oh?"

She said, "I saw a day in a time yet to come. I saw people who will not be born yet for hundreds of years, telling our story as a legend of long ago. I saw the road ahead."

"That's great! How do we vanquish the curse?"

"I didn't see."

Shadboyut fingered the unlit pipe at his belt. "Uh-huh, well, do we survive? Or do we perish in glorious heroic deaths?"

"I don't know."

He put the pipe in his mouth and gnawed on the stem. "So, you've seen the trail and no farther? What should we do when we get there? Do we need weapons? My papa chopped at the creature with a woodsman's axe, you said. Do we need something larger? What's larger? The saw blade of a lumber mill?"

"We'll be together. We must be strong. Don't be afraid."

By then, she had regained enough strength in her limbs to dress herself. The tent's interior was not as warm as it was the night before when the two of them shared the nest of woolen blankets. Goosebumps prickled her cold arms until she slipped overhead the blousy linen chemise that covered her from neck to knees. She pulled up her knitted leggings and two layers of linen-wool skirts over her legs. She wriggled into the sleeves of her wraparound tunic and secured the overlapping front panels with a thick leather belt. With no time for a thorough combing of her hair, Aya gathered her tangled curls into a kerchief cap and secured the headband's drawstring knot at the nape of her neck.

Shad reached for the flap of the tent. "Let's bargain with Lace for the use of these canvas tents, water bags, food and walking sticks. Maybe we can coax out some advice for the trail ahead."

Aya maneuvered onto her hands and knees, making ready to crawl out of the tent behind him. Barefoot, she reached to pick up her fringed buckskin boots.

Shadboyut lifted a corner of the tent's flap but moved no farther. "Oh, mercy on us."

"What is it?"

A commotion of voices sounded outside along with the footfalls of heavy boots on the flagstones of the trading post. Aya caught the sound of words and fragments of phrases that were both foreign and familiar. She recalled her mother's gentle voice speaking in the same guttural, aspirated consonants but these were not women's voices. Their words rumbled like drums in a thunderstorm, bellowing to announce their arrival.

Shadboyut dropped the tent's flap and spun about to frown at her. "Mercy be on us, it's Mountain People!"

Nineteen

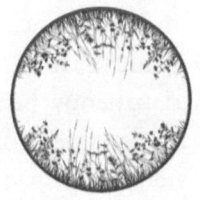

AYA LUNGED EAGERLY at the tent's flap. She half crouched and gazed outside for her first look at her mother's kinsmen. Stories and rumors told by the valley people swirled in her mind like a whirlwind of autumn leaves.

Two broad-shouldered, long-legged men swaggered into the yard. They wore dark-colored garb in a mixture of leather, buckskin, and wool. All she could see of their faces was the stubble of brown beards. Felt caps covered their foreheads inside the hoods of fur-lined leather cowls. Gloves concealed their hands. Knee-high gaiters with fur trimmed cuffs topped their thick-soled shoes. Everything about their unfamiliar style of garments had the appearance of layered heaviness, like trees overgrown with creeping vines and leafy branches: wool cloaks over buckskin tunics, wool aprons draped over burlap trousers. Their wide leather belts were burdened with a variety of knife sheaths and small axes. Yet, by the powerful strides of their long legs, they moved as easily as if they were nude.

The trading post's pair of sentinels greeted the new arrivals. Four men stood facing off each other, their thumbs hooked in their belts and chests puffed out with pride.

"Hey now, you flat buttocks," said one of the mountain men.

"Ye low-foot," said the other.

One of Lace's sentinels answered in their language, "Well met, ye rock brain. You're late! Been too busy fucking your *buan*?"

The other sentinel nudged his partner with an elbow. "Envious they've got something to fuck?"

All four men laughed heartily. The insults aroused no offense and only appeared to endear them all to each other. Aya frowned, confused, wondering if she misunderstood the nuances of a language that she had only heard her mother speak inside the home.

One pack animal loitered patiently behind the new arrivals. Aya recognized it as a *buan*—the long-legged cousin of farmers' goats that inhabited the high mountain crags. She had seen their shaggy pelts on sale on market days, but she had never seen a living *buan* before. The beast was larger than she imagined. Its haunches were as high as the oxen that pulled the travelers' wagons. It had the narrow snout and floppy ears of a goat but no horns. It had swine feet instead of hooves. Its tail was a hairless cord that ended in a fluffy tassel. Satchels, baskets, and jugs were piled on its back but, like the men it followed, the animal showed no signs of weariness for all that it carried.

"Mercy be on us," Shadboyut whispered close to Aya's ear. "The four of them are friends. Can you understand what they're saying?"

"Yes," she answered in a whisper. "They are, uh, greeting each other."

Lace emerged from the trading post's front door. She leaned on a cane. Each step that she took appeared to be laborious. "Dorrith! Jurrid! You're late. We expected you to arrive last night. I was saving the stone bed for you."

Should I translate? Aya briefly wondered how her companion might react to being deceived. Lace had relegated them to sleeping outside in a tent because she anticipated these travelers descending from the mountaintops.

One of the two arrivals strolled closer to the porch steps, in no hurry to respond or apologize for his tardiness. "We don't answer to you, Ogga. We get here when we feel like getting here. Be glad for what we bring you."

The woman Ogga, known to the lowlanders as Lace, raised the tip of her cane to point at the man in the yard. "Market days are coming up in the valley lands, Dorrith. You'd best think about serving the needs of the clan instead of filling your own belly with drink!"

Aya noticed that the woman spoke in a mixture of languages, throwing in mismatched words for market days and valley lands.

While she scolded Dorrith, the other fellow continued conversing with the two sentinels, like misbehaving children speaking behind someone's back but right there in front of her face. "We got a late start packing up the *buan* because Ula wasn't ready with the smoked meat," Jurrid said. "Then we didn't feel a need to hurry. It's not snowing. It's springtime. It's good to be outside under the sky, yeah? We got to the avalanche bluffs by late afternoon and, it being so close, thought we'd down to rest our feet. We decided to have a drink and try out the quality of the mead we're bringing down for trade. Then we had a little more and a little more. Then we got to laughing and fell asleep on the ground as the sun set. It was too late to walk down the rest of the way in the dark! So, we stayed."

The sentinel prompted, "And woke up with a hangover in a puddle of your own piss and vomit?"

"Again, as usual, ye drunken trout," added the second sentinel.

Jurrid laughed at both of their disapproving faces. "We had to take time to undress and wash ourselves in the waterfall. Fuck a goat but that water's cold!"

Aya smiled as her trepidation melted away. They sounded like merry fellows, not much different from farmers in the fields except for their language and their clothing. *To think, all my life I've been taught to avoid these men and be afraid of them. If a matron with a cane feels bold enough to chastise them, why should I fear approaching?*

Shadboyut put a hand on her shoulder to suggest restraint as she made a move to emerge from the tent. His dark eyes flashed in the sunlight that pierced the gap in the tent's opening. In that moment, he had the fearful expression of the eight-year-old boy that he once was, a child frightened for his life in a high mountain cave.

"Don't be afraid, Shad." She spoke in soothing tones as if comforting her younger sisters to go to sleep. "This is what we came for. Isn't this a welcome turn of events? We don't need to go searching in the heights for my mother's people. They've come to us."

"Yeah, like bears pouncing from the bushes."

Aya crawled outside and rose to stand proudly before her mother's kinsmen. She called out in greeting, "Brightness upon us." Her heartbeat quickened at the thrill of speaking her mother's language aloud in the open air, not in hushed tones behind the closed door of a cottage.

Dorrith whirled on his heel to face her. His mood turned dark as quickly as bolting the shutters of a window. "Do you speak to *me*, mud-foot, in the words of my fathers?"

She extended her arms, palms forward, in a gesture of welcoming and friendship. "I am the child of a clan daughter—"

Dorrith glanced back over his shoulder to the matronly woman on the porch. "Yours?"

Lace shook her head. "Not mine. She walked uphill last night with him."

"Him? Who?"

Shadboyut rose out of the tent's flap and stood beside her. "Don't make any sudden moves, Aya. Whatever you do, don't mention your—"

She said to Dorrith, "My mother was named Aho."

Both men stiffened their backs at the sound of the name. They raised their left hands in unison and made a gesture of prongs with their fingers.

"She lived in the 'valley lands' and she died."

Dorrith took the lead of stomping across the yard. He came to within a body's length of where she stood. His shadow extended from his boots and connected to her bare feet.

"Child of the Shunned One," Dorrith growled. "You dare to trespass on the soil where my fathers have walked. Dare you bring the taint of your sow's shame to the foothills of the true people's land?"

"I... uh...." Aya searched her memories for the best phrases and words to respond. Her knowledge of the language fell short. Her mother had never taught her the etiquette of how to beg forgiveness according to the customs of the mountain people. Even in their home, Aho's children used only the valley-dwellers' words to say, *I'm sorry, I regret the trouble I caused, please forgive my missteps.*

Shadboyut stepped forward and tried out his best showman's grin. "Hello, friend."

Dorrith pointed at his face with a finger like the tip of a spear. "You! No." Those simple words in the valley's language, although pronounced with a harsh accent, were clear enough in their meaning.

"My apologies, fellow traveler. I meant no offense."

Aya tried again. "I bring my mother home."

Dorrith cocked his head to the side. "What do you say? How can you bring home the Shunned One if you say she died?"

"I bring her bones," Aya said. "I ask to—"

"Her bones belong in the swamps of the valley below. Her ghost deserves to wander without rest in the muddy flats of the bogs where she chose to go. The Shunned One has no place in the land of my fathers."

"Can I...? How can I change that?" she asked.

"You can't!" Dorrith turned to walk away.

Aya took a few steps, dogging his heels. When he sensed her movement, he wheeled back around. One black-gloved hand shoved her chest and broke her forward momentum. Aya spun off-balance, tumbled sideways and dropped onto the bare ground.

"What a bully!" Shadboyut bent over her to ask, "Are you hurt?"

Aya grasped the bare hand offered to help pull her to her feet. "I'm fine. He pushed me, that's all."

Hands clasped, they stood together. Silence chilled the yard. Even the morning songbirds paused in their chirping.

"Oh no." Shadboyut quickly retracted his hand, but it was too late.

Everyone had seen it. Everyone saw them touch.

Dorrith pointed with the fingers of both hands. Jurrid lost his grip on the buan's tether rope. The two sentinels stepped backward as if a venomous snake lay in their path. Lace dropped her cane, and the stick rattled on the flagstone steps.

"Child of the Shunned One," Dorrith said. "How can you be blessed free of the curse?"

Aya squared her shoulders and raised herself up proudly. "Take me to your father. I will tell my story to him and him alone."

Dorrith nodded. "I will but the bones of the Shunned One must remain behind here. Only the father of our clan can give the word if that filth can be buried with the bones of our ancestors. It is not for me to say."

"I understand." Aya turned to face her companion with a smile. "Shad, they've agreed to guide us up the mountainside. Isn't that wonderful? We can tell our story to the elder in charge of their group."

"I wouldn't call it wonderful," he said. "But at least their mood changed. There's a fair chance they won't skin us and roast us for supper now."

She leaned forward and worked to cinch up the lacing straps on her boots. "Don't be silly, Shad, they're not going to harm us. Everything will be straightened out as soon as we can speak with someone who is older and wiser."

"And sober," he added.

Lace called out, "You lying taleteller, you withheld this miracle from me? You owe me a story, Shad!"

"I will, I will," he answered. "It's still being written, though. Hold our belongings secure until we get back?"

Lace grunted her wordless affirmation as she bent over to pick up her cane. Meanwhile, Jurrid and the two sentinels hurriedly unloaded the buan's load of satchels and jugs. In exchange, they picked up a number of bundles wrapped in oiled sackcloth and cedar trunks held shut with leather buckles.

Aya spared one last look at the ceramic urn stored in the tent. *Wait for me, Mamma. I'll be back for you soon.*

Twenty

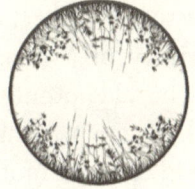

AT FIRST, the trail offered easy progress uphill with a pathway broad enough for two people to walk side-by-side. Jurrid led the buan by the harness. Dorrith guarded the rear of the group, leaving Aya and Shadboyut to march together behind the animal's dangling tail. The path had no wagon ruts. No wheeled vehicle had ever rolled up this trail before.

The ribbon of bare, trampled ground rose at an angle into the hillside. A narrow clear space cut between the trunks of hardy evergreen trees. Springtime was still new. To either side of the path, Aya catalogued the stalks of flower bulbs yet to show blossoms. Tufts of grass reached up to ankle height. Spotted mushroom caps grew in clumps out of the base of trees.

Before long, the pathway looped sharply and folded around on itself. They continued ascending the hillside but now with the morning sunshine at their backs. Fallen birch logs with white bark resembled the thigh bones of giants. Three or four switchbacks later, Aya began to feel winded but the thrill of seeing her mother's homeland energized each step. She lost count of how many times the trail turned about like threads on the frame of a loom.

A cluster of dark granite boulders jutted out from the hillside. The pathway narrowed into a shelf that curved around the obstacle. One misstep and they risked tumbling down the hillside to where they began.

"Be careful." Shadboyut held back in single file behind her.

"Thanks." She hoisted the hemlines of her layered skirts and tucked the excess in her belt. At first, she thought it would make walking easier, but the bulky swag of fabric caught on the edges of rocks and in protruding thistles. She expected Dorrith, at the rear, to voice a mocking comment about the inefficiency of a villager's clothing. Yet as they continued to progress uphill, he said nothing.

A hidden waterfall trickled down a hollow cleft in the rock face. Fringe tassels of white water in constant motion fluttered over the black rocks. Aya spotted an area where ferns were pressed flat, where fallen leaves and loam were piled into a pair of thick mattresses. Nearby trees showed the scars of rope burns. *Here is where they slept off their drunkenness last night,* she thought.

"We cross here!" Jurrid called out in the villagers' language. His tongue lapped at the words with effort.

"Did he say we're crossing the creek here?" Shadboyut asked.

"Yes, he did," Aya said.

"His accent is quite thick. I wasn't sure if he was still speaking in the mountain's tongue or not."

Jurrid led the buan to a crude bridge that spanned the creek. A few roughly hewn logs extended over a narrow section of the flowing waters. To either side, the current rippled between an array of mossy rocks.

The animal plodded into the water which turned out to be not too deep. Jurrid kept hold of the harness and walked the log bridge at the animal's side. Aya followed him across and, once she had reached the other side, she looked back for the other two men. Shadboyut made the crossing easily. His waist-length free-flowing hair and the fringes of his garments' seams all swayed together like the fronds of ferns. At the rear, Dorrith moved as a stealthy monolith with an expression like a stone mask. He kept one hand hooked on his belt within easy reach of either his broad knife or his hand hatchet.

Jurrid did not pause to rest on the other side of the creek, bringing the docile animal along with him. Aya followed the buan's tail and listened to the footsteps of the two men hiking behind her. The hours wore on as the group continued up the incline. The rest of the world slowly sank away below their feet.

By midday, the lofty trees became sparse. Wind stirred the dry branches overhead and sounded like distant voices whispering gossip. Burrowing pecker birds knocked at the tree trunks, the click-click reminding Aya of a barrel maker at his labors.

More blocks of granite popped up randomly about the trail like stone walls that had long ago crumbled. The pathway rose and fell, with switchbacks and curly curves, in an ever-ascending course. They looked over the tops of pine trees that they had passed through a few hours earlier.

"This isn't the path that we followed when I was a child," Shadboyut said. "My papa's group took another path, farther to the east, that had much less rocks."

"I've seen many trails up to the heights," she told him by looking back over her shoulder. Their gaze connected briefly and the unspoken —in my dreams—was understood. "I'm sure they know all the ways to go up and down the mountainside."

Jurrid called out, "We stop here. Eat. Drink."

"Oh, mercy be!" Shadboyut chose a fallen log for a bench. He hugged his raised knees and rolled his ankles. Soft-soled buckskin boots flexed like his own skin.

Aya sat on the log next to him. She busied her hands with pulling out the brambles and twigs from her linen skirts.

Dorrith settled cross-legged onto the ground and his partner soon joined him. Jurrid drank the first gulp from a leathery water bag then placed it on a rock. The other man picked it up and drank his fair share.

There followed a brief silence when the two men from the mountains stared at the two strangers. Dorrith held onto the water bag in his lap.

Aya asked in the mountain people's language, "Will you share water with us?"

"Show us again," Dorrith said.

Aya caught his meaning in the somber frown and the narrowed eyes that focused on their bare hands. "Shad, he wants to see it again."

"Let's hope that a clasp of hands is all that he wants to see us do."

"Don't be silly, Shad."

She reached to the man at her side and gently laid her palm on top of his knuckles. Their fingers crossed like the threads of a loom. Shadboyut lowered his head and turned his face away, as if he felt ashamed to display their secret of skin-upon-skin.

"Why?" Jurrid asked in the language of the villages. "Why you?"

Aya called up the memory of her mother's voice scolding her sisters for being naughty. Only a full-throated voice gave proper breath to the harsh consonants. "That is for your clan father to ask. I will answer only to him."

Dorrith tossed the water bag. She caught it with both hands.

Rather than wasting the time to build a fire, the mountain men shared cold food taken out of the buan's satchels. Smoked venison jerky, roasted walnuts, and dried mushrooms gave them enough sustenance to continue. Shadboyut fingered his beltline where he carried his pipe and the pouch full of lavender weed.

From that point, the trail continued its steady upward incline. They passed random patches of snow laid out like throw rugs of white wool tossed against the brown hillside. Trees grew thinner and rocks grew bigger. The trail became less of a walking path and more of a long stairway of broken, crumbled steps that ascended to points ever higher. With each bend of the trail, Aya felt they must be getting closer to the crest. Yet each time they turned the corner on another rocky outcropping, the ground continued to rise ahead.

The sun's course journeyed to the west as the hours trudged by. Shadows grew longer across the crags of lopsided rocks. Wind blew steadily now, a restless, unrelenting cold breath that chilled her fingertips and her cheeks. Aya's chest ached and burned in the frigid air. She began to develop a headache, although it was not as crushing or severe as the pain she felt at returning to her body after her spirit took flight.

"Are you feeling it too?" Shadboyut asked. "The air is thin at these heights. Would you ask them if we can rest again?"

She called ahead to Jurrid's back. "Let us stop again to rest and eat? Look at the sun falling lower in the sky."

"We're not stopping," Jurrid said. "It's too close to home."

"How close?"

He pointed to a gravel scree like a frozen waterfall of pebbles in between the cleft of two granite outcroppings. Snow in the rock crevasses made the black stone look like marble. "Up and over that rise is the approach to our home cave. If we stop here, some hunters might wander by and call us lazy. Do you want to be called lazy again, mud-foot?"

Aya told her companion, "He said no. We're too close."

"Oh, are we now? I hope so."

Slowing her pace, Aya turned left and right to gaze at her surroundings. From ground level, it looked different from what she had experienced in her dream visions. She recognized enough of the landmarks to know their location on the mountainside. Behind them was a panorama of all the world spreading to the distant horizon of bluish haze. The village where she had spent her entire life was a flea speck on the greenish brown carpet of the grasslands below. Granite cliffs blocked their view of the course ahead, but Aya remembered her dream. Once they ascended this last stack of boulders, the land would top off in a grassy meadow.

"Yes, yes, we are close!" Aya walked slightly sideways to cast her optimistic grin in his direction. "Try to find your breath, Shad, and push ahead. Just a few more steps. Just a little more! Think of how good it will feel to arrive at our destination..."

"Where the elder is going to make his inquisition and judgement of us."

"...where we can explain everything and ask for their help. I'm sure they'll forgive my mother's transgression if I can tell them what must be done to cure us all of this affliction."

Shadboyut paused to gulp a few deep breaths. Jurrid and the pack animal hiked farther ahead on the path. Dorrith, at the rear, hollered to their backs, "Go!"

Aya took hold of her companion's hand as a friend or as a lover would do in the days before the blight. Unashamed of their ability to touch each other's skin, she walked forward and gently pulled the man along with the guidance of her own strength.

"You can make it, Shad. It's not far now, I promise. Everything's going to be all right."

"What if you're wrong?" he asked, huffing for breath. "What if they condemn us?"

"They won't. They can't! I'll make them listen. Don't worry."

"Ugh," he grunted. "When did you get so reckless?"

"When did you get so timid?" she asked.

"Oh, let me think... Yeah, how about when they broke my papa's leg and turned him into a cripple for life and tried to throw us to our deaths in a bottomless chasm!"

"The chasm is not bottomless." She tugged at his hand to help him up the last few blocks of stone.

"That's not the point! You're not listening to me, Aya. These fellows are wild brutes like ravaging springtime bears who would rather—"

"Hey!" Dorrith barked. "I'm feeling sick to my stomach at all this *sho-sho-sho-shee-sho* yapping of yours. It makes my ears hurt worse than the ringing! Shut your mouths. Clap your lips and keep walking!"

Aya began to translate for her companion, "He said..."

"I can guess." Shadboyut glanced over his shoulder at the frowning man. "No more talk?"

"No talk!" Dorrith growled.

"Yes, sir."

The last pile of boulders rose sharply. Aya had to crouch over and use her hands to ascend. Her fingertips scraped raw on the stone. Her soft-soled boots fumbled to find toeholds in the rock. So it was that she was on her hands and knees, with her fingers digging into the gravelly soil, that she cleared the final edge of the rocky overlook.

Aya stood up in the shallow grasses that spread before her. The mountaintop's meadow put her off-balance for a moment, as she had never seen a field of lush grass not surrounded by a fruit orchard or the wattle-and-daub structures of a village. The grass-covered plateau ended sharply at the cliff's edges like a felt rag covering the top of a workman's bench. Pebbly soil was not suitable for farming and yet it felt more like a home than Aya had ever known in the valleys.

Jurrid and the pack animal were already far ahead. A lopsided mound swelled out of the alpine meadow. She raised herself upright, shoulders back, and beheld with awe the majesty of the cave's gateway. A cleft in the peak's tip resembled a pair of fists made of solid rock. In the hollow, the darkness invited her to come and share in its secrets.

"I told you," Shadboyut said quickly. "They live like cave bears."

Jurrid and the pack animal strolled into the jagged archway and were soon lost to view.

Dorrith nudged them from behind with his gloved hands. "Go."

* * *

Aya entered the gateway of shadows and immediately felt a rush of warmth that she did not expect. *Shouldn't mountain caves be cold?* A short tunnel sloped downward and Aya imagined being swallowed into the throat of an enormous stone beast. Gray gloom replaced sunlight and blue sky.

Hands to the wall, blinded by the sudden plunge into darkness, she felt rather than saw the passageway. Rock had the texture of toasted bread. Before long, the tunnel curved abruptly to the left. When she rounded the corner, light radiated from a chamber at the end of the passageway. Now she could see the mineral colors that streaked the walls in veins of yellow, blue, green, and violet.

The tunnel ended at a drop-off like a fountain's rim around a vast open chamber.

Aya stopped in her tracks, overwhelmed by the grandeur of the scene that expanded before her. The lofty cavern hollowed out the mountain in a natural vault far beyond the magnificence of any threshing barn or mill house human hands could construct. Spikes of waxy stone protruded from the high ceiling. A crust of iron pyrite glittered all over the walls, reflecting in silvery rainbows the campfires that sparkled at the cavern's base. The level floor was an expanse of sand-filled craters rimmed by green marble. Stalagmites of varying sizes resembled tree stumps made of stone.

Dorrith pushed ahead and jumped the last step into the open cavern. He hollered out greetings. His deep voice echoed among the stalactites of the high ceiling.

People—more people than she had expected to find—milled about their chores in preparing the evening meal. Small groups collected around boxy canvas tents erected in the deep sands of each crater's pocket. Aya lost count of the hairy heads in constant motion, perhaps forty-five or fifty adults and children. The inhabitants of the cave all wore leathery trousers but no shirts. Men and women dressed alike and grew their hair to waist length. Women were as tall and hardy as most of the men, so from behind, Aya could not distinguish between the sexes.

Dorrith bounded a zig-zag trail between a few clusters of canvas tents. He skirted around a stalagmite pillar as tall as himself. He arrived at a dwelling spot that appeared to be much the same as all the others. By his enthusiasm and eagerness to get there, this one had a special meaning.

A woman with pumpkin-colored hair tended a stew pot suspended over a circle of glowing logs. She smiled at his approach. A child of perhaps five years of age stood up from the woman's side. Grinning, the child playfully raised a kindling stick as if it were a spear. Dorrith feigned terror then playfully drew his hatchet from his belt. The man and the child briefly engaged in a crossing of stick and hatchet, a bout of sparring with ferocious-sounding growls and barks. It ended when the woman at the fireside called out as only a mother would admonish her misbehaving family.

Aya could not hear the words distinctly from the distance and the murmuring of others in the cavern that echoed all around to the ever-present whistling whine of the blight ringing in the deepest bones of her ears. Yet she did not need to know their words to see the precious rarity of their affection; the woman's smile tarnished by the melancholy in her eyes; the child's pleasure at the game dimmed by the wariness of caution. *Don't go near. Don't embrace. Don't touch.* The man named Dorrith at this moment was a vastly different person from the man who had shoved Aya to the ground that morning. He had a family he loved and that he could not lay his hands upon.

Aya blinked at the tears welling in her eyes. More than ever, she was determined to find the cause and put an end to the suffering of the world.

"Come this way." Jurrid passed the pack animal's halter into someone else's care. Near the far edge of the cavern's wall, an array of thick ropes formed a pen that contained half a dozen more buan.

"Are we going to meet the father of our clan?" Aya repeated the phrase that she had learned that morning.

Jurrid frowned but did not respond. He removed his hooded leather cowl and felt cap. Shaggy blond hair tumbled loosely across his shoulders. His routine of undressing was like a farmer coming indoors from a day's work in the fields. Yet clearly he was no farmer. Those upright shoulders bore no signs of carrying heavy burdens or performing back-breaking labor in the fields. Aya marveled at the man's supple movements even after a full day of hiking uphill.

"Come," Jurrid said again, this time in the villager's language.

He led the way, and they followed him up a gradual incline that formed a ramp. Slanted stone was smoothly polished by the foot traffic of centuries if not millennia. Aya could not be sure if the ramp had naturally formed by ancient upheavals of the earth or if the ancestors of these mountain men had carved it out of the rocky floor.

They ascended off the cavern's floor to the height of a threshing barn's roof. Now at the high ledge, Aya gazed down at the village of canvas tent tops sheltered in a stone dome. A few of the people glanced up curiously but most of them carried out their daily chores. The fabled wild people who inhabited the vast mountain ranges of the north kept to themselves, bred among themselves, spoke and sang their own secrets to themselves. No villagers had ever journeyed this far or had lived to tell the tale. These were her cousins, the blood relations she had never known, and yet they did not feel like family. She did not feel at home yet.

The ramp ended at a yellow linen curtain that covered a natural arch. Waxy stalactites pointed their spiky tips down at the tops of their heads. Wooden pegs hammered into the cavern's wall held up the curtain rod. No walls. No door. Only the panels of dandelion yellow linen concealed the chamber from onlookers.

Jurrid called to the curtain, "Father, may I greet you in the light?"

A man's bare hand pulled the curtain flaps aside. "In the light, my son, do I see you. Enter my chamber. Tell me, what news have you brought from outside?"

Twenty-One

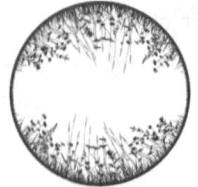

"I BRING these two from the lands below." Jurrid made a sweeping gesture with his arm to usher Shadboyut and Aya into the curtained chamber. Beeswax candles cast a honey-scented light around the simple furnishings of a pine log table and a cedar storage chest. Dominating the space was a stone bed covered in wool blankets and bearskins.

The sole occupant of the room stood back from those who approached. "What value do they carry that you should bring mud-foots here, Son?"

Jurrid said, "They can show you, Father, what my words cannot."

"Show me what?"

Aya faced the man they had journeyed all day to meet. In that moment, her mouth could not form words. Her throat went dry. Her eyes drank in the sight of a man like no one she had ever seen before.

Kyrggh wore no trousers, no shirt, and no shoes. Only a scarf of gray linen wrapped his loins and tied into a knot at the front. His bare legs showed the strength of one who had spent a lifetime hiking up and down the challenging mountain bluffs. His belly had ridges of muscle like a washboard. His light-skinned freckled shoulders had the bulky broadness of oxen. A leather thong necklace with a bear claw and glass beads encircled his throat. Flaxen hair was more pale-colored and straighter than anyone's hair that Aya had ever seen. Though he had a full beard, he had chopped the blond stubble close to the jawline. Narrow eyes had irises as gray as leaded glass with a stern, commanding expression. Such a man could snap her thin frame in half with his bare hands. He lived in these forbidding wastelands where most feared to travel, a man as wild and fierce as the cave bears themselves.

Shadboyut cleared his throat and that broke her out of her reverie. "Hello, sir, it's an honor to meet you. My apologies for I do not know the language of your people."

"My name is Kyrggh. I am Father of the Black Bird Clan." The father spoke in the language of the valleys with an accent that clipped off vowels and aspirated the consonants. Yet his diction was less garbled than Dorrith's or Jurrid's speech.

Aya understood that it was an honorary title as Kyrggh did not appear much older than herself.

"Kur-ri-gue?" Shadboyut struggled to repeat the unfamiliar name.

"What can you show me?"

"This." Shadboyut grasped her hand. Their fingers intertwined. Aya held onto the warmth of him. She clutched onto that reality of his skin pressed against her skin. They stood utterly still to allow Kyrggh his moment to react.

"Who are you?" the father asked.

"I'm a simple traveler. My name is Shadboyut."

"Shad-... Shad-bo-..."

"Yes, you may call me 'Shad,' if that's easier for you, sir."

He turned his steel-gray eyes to Aya. "And you, woman? Who are you?"

Jurrid blurted, "She is the daughter of the Shunned One!"

In reaction, the father clenched his jaw. Both men formed the pronged gesture in unison with the fingers of their left hands.

"You... you..." He switched languages to the words of her mother but growled with the deep-throated bellow of a cave bear. "So, it is by the blood of treachery, the brother-killer's child has made a pact with the *demons* of the netherworld?"

"No—" Aya had no time to explain before the man lunged forward.

He clutched Aya's bare hand. His large fingers clamped over her knuckles and held her in a vise. Pain blazed up her forearm, a fiery agony that sharply raked into her flesh but drew no blood. Tears dribbled out of her eyes. Aya struggled to breathe. Magenta, green, and purple sparkles filled her sights. Dizziness swirled in her head, and she feared she would faint.

Contact only lasted a moment—what felt like hours—before the father released his grip.

Aya sat back on her heels and hugged her belly with her numbed arms. She snorted up the phlegm clogging her nose and swallowed the lump in her throat. *Be strong. Be strong.* Though her jaw quivered violently as if she stood barefoot in a snowbank, Aya found enough strength in her neck to raise her head. She gazed up at the stern eyes of Kyrggh once more.

He sat on the edge of his stone slab bed piled with layers of bearskins and wool blankets. He flexed his right hand weakly; it appeared numb. Fingertips had turned blue.

Jurrid made busy at a table against the wall. He uncorked a ceramic jug and poured amber liquor into a flagon. The odor of sweet honey and herbal spices wafted through the chamber. Not daring to risk contact, he placed the flagon on the corner of the stone bed. The father picked it up with his left hand and loudly gulped.

Shadboyut enveloped her in his gentle embrace. He massaged her forearms as if warming someone who had come inside from the cold. "Why did he do that? What cruelty!"

Aya explained, "They accused me of withholding a cure to the blight. Something about a... a word that I don't know for some type of predatory animal, or not an animal, that dwells in the netherworld."

"Oh, I see. Dark spirits and imaginary creatures from ancient legends, eh? Just what I expected from these bear-skin-wearing brutes—"

Aya squeezed his hand urgently and hoped that he understood her unspoken meaning. *Do not tell them you were there too, Shad. Do not mention your papa. Do not confess to trespassing in their forbidden place!*

Shadboyut fingered the pipe in his belt. "If we wished to keep it secret, why have we journeyed uphill? Why did she leave the valley? Why am I not riding with my caravan friends to the market days elsewhere? We've come to help you! Can you understand that much?"

In the pause, the ambient mood in the room shifted and the thunderclap of outrage faded into silence.

Kyrggh nodded soberly. "I accept what you say."

Jurrid murmured, "They could still be demons."

"Demons would be smarter about hiding themselves, my son. Or she would have attacked me when I grabbed her."

Aya sighed relief and quickly translated for her companion, "They've decided we are not netherworld creatures after all, if we did not respond when provoked."

"Oh I see, well, then hurting you was worth it?" Shadboyut's jaw flexed as he frowned.

Kyrggh made a half-pointing gesture in the direction of their hands. "You can touch," he said in the language of the valleys. "Why?"

"We don't know," Aya said. "But it's only the two of us. Only each other. No one else."

He asked, "Is there more you can do?"

Aya raised her back up straight, sitting tall on the cushion of her heels. She chose to speak the mountain's language in the hopes that Kyrggh would understand her more easily. "In my sleep, my spirit flies away from my flesh. I see places where I have never walked. I see days that passed long ago. I see days that have not yet come."

"Mud-foot lowlanders, heads full of sawdust." He slurped off the last of the mead in the flagon. "The burned gods have bestowed your spirits with the powers of air and wind. Why have they infused you with their grace? Why has the daughter of the Shunned One been chosen, not someone else more worthy?"

Shadboyut asked her, "What's he saying?"

Aya blinked to switch her thoughts back to the language of the valleys. "I told him that I dream. He understands the lore that you mentioned about burned gods and spirits. He is asking why it's happened to me."

Shadboyut unfolded his legs and rose off the floor to stand tall. "You understand the lore, you say? You believe her tale of flying away in her dreams? What else do you know?"

Kyrggh pointed at them while still holding the mead flagon in his hand. "We call you *n'ndrh-harhim*, how do I say it?"

She wagged her head in puzzling to form a translation in her mind. "The children who carry a light. No, the ones who are a light."

"Shining Ones," Shadboyut suggested. "Plural?"

"Yes," she said.

"Does he mean both of us are shiny?"

"Yes, Shad, I think he does mean that."

"Your soul is bright," Kyrggh added. "You can touch her. You are *n'ndrh-harhim* the Shining Ones."

Shadboyut opened the pouch at his belt. His nimble fingers worked to pack dry weeds into the bowl of his pipe. "I need a smoke. May I borrow a light from that candle?"

At the father's nod of permission, Jurrid carried over a small candle for the man to light his pipe. Eyes lowered, saying nothing, he puffed up thick clouds of lavender smoke.

"The Shining Ones are always two." Kyrggh gestured as if grasping at words in the air. His brows furrowed in frustration, and he switched back to his native language. "Your kind always travels two-by-two, never alone. One spirit takes flight. One spirit is tethered to the ground. Wings and feet, two limbs of one creature. Why do you not know of this lore? Do the mud-foots in the lower lands know nothing of the spirit world?"

Aya turned aside to translate. "He says we are like the wings and feet of a bird. It's the two of us together, Shad."

Puffing on his pipe, he softly sang a verse of epic poetry. "*We are children of the light. The spirits of our ancestors haunt the silver clouds. We are one...*" Wisps of smoke leaked out of his nostrils. She wondered what thoughts were going through his mind for she had rarely seen him so introspective for so long.

Kyrggh asked her, "You say that your sleeping eyes can see things that your awakened eyes do not see?"

"Yes."

"And him..." He switched languages to address Shadboyut. "You? Singing man? Do you call the spirits of water, or stone, or wood?"

Without saying a word, Shadboyut raised his hand to cup the air around the bowl of his pipe. On the next inhale, the embers glittered brightly and then flew upwards. In a swirl of glowing fireflies, the sparks laughed soundlessly. *Let's play! Let's play!* They twisted and wove themselves into a shining strand in a column that rose straight out of his pipe and reached for the melted-rock ceiling. The shine glittered in the crystalline veins of the walls.

"Oh, Father!" Jurrid exclaimed.

"Be not afraid, my son. Let's see if the lowlander can harness the forces he has unleashed."

Shadboyut turned his wrist and extended his arm, aiming his palm outward. The spray of sparkles poured outwards in a horizontal stream. Fire blazed a streak up the middle of the bearskin throw rug. Fire splashed into the rock wall and, finding nothing to consume, crawled up to the ceiling.

The roots of an outside tree had penetrated over the centuries into the stone of the mountain. Roots dangled like petrified fringe overhead. Fiery sparkles took hold. Their glittering mouths chewed at the woody roots and began to work their way upwards.

"Huh," grunted Kyrggh. "Appears he can't."

Jurrid remarked, "It is the fable of Proggok and Glycha at Avalanche Lake..."

"When the waters ran amok," the father added.

Aya tapped her companion's shoulder. "Stop them, Shad. There's a tree above us on the outside! They'll burn it up from underneath the roots and start a larger fire that may consume the entire alpine meadow!"

"Sorry." He called out to the glittering swarm at the ceiling. "Hey, you! Come, stop now."

They only giggled and burned all the brighter.

"Shit." Shadboyut unfolded his legs and stood up tall. "I said, hey, stop it. Naughty little things, I'm telling you to behave!"

Kyrggh strolled a few steps across the room to where a cedar chest lay on the floor. He raised the lid and rummaged about for an object wrapped in velvety cloth.

Aya clasped his hand. "Perhaps if we work together somehow..."

From the cloth, Kyrggh drew forth a long fork of two silver prongs. Aya gasped in recognition at one of Gerrie's tuning forks.

Kyrggh tapped the prongs on the edge of the cedar chest. Then he pressed the pommel of the handle against the rock wall. The whole chamber became a ringing gong that reverberated a single bell tone deep into the marrow of Aya's bones. Ringing made the air shimmer like ripples on the surface of a pond.

Fire sprites whimpered and faded out; their little eyes shut tight. Whispery voices hissed, *Don't hurt us. We just wanted to play.*

Twinkles sank into the flickering tongues of flame on the beeswax candlesticks. They obediently snuggled into the light and fell silent. Aya murmured in her thoughts, *hush hush,* as if soothing her younger sisters to sleep when they were small.

"I'm sorry about your rug, sir," Shadboyut said.

Kyrggh let out a short burst of deep-throated laughter. "He summons the spirits of fire but let's them run amok like rutting buan."

"You're being rude," Aya confronted him in the language of the villages, for her companion's sake, but the soft-lisped consonants and lyrical intonations fell short of conveying her indignation. "If you insult my husband, then do it in words that he understands."

"Husband?" Shadboyut repeated. "So, I'm your husband now?"

She cast him a sideways glance. As in the ancient legend, he had been her husband before they ever met.

Kyrggh nodded to her in acknowledgement. "Shining One, you call up fire spirits. They ran wild. I laughed."

"If you're apologizing, then I accept," Shadboyut said. " Laughter is certainly not the worst insult I've heard in my life. And I can't deny that I'm not a particularly good shepherd of the little sparklers, am I."

Aya squared her shoulders and addressed him in the language of her mother. *Be strong. Be strong.* "We stand before you in the light. We are Shining Ones with the power of dreaming and the power to summon the spirits of fire. We have seen the source of the curse. We come to you with the answer for how to end the pain of the world. Will you listen to us, now?"

Kyrggh opened his naked arms wide in a gesture of welcoming. "You will eat and drink and wash yourselves. You will sleep here tonight with me. We will talk of your dreams, Shining Ones, and the hope that you bring on this day."

Twenty-Two

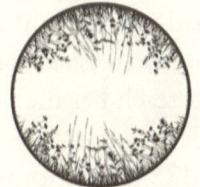

JURRID MADE the rounds of the tented groups in the expansive open cavern. He collected a sampling of food from each hearth fire and pantry basket. Soon, his arms could not hold it all. A few of his kinsmen stepped up to help him carry wooden platters, wicker baskets, gourd bowls, kerchiefs, and ox horns. Children carried glass decanters, ceramic jugs, and leathery water bags. They formed a caravan to ascend the ramp jutting out from the wall and brought a feast enough for a dozen people to lay at the feet of the Shining Ones.

Kyrggh tugged on leather trousers and tied back his long flaxen hair with a rawhide cord. As his people arrived with the platters of food, the Father of the Clan drew aside his yellow linen curtains. The alcove chamber revealed itself as a theater stage to be viewed from the larger cavern beyond the jagged edge.

"My children," he said. "As the rain feeds the lake, and the lake returns its waters to the sky, so will your generosity be returned to you. Behold here, the Shining Ones who have come to bestow their wisdom and mercy in our time of greatest need."

His voice projected beyond the edge of the alcove and echoed up to the arched cathedral ceiling of the larger cavern. Faces on the cavern floor turned upwards like flowers drinking in the light of the morning sun.

"Bring forth music and song, my children. This is a night of celebration. We have called out to the ghosts of our ancestors. At last, they answered. The time of pain is near an end!"

To those who laid food at her knees, Aya wished to express her gratitude, but her knowledge of their language fell short. How odd, she thought, that her mother had never taught her the proper etiquette of her people. Or perhaps Aho had wished for her to integrate with the villagers and saw no need to teach her the nuances of *please* and *excuse me* and *thank you*.

"This all looks delicious!" Shadboyut smiled as he eagerly surveyed the array of roasted drumsticks of geese, cubed pork loin of wild boars, strips of venison, elk, beef tongue, rabbit, and ribs of lamb. Bowls contained a steaming hot porridge of buckwheat groats seasoned with flecks of grated nutmeg. Beets, yams, carrots, onions, and mushroom caps on skewers showed the charring of wood fires.

A woman with tawny hair and brown eyes kneeled on the floor. She faced him so closely that even Aya sitting cross-legged at his side could inhale the scent of wood smoke in the woman's thick hair. Her bodily scent, like anise oil, wafted from the skin of her shirtless torso. The woman's smile mirrored his jovial expression. "Good food?" she asked.

"Yes," he answered, not looking at the meat and vegetables anymore. "It's very good food."

A glint of interest shined in his eye that soon dimmed with the ever-present melancholy Aya had seen in every villager's eye since the chime struck.

"In the lowlands, they say, 'thank you' when receiving hospitality," Shadboyut said. "How do your people say thanks?"

The woman, still smiling, shook her head to show that she did not understand the question. "My name is Ula."

"Hello Ula," he said. "My name is Shad."

"Zhjodd?"

He laughed softly. "And to think I've been afraid of you people my whole life."

Aya hiccupped a cold breath as jealousy banged her chest. She thought of pinching him or nudging his shoulder but restrained herself. *So, I'm your husband now*, he asked with a lilt of surprise. Now she understood; despite the tender and passionate moments they had shared, it had only been a brief time since they became acquainted. They had not exchanged a pledge of fidelity. Their names were not written in the record books of the village. Aya put a hand across her own belly that gurgled hunger, but she felt no appetite for the feast spread on the ground before her. *If he could touch anyone else, would he have chosen me as a lover? If we cure the world of the blight, and if he can touch anyone else but me, will he continue to stay at my side?*

Jurrid standing at the curtains called out to the woman. "Ula? Come away now. Stop bothering them. Let them eat."

"As you say, Brother." She rocked back on her heels and smoothly sprang upright to her feet. Ula strolled away, back down the ramp with the others but spared a moment for a backward glance over her shoulder.

Shadboyut waved goodbye one last time, then he dug into the heaping platters and bowls spread on the floor. "Did you try these lamb ribs, Aya? They're amazing. Is this rosemary or oregano? I can't be sure."

Aya nibbled a spoonful of the porridge.

"Y'know, it might be the dandelion wine, or the beer, or the honey mead but I'm feeling much more at ease than I felt an hour ago. I should be curled up in a sniveling ball of weeping like a child with all these confrontations and surprises. Truth be told, I've never had more peace of mind."

Aya looked down at her own hands resting in her lap. Surrounded by joyous people, she had never felt more alone. Questions roared like a thunderstorm in her mind. *If we are immune, can we save everyone else? Is the entire world still doomed but for the two of us?*

Outside in the open cavern, musicians struck padded mallets onto a rack of wooden tubes. Clear tones rang from the earthy chimes, unlike metallic bells, and the harmonized waves of pitch echoed in the stalactites on the cathedral ceiling.

"Mmm," Aya hummed along to the music of her mother's people. She closed her eyes but still saw colors flashing inside her eyelids. Vertigo swept over her head, and it felt as if the solid ground lurched and turned. Her sights lingered in a swirling swarm around them both, floating and turning to view herself and Shadboyut from a thousand different angles, behind, below, and around, removed and separated from the rising tones of color that quickened her blood and raised a fever to her skin. Harmonics of a thousand tones vibrated in airy silver strings. The tones intensified, merging into a unified clanging—the scream of all colors blending into white. On her last exhale, all sound hushed, and all the whiteness turned black.

Her soul broke free and slipped outside of herself.

* * *

Aya dreamed of being at the trading post in a different season. Dry brown leaves scattered around the yard. Trees displayed a colorful palette of red, yellow, orange, and green. On the porch, a mountain man held the harness of a buan while another worked to unload the parcels and satchels from the pack animal's back.

The matronly woman who would someday be known as Lace was a child version of herself. She dressed in a mixture of garment styles: the fringed trousers of the traveling peddlers, the linen-wool tunic of a village farmwife, and the hooded leather cowl of a mountain man. A crocheted shawl looped around her head and neck.

"Ogga!" The elder owner of the trading post, resembling the matron that Lace would someday grow up to be, called out to the young woman.

"Yes, Mamma?" Lace answered in the mountain people's language.

"Come hold the buan for our guest. She wishes to go make a bargain in the yard. Hurry up now. Lazy girl!"

Aya's spirit was distracted watching Lace reluctantly obey. She nearly missed it. When Lace took hold of the buan's halter, the mountain people turned and brought their faces into view. Beneath one's hooded leather cowl, Aya saw the younger version of her own mother's face.

Mamma!

Another person—a traveling peddler dressed in fringed clothing—loitered with a two-wheeled cart by the firewood stack. His wavy brown hair flowed loosely down to his beltline like skeins of frazzled yarn. Gerrawgon looked no different here than he had on the day Aya met him... or would meet him, more than twenty years in the future.

"It's good to see you again, Aho, daughter of the Black Bird Clan." Gerrawgon smiled to welcome her approach.

"You as well, Gerrie." Aho called back to her brother, "Go have a drink and a meal. I shall return soon."

The other mountain man was almost finished unloading the animal's burden. "Don't bother to rush your fucking, Aho. It's nightfall soon because you delayed our descent, and now I must pay for a spot on the stone bed. I'm not paying for you too! You can sleep in the woodpile with that mud foot."

Aho jabbed her finger at the air in his direction. "You delayed our descent just as much with insisting on taking the wrong trail and we had to double-back *twice* to find the waterfall. Rocks for brains! You couldn't find a trail if you turned around and saw your own footprints in the snow."

"So says the hawk among sparrows, who is always cutting a new trail, always walking off to the wild grasses where no one has ever trodden before, always restless and selfish." For the last satchel, he threw it forcefully to the ground. "Sharing a trek with you at my side, you'll be the death of me someday!"

Gerrie slipped his arm around Aho's waist and hugged her close to his side. "Come now, you two, don't argue. Your lives are too brief to waste time shouting at each other."

"He's such a sack of boulders!" Aho fumed.

"Stubborn she-boar!" her brother barked in response.

"Hush, hush," Gerrie soothed. "Let's go find a quiet place in one of the sheds where I can help you make all of this anger go away."

Aho rotated within his grasp and looped her arms around his neck. She was a tall woman, even for the mountain people. She did not need to raise her chin very far to bring her lips to meet his.

Even as a spirit, Aya shuddered with the shock of realization. This man had known her mother intimately. The man who did not age, whose inhuman soul had dropped from a jeweled sanctuary in the clouds, was undoubtedly her father. Unlike her sisters who had ordinary villagers as fathers, Aya was a hybrid creature. Because of the fallen immortal's blood in her veins, her soul had the ability to break free of her earthly flesh and soar into other places or other days.

"Ugh!" grunted her brother. "I'm going to vomit."

The child named Lace said to him, "We have beer."

"That's a good drink." He tied the buan's harness to a post and followed Lace inside the wooden building.

The matron of the trading post called out to the pair, who were still deep in the throes of kissing. "Say there, you two! I bolt the doors at the fall of night. If you choose to revel and cavort in my shed past twilight, then you've made your choice."

Gerrie broke the kiss long enough to respond. "Thanks, Madame Trader but we'll be fine out here under the stars."

Aho nuzzled his neck and suckled a deep, long kiss to the soft spot underneath his earlobe. "Mmm," she murmured into his skin. "Grab your blankets. Let's go."

"Yes, lets."

Gerrie turned toward his two-wheeled cart and came to face where Aya's spirit stood. Her translucent feet, like wisps of smoke, floated slightly off the ground. His eyes widened, startled at the sight of her.

Why did you never tell me that you are my father? Aya's voice emanated from her closed lips. *All the hours that we spent talking and you never told me the truth. You asked questions about my mother. You knew! You lied to me about who you are.*

"You're being very rude, my child. Where I go, what I do, and what I choose to say or not say is entirely my choice. It is not for you to demand confessions from me." Gerrie's expression darkened in a sour frown and a harsh slant of his eyebrows.

Aho looked around. "Who are you talking to?"

"No one, my love. Just the ghost of a child who is not yet born."

"Ghost?" Aho raised her left hand to form a gesture of her fingers as two prongs.

He laid his hand on top of hers and gently closed her fingers into a fist. "Don't be afraid. She's simply lost. She won't be staying long. Come now, my love, let's grab some blankets and go to the woodshed and forget all about everything and everyone except each other."

Mamma. Aya reached out for her but Aho's eyes darting from side to side clearly did not see her spirit form. The shape of her arms began to dissolve like swirls of cream poured into a pot of simmering onion soup.

Gerrie flicked his other hand as if brushing through cobwebs. "Hush, child. Go back to where you belong."

Aya's spirit lurched backward as if yanked by a string. She soared up the mountainside as the seasons of autumn, winter, spring, and summer tumbled around her in a whirlwind of colors. When she plummeted into the shape of her own body, she was tempted to hold her breath in the darkness and never awaken.

* * *

Shadboyut kissed her forehead. His lips felt hot on her cold skin. "Ah, there she is. You see? I told you."

Aya's ribs ached. The now-familiar headache throbbed as if musicians were beating upon her skull with padded mallets. Slowly, as her awareness of her own body returned, she realized that she lay upon a pallet of buan fleece and bearskins. Inhaling despite the raw dry lump at the back of her throat, Aya savored the odor of Kyrggh's skin and hair. His scent permeated the canvas pillow stuffed with buckwheat hulls, the fluffy fleece, and the wool blankets bundled at her side.

She opened her eyes that were half-glued shut with the crust of dried tears. To her right-hand side, Shadboyut caressed her cheek. To her left-hand side, Kyrggh sat at the edge of the stone mattress.

"You've been, uh, gone for a solid couple of hours," Shadboyut told her. "How do you feel? Are you all right? Can you sit up?"

His arm behind her shoulders helped to raise her upright. Aya felt her bones creak like a chair left outdoors to be warped and ruined by weather.

Kyrggh asked, "What did you dream, Shining One?"

"Wait. Just wait, all right? Give her time to catch her breath." Shadboyut lifted a glazed stoneware cup to her lips.

Aya drank a tepid brew that tasted of barley and mint. The soreness of her throat began to ease. Her headache still throbbed. Worst of all, the ache in her heart could not be soothed. Her chin quivered as the tears trickled freely out of her stinging eyes. *It's him. It's him.* The cart-toting vagabond who told silly legends of a drunken giant falling in a river was an immortal, ethereal creature of legend. And he was her father.

"There, there, shhh..." Shadboyut snuggled close to her side and wrapped his arm around her head to coax her into laying her cheek against his shoulder.

Aya breathed deeply the scent of her companion's hair that brought up memories of the wild forest and the open sky. His shoulder was as solid as a bedpost. *Mamma kept him a secret to her deathbed. Why? Why did she allow me to wrongly assume that my father was one of the mountain people? Did she know what sort of creature Gerrie is, or did he lie to her too? Did he love her at all or was she merely a moment's pleasure?* Aya gave up trying to be strong and sank all her weight against him. Weeping convulsed her. The only sounds that she could gargle were choked sobs and moans.

"The legends told by our ancestors say nothing of this anguish," Kyrggh said. We are only told that the Shining Ones command the elemental spirits and soar to dream beyond the limits of their own eyes. I am learning, on this day, that there is—as with all things—a cost to be paid. What is given must be returned."

"You, wagon man!" Kyrggh switched languages to address Shad-boyut. "The stories of my people do not know this. Her dream walk is not an easy trail."

"No, it's not." He stroked the back of her head. His lean fingers snagged in the tangles of her curly hair. Slowly, her sobbing lessened to an uncontrollable series of hiccups and gasps.

"What did you see?" Kyrggh asked again.

"Stop rushing her. Let her breathe."

"I can do it, Shad." Even to her own ears, her voice sounded foreign and strange, congested and hoarse.

Aya made the effort to raise herself off the man's shoulder. Legs out straight, she sat upright on her own strength. She lifted her skirt to wipe the moisture from her face. In that moment, with ruddy-colored linen pressed to her cheek, Aya decided to withhold the truth. What she had witnessed felt too personal to share with anyone. If she were to repeat what she had seen and what she now knew, she feared a resurgence of weeping. *It wouldn't be a lie, after all,* she convinced herself. *I'll still be sharing one of my true dreams.*

"In my dream I saw a large beast squatting in a pool," Aya began telling her story in the language of the mountain people.

Twenty-Three

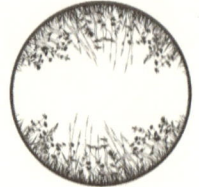

KYRGGH WATCHED HER INTENTLY, his gray eyes unblinking, as she related the tale of her dream. He drank in every word that came from her mouth and, no doubt, vowed to preserve her legend to pass on to future generations. She wished to have more eloquent skills at storytelling, especially in her mother's language. Her voice was a hoarse monotone, but Kyrggh did not seem to mind. Despite her wooden delivery, he appeared utterly entranced.

"It was a beast unlike any beast you know. It dwells in a cave filled with green rocks in a mountain peak. The cave is to the northeast, up the next peak. It is a high place where the snow does not melt."

Kyrggh nodded to show he knew of the place, and she continued.

"The beast is like a... a... I don't know your word for it. There is an animal at the seashore called a 'crab' that has many legs and eyes on top of its head."

Shadboyut interrupted. "Wait, you're telling him about the screaming crab in the cave? That's an old dream, isn't it?"

Aya held out her empty cup. "Could you refill my barley tea, please?"

"Why aren't you telling him what you saw just now?" Shadboyut cocked one eyebrow. "What did you see? Or was too private to share?"

Kyrggh asked, "What is this word, 'private'?"

"Did you dream of *him*?" Shadboyut pressed.

Aya felt a blush warm her cheeks. She thought again of the indignation in her father's expression, his stern rejection, and his admonition. *You're being rude, child. It is not for you to demand confessions from me.* Tears welled up and she feared she might begin weeping again.

Shadboyut chuckled softly and kissed the corner of her eye. He licked his lips and drank her tears. "Oh, come now, don't be shy. I'm not the jealous sort."

"What? What do you mean?"

Her companion tilted his head in Kyrggh's direction. "He's gorgeous. C'mon, tell me, did you dream of a future day when the curse is lifted? Do the two of you, or better yet, the three of us—"

"No," Aya said bluntly.

Shadboyut grunted his exasperation and rose to go refill her barley tea from a jug. "Say no more. Go on with your tale of the screaming crab, then. Don't mind me."

"The source?" Kyrggh repeated in the language of the mountains. "You have seen the source of the curse?"

"Yes, it is a 'crab' in a high cave. A few months ago, it began to scream." Aya withheld the details of Shadboyut's father attacking the creature with an axe. Better not to raise more questions about the timing of things. "It squats in a pool of blue slime that is not water. All around, the stones of the cave are pure white like icicles."

"You have seen the forbidden place?"

Aya nodded. "You're aware of this creature?"

"The Clan of the Black Bird serves as the guardian of the place where no one may tread. We call its resident The One Who Sleeps."

"It no longer sleeps," she said. "It is awake and constantly screaming. The stones ring with the sound of it. As long as it cries, the sound of its voice ripples the air. The sound goes into our bones, into our heads, into our blood, into our skin."

Kyrggh rose from the bed and turned his back on them both. He stood facing the yellow linen curtains. Once more, the panels were drawn shut and concealed them from the view of everyone else in the cavern. Candlelight illuminated the contrast of his dark leather pants and his pale torso against the yellow backgrop.

"How do we stop its screaming?" His voice echoed dully against the wall.

"I don't know." Aya drank the second cup of barley tea that her companion had brought.

"He knows the trail, does he?" Shadboyut asked. "He knows about that beast?"

"Yes, Shad. I think they have a reverence for it. The clan guards the place."

"Oh, they guard the mountain cave, do they?" As a storyteller, he did a fairly decent job of feigning surprise.

"He believes me. He understands."

Kyrggh said, "With the springtime should come a renewal of life. Bears awaken from their sleep and emerge from the caves to forage for food and nourish their cubs. It should be a time of the celebration of life but for the first time in the memory of our people, we are not celebrating the blooming moon. In the passing of four full moons, I have blamed the lowlanders for some transgression against the gods of the mountains. How could I know the source is here with us? What have we done? Have we not kept the ways of our ancestors as well as we should have?"

Shadboyut looked to her expectantly for a translation. Aya felt too enthralled with the man's monologue to make the effort of mixing up the words in her mind.

"I have devoted my life to guarding the secret of these mountains. I keep the singing rods passed down, father to son, from the time of my ancestors. And yet I have failed to prevent whatever offended and awakened The One Who Sleeps... Shall I call it now The One Who Screams? We suffer. We all suffer. The mountain clans, wagon men, and dirt-eaters of the lowlands alike. If punishment is meted out to all without favor, then how can my people earn redemption?"

Once more, Shadboyut sat down on the stone mattress beside her. "Excuse me that I don't understand exactly what you're saying, my friend, but I can tell you're sounding a bit maudlin."

Kyrggh half-turned and gazed over his shoulder. "What is this word, 'maudlin'?"

"Don't give up hope. You've got us now!" He smiled and slipped his arm around Aya's waist to cuddle her. "Where I've traveled, down to the seashore, do you know what they do with crabs? They cook them! Yes, that's right. They cook them and eat them for supper."

Aya gasped. "Do you think we could, Shad? Could we ask the fire spirits for help?"

"They're mischievous little bugs. I'm sure they'd help."

She smiled for the first time in hours, if not days, if not her entire life. Her cheeks ached to stretch wide. "Oh, mercy be, Shad, that sounds like a real possibility!"

Kyrggh looked down at the scorched line burned into the bearskin throw rug. "I must meditate upon this question. You two may sleep here tonight in my bed. I will go to the Chapel of the Ancestors and pray for guidance."

"Thank you," she said in the villagers' language, for she was still unsure of the mountain people's etiquette.

Kyrggh shifted on his feet, appearing to be equally unsure of how to respond.

Shadboyut added, "It's a good bed. A good bed."

That put him at ease. Kyrggh nodded to bid them goodnight. Without another word spoken, he ducked through the curtain and left them alone.

* * *

The layers of furry bear skins and buan fleece pelts on the stone bed offered a comfortable and warm surface unlike any that Aya had ever reclined upon. Her neck and head settled into a canvas pillow stuffed with buckwheat husks. Soft blankets of felted fleece, not woven of wool, had the velvety texture of forest moss.

"Oh, this is..." Shadboyut settled himself under the blankets beside her. He rolled his cheek into his own pillow, mumbled a few more words, and immediately fell asleep.

Aya reached out to the bedside stool and snuffed out the beeswax candle with a pinch of her fingers. The only light in the room slumbered as deeply as the man at her side.

She closed her eyes in the darkness but sleep did not come easily.

In her head, thoughts whirled of all the events of the day since waking up that morning in the trading post's yard. Fresh faces and new stories filled her mind, replaying the most memorable details. Her heart pounded in the darkness as a series of emotions washed over her in colored stripes: the cool purples and blues of joy at seeing her mother's birthplace; the yellows and greens of discovery for all the questions answered and secrets revealed; and the fiery scarlets and burgundy reds of anger at the immortal man who had caused her to be born.

How many children has Gerrawgon fathered in nine hundred seventy years? Aya wondered. *How many children has he abandoned? How many lovers has he discarded?* She reflected on the twenty-four years her mother had lived in the valleys while Gerrawgon wandered masquerading as a peddler with his two-wheeled cart on the wagon roads. *Did Mamma know his true nature? Or did he maintain the deceit while taking his pleasures with her?* Even when her mother was dying of the wasting-away illness, Gerrie did not deign to descend from the hillsides to visit her on her deathbed.

She thought of Shadboyut's father again. *He only knew Mamma for a single day, but he loved her more sincerely than the ageless man who sired me.* A one-legged cripple, suffering from the wasting-away illness that had no remedy, had managed to crawl up this mountainside. He dared to engage in battle with a creature of mythic horror, in a cave that Gerrie was too much of a coward to enter. He sacrificed his life for her sake. Aho's name was the last name on his lips; her face was the last thought in his mind as he died.

Aya blinked in the darkness and her eyes were dry. She no longer wept. She was finished with all her weeping for the events of the past. Her thoughts turned to hope for the future and imagining the tasks for the day to come. *Tomorrow,* she promised herself. *Tomorrow, we will be strong. We will end it. We will save the world.*

* * *

Aya awakened in pure darkness and could not tell if her eyes were open or shut. Shadboyut slept beside her, breathing deeply into his pillow.

How many hours had passed, she wondered. If morning had arrived, she could not see through the rock.

In sitting up, she felt a pressure below her belly to relieve herself of all the soups and drinks she had consumed the night before. Frowning in thought, she worked to remember what she had seen of the meager furnishings in this room. A cedar storage chest, a bedside stool, and a worktable gave her no option but to seek outside the room for what villagers called a soil box.

She lowered her bare feet to the floor and expected it to be cold, but the waxy slate felt as warm as hearth bricks. Wearing only her knee-length chemise with a drawstring neckline, she ventured down the length of the stone mattress towards the direction of the curtained doorway.

When she emerged from a slit in the drapes, a sepia toned panorama welcomed her eyes. At the clusters of canvas tents, in scattered spots, small fires were rising to life. The telltale clicks of steel on flint echoed softly in the vast cavern. Inhaling, she savored the faint odors of sausages being roasted and the starchy steam of buckwheat groats.

Aya descended the narrow ramp that brought her to the base floor of the cavern. She walked to the nearest tent where a woman squatted on her heels and worked to feed sticks into a growing fire in a circle of round stones.

"Hello?" Aya said to the woman's back.

The woman rocked onto her heels and smoothly rose to stand tall. Her brown eyes were a striking mismatch in contrast with her tawny hair. "Hello, Shining One."

"My name is Aya."

"I'm called Ula," said the woman who had exchanged flirtatious smiles with Shadboyut the night before.

"Yes, I remember." Aya gestured to herself. "Is there a place where I can, uh, let out my water?"

"Here." Ula raised the corner flap of her tent and extended her hand to welcome the guest inside.

Aya ducked under the frame. A tightly woven straw mat created a sturdy floor. Ula's blankets had already been rolled up, tied with a strap, and hung from a crossbar overhead. Furnishings were similar to what

Kyrggh owned but in a smaller space: a cedar storage chest, a short-legged table, and beeswax candlesticks.

In the corner of the tent was a bucket with a lid. Ula dropped the tent flap and allowed Aya some privacy to use it.

When she emerged afterwards, Ula had readied a basin of warm water, a linen face cloth, and a cake of soap.

"Thank you." Aya sat down on a block of stone padded with buan fleece pelts. She proceeded to wipe her hands and face of all the trail's soil from the day before.

Ula squatted on her heels to stir porridge simmering in the iron pot suspended on a tripod above the firepit. "I can show you the passageway down to the hot springs pool, if you want."

"Hot springs pool?" Aya repeated. "I don't know what that is."

"A pool is water. You sit in the water."

"I don't understand. How do you heat the water?"

Ula smiled, compassionately perplexed. "The mountain heats the water."

Aya braced herself, ready to be admonished. *You ignorant mud-foot villagers, don't you know anything?* What she feared did not come.

The woman matter-of-factly scooped up a serving of porridge into a gourd bowl. She placed it on the stone bench near Aya's hand. As always, both women were careful not to get too close so as not to risk a touch.

Aya used the ox-horn spoon to savor the first mouthful. Cinnamon and honey enhanced the earthy, nutty flavor of the buckwheat groats. "This is very good. Good food."

That raised a genuine smile in response. Aya realized that the mountain people expressed their gratitude to each other without formal words of thanks and promises of reciprocation. It was enough to acknowledge that the offering was appreciated, that the food which Ula had worked to prepare met the needs of the one to whom she offered it. Task well done; task competently accomplished.

Ula poured boiling water from a small kettle into a tin cup. A dried black mushroom at the bottom of the cup swelled and released its aroma. She took a sip, then offered it to Aya.

"Do you have another cup?" Aya asked.

"No."

Aya looked down at the porridge in her lap. "Do you have another bowl?"

"No."

"Why?"

"I am only one."

She placed the bowl to the side on the stone bench. "Come sit with me. Eat with me."

"As you say, Shining One." Ula rose to take a place on the stone bench, within reach of Aya's hands but restraining her movements so that they did not risk a touch. They took turns at the spoon and the cup. Aya's belly filled with the warmth of the food and the woman's companionship. *This is how Mamma lived, sharing food and fire with her sisters and brothers. Why was she so restless? Why did she ever wish to leave?*

"How many other clans inhabit the mountain ranges?" Aya asked.

Ula was quiet for a moment in thought. "There are nine fathers."

"Nine," Aya repeated. "I see."

"Our father is the guardian of the forbidden place wherein dwells The One Who Sleeps."

"Do the other clans guard other things?"

Ula tilted her head aside. "No, there is only one forbidden place. The Black Bird Clan has the duty to keep all others away. So it has always been. So it will always be."

Aya looked around at the broad cavern with its high cathedral ceiling. More people gathered around their cooking fires for the morning meal. The irregular surface of the floor formed natural barriers between the dwellings. Rocky mounds as large as sleeping oxen encircled the sunken areas. Stalagmites jutted out of the irregular ground like teeth. Heaps of crumbled boulders were too large for human hands to move aside. Not having a smooth, clear field of vision made it difficult for Aya to count the number of tent cabins.

"How many people are in this clan?"

"Sixty..." Ula paused. "No, wait... Fifty... Fifty-one. Yes, it's fifty-one now."

A lump rose at the back of Aya's throat as she surveyed the small family groups once more. No one was older than forty or fifty years. Despite the early hour, no swaddled babies cried out for their mother's milk. Any children she could see were walking on their own and doing chores. Do they have a midwife, she wondered? Do they have a healer? How many elders or babies have died since the chime struck? Had any mothers died in childbirth? Had infants starved if they could not be suckled? Did the frail elderly stumble on the treacherous paths of the caverns or hazardous trails of the mountainside and no one's hand could save them? All these questions boiled in Aya's thoughts, but she had no heart to ask. There was no reason to ask, for the answers were plain to see.

She reflected on the words spoken a short time ago, when Ula had served her food. *Do you have another bowl?*

No.

Why?

I am only one.

Twenty-Four

BY THE TIME Aya and Ula finished their bowl of porridge and kettle of mushroom tea, more of the mountain men rose from sleep and consumed their morning meals. Conversations chattered and hummed like crickets that echoed in the high, lofty cathedral dome of the cavern. Aya wondered how they knew that morning had come when the sun's light did not penetrate this deeply into the hollows of the mountain.

More faces turned in her direction. Aya felt the staring eyes of her blood cousins from a faraway land whose names she did not know. She had no hope of melting into the scenery unnoticed. Although her linen chemise was soiled from the sweat of her body and the dirt of the trail, the bone-colored cloth was a stark contrast to the leathers and bear furs worn by everyone else.

Even more than her foreign garments, the people stared at her for being a Shining One with the legendary ability to soar outside of her own skin and witness visions of other places in other times. She reflected on Gerrie's words with a new sense of understanding. *Would you have worshipped me as a god? Or would you have shunned me or hunted me? Would you have cut my skin to see if I bleed?* On this morning, when she faced all the curious eyes of her mother's people, Aya wondered if she had been too hasty in revealing herself to Kyrggh so soon.

Jurrid strolled over to Ula's firepit. Fully dressed with the hood of his cowl tossed back, his belt sagged under the weight of pouches, knife sheaths, and a short hatchet. His close-cropped beard obscured the lower half of his face. Aya could not read his expression.

"Kyrggh is summoning all of the hunters," he said to Ula.

"We meet where?"

"In the Chapel of the Ancestors."

Ula ducked into her tent. There followed the sounds of a cedar chest's lid creaking open and the woman rummaging about for her clothing.

Jurrid looked past Aya and up to the curtained alcove. "Is the other Shining One awake?"

"I don't know," she said. "He drank a lot of mead and beer last night."

Aya fingered her hopelessly tangled hair. The curls had matted into a thick wad of felt at the nape of her neck.

Jurrid asked, "Do you wish to bathe in the hot springs pool?"

"No," Aya said. "There will be time to bathe when the work is done."

He nodded with a slight grunt. Aya could not tell if he appreciated her dedication or expressed disdain for her unkempt appearance. Perhaps it was a mixture of both.

She added, "Could someone go wake up Shad and feed him the morning meal?"

"Someone?" Jurrid repeated. "Not you?"

Barefoot, in nothing but a linen chemise, Aya squared her shoulders and stood tall. She raised her chin slightly to look him straight in the eye. "I'm going with you to Kyrggh's meeting."

"With me? But..."

Ula emerged from the tent. Now she wore garments similar to Jurrid's: the dark buckskin tunic over a linen undershirt, a wool apron that draped from her hips, a hooded leather cowl, and a thick leather belt. She carried boots in one hand, a longbow in the other, and a quiver of arrows hung from her left shoulder.

"We are honored for you to walk with us, Shining One," the woman said.

"It is my honor."

* * *

Roughly a dozen men and women of similar age gathered in a round, domed chamber at the end of a tunnel. It felt to Aya that they had traveled deep into the conical mountaintop's core. A narrow waterfall trickled out of a fissure in the ceiling. Sunlight beamed into the room from that water-giving hole. Iron pyrite and rainbow-colored gemstones encrusted the walls. Light glittered from every direction.

Kyrggh stood at the center of the chamber. A waist-high cylinder of white marble encircled a dark hole in the floor. Aya approached him. No one objected to the Shining One who dared to draw near to their sacred altar. She chose to stand at Kyrggh's side with marble blocks like a hollow tree stump between them.

The best and strongest hunters lowered themselves to genuflect on their left knees. They crossed their wrists and draped their hands off their kneecaps. All together, they bowed their heads in obedience and waited for Kyrggh to speak. Aya marveled at the unison of their movements and postures; she had never seen anything like it, even in the villagers dancing at seasonal festivals.

"My children," Kyrggh began. "I have meditated overnight and prayed for the ghosts of our ancestors to give me guidance. My prayers were answered. Knowledge and understanding have come to me. Listen to what I tell you now."

The group humphed and hummed and grunted still with their heads bowed. Aya saw no faces, only their broad shoulders and shaggy fronds of brown hair.

"In our time of need, the Shining Ones of legend have come to us. They offer deliverance from our suffering. The trail is ahead. We will journey on this day to the Forbidden Cave where the Shining Ones will confront The One Who Sleeps. It sleeps no more! It is awake and screaming. The scream is the source of all our pain. The task is clear. When its voice is silenced, our suffering will end."

Kyrggh paused to allow the group a collective gasp of surprise and hope.

Aya rested her hand against the flutters in her own belly. *I hope it's that simple.*

"I will guide the Shining Ones to the gateway of the Forbidden Cave. I ask for three more willing to join us on the trail. Stand, if you—"

All fourteen of them rose to their feet.

"No," Kyrggh said. "I will only risk three of you to trespass in the forbidden place. It is dangerous and I will not sacrifice you all. If you cannot choose yourselves, then I will choose."

Aya looked aside at his hesitation and, in his profile, saw the flex of his jaw underneath his closely-chopped beard. *That place cost Mamma and Shad's father their lives. It is called the Forbidden Cave for a reason.*

"Dorrith? Jurrid? You first encountered the Shining Ones and brought them to us."

Both men nodded.

Aya scanned across all their willing, eager faces, their eyes sparkling with hope. Choose me! Choose me! She settled on the face of the brown-eyed woman with whom she had shared a morning meal.

Kyrggh, after a brief sideways glance, pointed at the woman. "You, Ula."

Aya felt a chill shudder down her spine. Ula smiled and squared her shoulders with pride.

"Pack what is necessary," Kyrggh said. "We carry it all ourselves—no animals. We leave as soon as we're ready."

* * *

Aya hurried back to the alcove chamber where she found Shadboyut sitting half-nude on the stone bed. He hugged a flagon of tepid barley tea against his bare chest.

"Hurry up!" she said. "Get dressed. We're launching onto the trail as soon as we can get our boots on."

"I feel sick. I ate too much meat."

"No time for that, Shad." She scrambled to pull on her two layers of linen skirts, her wraparound wool tunic, leather belt, and ankle-length hooded cloak.

"Do I have time to smoke a pipe?"

"No, you don't."

"How long have you been awake?"

"A while," she said.

"Why the rush? We've been suffering for months now. Is one more day going to matter?"

Aya pulled aside the curtains and opened the view of the entire cathedral cavern. "Yes, one more day is going to matter. Look at them! They don't complain but every day that passes is a day that a mother cannot hold her own child, or lovers cannot embrace each other. The world is dying, Shad! How can you bear to wait one more day...one more hour?"

With head lowered, his long black hair fell in a curtain that concealed his face. "I've scorched a rug. I've charred the pages of a ledger book. Mercy be on us, Aya but we've never tested how much the little fire sprites will do."

"You're afraid?" she asked.

"Yes," he said quietly. "Don't tell the mountain boys but yes, I'm afraid. How big did you say that crab creature is? The size of a peddler's wagon? My papa attacked it with a woodsman's axe and all he managed to do was make it angry."

Aya came to sit on the bed with him. "My spirit has traveled to the days that have not yet come. I'm confident that we will vanquish the creature and end the suffering of the world."

"How?"

"I don't know, Shad but I feel that we will succeed. We must!" She kissed his cheek and felt the scratch of his morning stubble. He rotated his face and allowed their mouths to meet in a warm, leisurely kiss.

"All right," he sighed. "Help me find my pants?"

* * *

Dorrith lugged a large tin bucket filled with smoldering chunks. Jurrid carried a burlap sack filled with small logs and dried cakes of buan manure to feed the fire. Ula brought a glass decanter filled to the cork with lamp oil. Those three followed in single file behind the pair of Shining Ones who walked on the heels of Kyrggh the Father of the Clan.

No footpath marked the trail. Only by the position of the sun and the angle of the mountainside did the man lead their course. The weather was clear. The mountain set the pace but allowed them to make substantial progress in the first couple of hours. The group made it to the crest of a narrow ridge that extended between one lopsided pyramid and the next.

"There." Kyrggh pointed to the far end of the ridge that connected to the point of the next mountain's peak. Clouds swathed the peak in furry vapors. Streaks of snow marbled the gray granite.

"Yes." Aya gazed into the distance to where she knew the hole in the mountainside to be.

Everyone paused to drink from the flasks or water bags that hung from their belts. Jurrid passed a few sticks of smoked venison up the line of gloved hands. Dorrith fed the smoldering fire in the tin bucket that he carried. Fierce, swift winds poured over the ridge. Dorrith coddled the fiery bucket as if it were a newborn infant.

Shadboyut pointed to a jagged line of trees farther downslope and to the southeast. "Years ago, we came up that way. As a child, these mountain ranges felt so enormous and seemed to stretch on forever. Now, to see the world from this angle, they feel even higher than I remember."

Aya told him, "The world is even bigger than what you can see from here. Beyond the mountains, beyond the oceans to the west and the south, there are other lands and other peoples who know nothing of what we're suffering or what we will do here today. Until now, our lives have been spent in a small patch of land."

Kyrggh furrowed his brows in listening to her speak in the villagers' language. How much he understood, she could not be sure. As soon as their eyes met, he turned away.

"Let's move on."

The group continued walking, single file, on the hatchet's edge of gravelly earth. To either side of their boots, the ground sharply dropped away. Treetops seen from above were a distant fuzz, like a throw rug. One slight misstep would send a walker tumbling uncontrollably down the gravelly scree to be lost in the boulders and waterfalls of the forest below.

She looked up to the sky. Eagles soared with wings outstretched, drifting lazily between the clouds. *I've been where you are. I've seen what you see.* With each springing footstep, she wished to leap into the sky and join the eagles in flight. Vertigo sparkled purple and magenta colors in her eyelids; Aya shook it off. There was no time to launch into a dream.

"Are you all right?" Shadboyut asked from behind.

"Yes."

"Is the air too thin? Are you feeling dizzy?"

"I'm fine," she insisted.

"Don't faint again. Not here."

Aya spoke across her shoulder. "I won't. I almost did but I controlled it. I think I'm learning to control it."

"That's good to hear. Every skill takes practice, yeah?"

"Yes, Shad, yes it does."

The sun's course across the sky advanced by a finger's width or two by the time the group arrived at the next mountain peak. The narrow ridge broadened and spread out to a crescent-shaped cliff that wrapped around the jagged cone. Stacks of rocks on either side of the trail's end marked a sort of gateway. A bear's skull was mounted on a tarnished metal pike; its bleached forehead painted with symbols of interlocking triangles and spirals.

Aya pointed forward with her whole arm outstretched. "There! The cave's entrance is around that turn."

Vibrations in the stone throbbed at the soles of her feet as she launched ahead of the group. She took only a few steps before she had to stop. Pins and needles of tingling seized her calves and shins.

"What is it?" Kyrggh asked.

Shadboyut rushed to be at her side. As soon as he came near, he also stopped abruptly. "It stings!"

Kyrggh jogged the short distance to join them. He halted in front of her, bowed his head and grunted. "Yes. It hurts."

Jurrid cried out, "Father?"

He raised his palm to signal restraint. "The mountain screams, my son."

Shadboyut grasped her hand. As their skin connected, the thorny burning in her legs reduced to a bearable discomfort.

"It's like the curse," she said. "The two of us..."

Kyrggh shuffled backwards stiffly until he reached the bear's skull marking post. "When the father before me showed me this sacred place, it did not feel like this. The mountain has changed. Indeed, it must be The One Who Screams who is now awake."

"Shall we go forward?" Dorrith asked. "

"No," Kyrggh said. "The Shining Ones must go on."

Jurrid dropped fuel into the fiery bucket to make the flames grow brighter. "We can endure it, Father. We can accompany the Shining Ones into the forbidden place."

"No, my son. If this is the first obstacle, we should not risk unknown dangers ahead. Our trail ends here."

Ula handed over the glass decanter full of lamp oil. Aya received it and hooked the leather thong strap over her shoulder.

Shadboyut tapped nervously on the stem of his pipe stuck into his belt. "All right, mountain boy, hand over the fire bucket. Looks like I'm going to carry it from here."

Twenty-Five

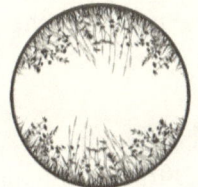

BY HOLDING HANDS, they were able to traverse the clifftop. With some difficulty but it was not unbearable, no more than walking barefoot in the snow. *Be strong, be strong*, Aya told herself. The distance would not be so far, she hoped.

The cliff's narrow ledge wrapped around the mountain cone's peak like a platter underneath a loaf of bread. Aya trod cautiously in single-file behind him while holding onto his free hand. She made sure of each step as she put one foot in front of the other. Coming around to the shadowy side, the cliff's surface was glazed with a layer of slick black ice.

"Careful, don't slip or fall," Shadboyut said.

Turning the gradual curve around the peak's base, they encountered a colossal obelisk that blocked their way. Shadboyut held the fire bucket in one hand and Aya's fingers in the other, so he could only point in the southeasterly direction by raising his chin.

"There," he said. "That's where we came from when Papa and I fled up the mountainside to this very spot."

Aya looked over the cliff's edge to the sheer drop. Vertical walls of granite slabs offered few hand holds. To ascend would be to crawl like a squirrel on a tree trunk by one's toes and fingertips. *The one-legged man came this way*, she thought.

"Where is the cave?"

"Here." Shadboyut led her straight to the obelisk's smooth face. As they approached, Aya perceived a subtle variation in the depth between one panel of rock and another. Drawing nearer, it became clear that the cave's entrance could only be viewed at an angle by standing directly on its threshold.

They stepped together into the hollow and turned the corner. Symbols were carved into the obelisk at the rear—a simple crisscross of five diagonal lines.

"This is it," he said.

Aya squeezed his hand. He squeezed back.

Darkness was not silent. Stone walls chimed a constant drone. The tone's pitch matched the ringing inside Aya's ears that she and everyone had suffered since the chime struck. The tones reverberated in all the octaves at once. A single musical note was duplicated in all its flavors: an inaudible deep, a rumbling deep, a medium hum, a high whine, and a shrill whistle.

Shadboyut squinted his eyes. "Mercy! Do you hear that?"

"Yes."

"It wasn't like that before!"

"Of course not," she said. "It's what we're here for."

The passageway narrowed. The two of them could not walk side by side. Shadboyut went ahead carrying the fire bucket. The deeper they ventured into the core of the mountain, the dimness gave way to a jade glow radiating from the rocky walls. Everything within Aya's field of vision turned to an eerie, unnatural color. The man's brown-toned clothing and her own russet skirts transformed into the same gray hue. Only the smoldering embers in the bucket retained their orange glow.

The tunnel ended at a circular domed chamber. In contrast to the melted-wax walls of the clan's home cavern, this cave was a stockpile for crystalline logs of white, green, and blue quartz.

Shadboyut stood with reverence on the spot where Aho's brother had shattered his father's leg. He looked aside to the sparkling waters that trickled down from a dark crack in the ceiling.

"I'm sorry, Shad but we don't have time to dwell on memories." Aya pulled him by the hand to the rim of the rocky ledge.

Down below—but not as far down as she had feared it would be—a tourmaline green glow illuminated the base of the rift. The ledge upon which they stood overhung an identical chamber directly below.

"All right, you win," he said. "It's not bottomless. But it wasn't glowing like that before, either."

"The crab's screaming makes it glow," she guessed. "We're close. How do we get down there?"

Shadboyut gently tugged her hand. He led the way to the left-hand side of the ledge where the shelf ended and met the dome's base. Blocky boulders offered a rough-cut stairway that descended in a spiral to the chamber below.

"Dare we let go of each other?" he asked. "I need both hands."

Aya opened her grip. The vibration in the soles of her feet grew stronger but it was not as painful as it had been outside of the cave. All around them, the air rippled with the constant drone of harmonics. It all diffused into a bearable discomfort.

"Let's hurry," she said.

He went first, carrying the handle of the fire bucket. The gigantic blocks were too large to descend in one step. He had to sit down on each block, slide forward, and drop to the next level below. Aya hugged the glass decanter of lamp oil close to her side. The last thing she wished to happen was for the glass to shatter and spill its flammable contents. Not yet.

The green crystalline glow of the lower chamber was unbearably bright. Like stepping from darkness into the afternoon of a summer's day, it took a moment of blinking for their eyes to adjust.

Glittering silvery sands encircled a pool of blue lava. White quartz pillars enhanced the burning chill. *There it is*, she thought but dared not speak aloud.

In the pool squatted the crab-like creature with a shell as large as a caravan wagon. The opaque gelatinous shell hinted of inner gills or guts flexing within its monstrous body. Tentacles spread out in all directions like white ropes that draped over fallen logs of crystal scattered on the silvery sands at the rim of the pond. Its bulbous eyes had no lids to blink. It had no mouth and yet it screamed.

"Does it see us?" Shadboyut whispered.

"I don't know."

"Let's hurry then." He set down the fire bucket and twisted it slightly to secure its position in the silvery sands.

Aya looked past Shad getting busy with his task. The gigantic creature loomed before them both. Oddly, she felt no fear; she had been here before; she had seen this scene before; she had seen the days yet to come when everything would be all right. She stood by serenely as if assisting her sister Dimylse with preparing supper at the hearth fire; she knew what the outcome would be. Chop the vegetables. Pat the dough into flatbread. Stir the stew in the cauldron.

Her gaze drifted beyond where Shadboyut crouched over the fire bucket. Against the left-hand wall of the chamber lay the desiccated remains of a man dressed in a mountain man's leathers that she now knew to be her uncle's corpse. *Mamma's shame; Mamma's regret.*

Not far beyond that corpse lay the half-decayed, deflated remains of his father Zhardohut who died more recently with a woodsman's axe in his hand.

"Focus on the fire." Aya took a step to her right to keep his attention away from the grim scene at the opposite wall.

"I am." Shadboyut waved his hand above the fiery bucket. "Hello there, little fire bugs? Hello? Come out, now. Do you want to come out and play? I've got a game for you."

Aya uncorked the glass decanter full of lamp oil. She used her kerchief cap to stuff into the bottle's neck and made sure the fabric dipped far down enough to soak up the flammable oil.

Tiny eyes blinked away in the flickering tongues of flame. *May we come out?*

He smiled. "Yes, yes, come on out."

No hurt us?

"No, don't be scared. The bad man with the tuning fork's not here. No one's going to hurt you. C'mon, come along, we want to play with you! We want to play very much."

He extended both arms. With fingers spread wide, he invited the sparks to rise out of the bucket. He flexed his hands in the grace of a master puppeteer pulling the strings and raised a column of shimmering orange embers that giggled with delight.

Fire sprites rose out of the bucket in an increasing whirl of sparkles that gained intensity. Shadboyut had to take a step back or the outer edges of the spiraling flashes might catch on to his long hair or the fringe of his sleeves.

"Focus," Aya said.

"Tell them what to do!" he cried out.

Aya dipped the bottle's wick into the swirling column of sparkling flames. The fire sprites eagerly jumped onto it. Underhanded, she flung the glass bottle towards the creature's shell. It smashed and glass shards glittered as they sprayed over its surface.

Shadboyut pointed with his outstretched arm. In response, the fiery column rushed sideways in a glowing stream. It poured out of the bucket with all the force and vigor of a stream's waterfall turning the wheel of a grist mill. The fire sprites crawled onto the back of the gigantic crab like sparkling hornets swarming onto a juicy piece of meat. Their glittering glow blanketed the creature from side to side, front to back, tickling the base of its tentacles and pinching its bulbous eyes.

The two held each other's hands as they stood there and watched. *Not long now*, Aya thought.

Fiery specks continue to ripple and flutter on the crab's back but the ringing in the cave did not change in volume or in tone. The stones beneath their feet continued to vibrate the same as before.

"How long do you think it will take to cook?" he asked.

"I'm not sure."

One of the crab's tentacles writhed to its right and whipped around to slap itself on the back. Sparkles splashed away, giggling, and winked out of sight.

"This isn't going well," he said.

"Wait."

The slimy tentacle slid over its own back and wiped the sparkles away. Ever so gradually, it rotated its half-submerged body in the shallow lava pond. It maneuvered a half turn to show the purple gash of a wound chopped in its right-hand side.

Shadboyut followed the creature's rotation and shifted his stance in a half-circle until he faced that side of the chamber full on. He saw the corpse slumped against the far wall.

"Oh, Papa?"

Fiery sparkles all vanished into puffs of smoke.

Aya tightened her grip on his hand. His fingers went limp. "Bring them back, Shad! It isn't finished!"

"Papa." His voice cracked on the word in a raw, grating tone.

The crab's tentacle whipped about the chamber again, swinging in their direction. Aya tugged on his arm hard, forcing him to duck. The gelatinous white cord whipped the air above their heads. It ended by slapping the wall. Chunks of the quartz pillars collapsed and buried the two corpses together in a heap of ice-colored stone.

Vibrations shook and rocked the chamber's floor. The tentacle coiled into itself and made ready for another swing.

"C'mon!" Aya pulled at his hand and Shadboyut had no choice but to follow. The two of them scrambled up the blocks from where they had descended. The tip of the creature's tentacle slapped the stones behind their feet.

Reaching the ledge, Aya leaped into the clear flat space where the creature's tentacles could not reach. She paused to gasp for a breath. Shadboyut put his hands over his face and moaned in between his fingers.

"I'm so sorry that you saw that." Aya stopped short of voicing the rest of her thought. *You had to know his body was lying here. You shouldn't have been surprised.* She wrapped her arms around him. Her hands soothed him into surrendering to the storm of tears he had been holding back until now. With his face pressed into her shoulder, he whimpered in grief.

"There, there, there." Aya's comforting hands rubbed his back through the strands of his long hair. *Am I being selfish,* she wondered, *to hope that he finishes weeping soon and we can make another attack on the creature?*

A force bumped into the rock beneath their feet. A crack opened in the stone platform. The two broke apart and looked down at their feet. The jagged split widened and deepened, splitting down the middle of the shelf upon which they stood.

No time to sniff up his tears, Shadboyut pushed her ahead to the passageway. Aya ran first, leading the way out of the darkness and rushing at her best speed toward the sunlight. The walls shook. The floor bounced. Silvery grit and dust sprinkled from overhead. Behind them, pebbles clattered and grew louder as bigger chunks of rock collapsed.

Aya jumped free around the entranceway's folded pillar. She reached back, grabbed Shadboyut's sleeve, and yanked him the rest of the way outside. The mountain's face cracked like an egg dropped into boiling water.

The soles of their shoes slipped and skidded on the black ice as they scrambled to get some distance. Boulders broke loose from higher up on the mountain's cone. A wagonload of gray rocks poured down the slope. Stones covered the cave's entrance, too large for even the mightiest oxen to haul. Gravel and stone reshaped that side of the mountain and forever sealed that trail off from anyone daring to ascend from the east.

Hand in hand to endure the painful vibration of the rocky outcropping, the two of them ran back the way they had come. They sprinted to rejoin the group of mountain men waiting at the bear's skull in expectation of their victorious return.

Aya dropped to her knees and gripped the artfully stacked stones that marked the edge of the forbidden zone. Shadboyut stood beside her, hunched forward and holding onto his own sides.

Kyrggh demanded, "What happened? Did you kill it?"

"No," she groaned. "We failed."

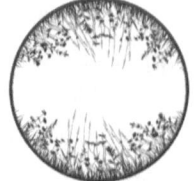

KYRGGH OFFERED Aya the water bag from his belt. "Drink."

Aya shook her head in refusal. "Did you hear me? We failed."

"I heard you," he said. "Drink."

Aya reluctantly took the pouch into her own hands. She gulped a few mouthfuls of tepid water flavored with ginger.

"It's my fault." Shadboyut accepted the offer of a drink from Ula's flask. "We threw fire at it, but it wasn't strong enough to get through the beast's shell. Maybe it would have been if I held it longer, but I couldn't sustain it."

The six of them reformed into a standing circle. Stray rocks still clattered off the rockslide in the background. Mountain winds stirred the furry edges of the mountain men's hooded cowls. The sun overhead had cleared its zenith and began its descent into the west.

Kyrggh said, "Failure is only failure if we do not get up and attack once more. We will not leave this mountaintop until The One Who Screams is silenced."

He turned aside and said, "Go again," in the villagers' language for Shadboyut's sake.

Aya stood as a lone pillar at the center of them all: the mountain-dwellers to her right-hand side and her vagabond companion at her left.

They all looked at her expectantly. At that moment, she felt self-conscious of her own youth and inexperience. She had never hunted animals. She had never battled to save someone's life. She had never held the fate of the world and all its future days in her hands. Yet, if it weren't her responsibility, then why have visions at all?

"In my dream, I saw another way to enter. Father, do you know of another passageway into the forbidden cave?"

The other three shook their heads despairingly but only Kyrggh remained still. After a pause, he admitted, "Yes, there is a secret passage taught to me by the Father of the Clan who came before and all the fathers who came before him. It has always been forbidden to use it."

Aya said, "We are past doing forbidden things, are we not?"

He nodded. "As the guardian of the sacred mountain, only I hold the tools and the knowledge to ask the spirits in the stones for their aid to enter the forbidden place. The problem I see now is that it will make a noise when I open the way. It is not a stealthy entrance. The One Who Screams will hear and know of our approach. But again, we have already lost the element of surprise. I see no other way but to make the breach."

"I agree." Aya briefly translated for her companion. "Shad, he knows another way inside."

"Fantastic. Then what? The fire bucket might still be smoldering, if the beast hasn't tipped it over. We weren't strong enough to get through the damned thing's shell."

"The underbelly." Kyrggh patted his own stomach so that Shadboyut could understand his words. "Every beast has a soft underbelly."

Shadboyut snapped his fingers. "He's right! If we could get the damned thing to stand up out of that pool."

Ula said, "When I hunt wild game, I flush them out of hiding. Can we coax The One Who Screams into exposing its underbelly?"

Kyrggh raised a hand to signal silence. "You are both saying the same idea, Shining One."

"We are?" Shadboyut smiled to the woman carrying a quiver of arrows and a longbow.

"It is a sorrow in my heart that I must say these words," Kyrggh said, switching back to his own language to express his thoughts to his comrades. "What we need right now is not a hero but a deceiver."

"He says we need a liar," Aya translated.

"A liar? Me? Well, I suppose you could see it that way. What is a storyteller, after all but a liar who tells lies to a willing audience? People enjoy my puppet shows because they want to experience the old legends brought to life. Not that they actually believe that ceramic faces and costumes stuffed with sawdust are actually the heroes of old but when my voice sings the old epics, there is that wondrous time when the audience sees what it wants to see instead of what is actually in front of their eyes."

Aya asked, "How do you think we could trick the beast into rising up out of that pool, Shad?"

"Indeed, what would entertain a monstrous crab and so enthrall him to his doom?"

Kyrggh translated to the other three. "How can we bait it?"

Dorrith asked, "What does it eat?"

"What treasure does it guard?" Jurrid added.

The woman Ula at the end of the line asked, "What does it wish to fuck?"

Shadboyut looked to Aya for a translation. After a pause to consider the most appropriate words, she said, "Ula thinks it's lonely."

"I see." He flashed a mischievous grin and then grew serious. "She could be right. Everyone, man or beast, has one primary drive that can be more compelling than pain, more compelling than the fear of death itself. Think of it! The poor old thing has been trapped in that cave, all by itself, for who knows how many centuries? Now it's injured and in pain and has no friends for comfort."

"Yes but where can we find another such beast?" Aya asked.

His dark eyes rolled slowly from left to right around the circle, making a visual inventory of everyone's layers of garments and cloaks. He looked to the bear's skull mounted on a pike. Then he kicked at the flaky pumice soil with his toe.

Kyrggh reached across the gap and came close to nudging Shadboyut in the chest with his fist. "What are you thinking?"

"My friend, let me show you how to build a puppet."

Twenty-Seven

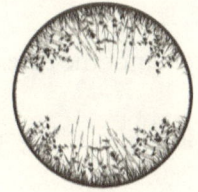

THE GROUP STRIPPED off their cloaks, their hooded cowls, their belts, and everything they carried. As the only one not wearing a cloak, Shadboyut removed his jacket and worked to slice away all the fringe strings dangling from the seams of the sleeves. The mountain men and Aya spread their cloaks on the stony ground and, with their supper knives to poke holes in the cloth, used the strings of fringe to stitch the panels together into a larger whole.

Shirt sleeves, trousers, and Aya's leggings that she wore underneath her skirts became tentacles. Ula's longbow and the others' walking staffs gave structure to the appendages. Bootlaces, waistband drawstrings, and every other thong or strap was tied end-to-end to create the web of strings for the puppeteer's manipulation.

"The body needs more structure," Shadboyut said more than once.

Aya contributed her two layers of linen skirts, her knee-length chemise with its blousy sleeves and drawstring-gathered neckline. Now shirtless, wearing only her under slip that wrapped around her hips, Aya's nude back prickled with little bumps like a plucked goose in the unforgiving mountain winds.

Kyrggh and his three kinsmen gave up their tunics and linen under-shirts. They jabbed knives at the garments' seams and forcefully yanked the panels apart. Aya kneeled on the ground alongside Jurrid and Kyrggh. All three of them worked with the fringe strings to lash together a second layer of the puppet's body.

Ula's collection of arrows jammed heads-first into a water bag, their shafts and feathered ends forming the spokes of a wheel. Shadboyut used the stiff leather quiver as an axel, then turned it upright. "Framework for the upper part of the shell," he explained to Aya. "Can you tell them?"

Dorrith pointed to the center of the base layer. "Put it there, Shining One."

Aya called over her shoulder, "He understands, Shad. Keep working."

Kindling sticks became pegs to attach everyone's thick leather belts to the small fire logs. The jointed framework radiated outwards from the quiver. Six pairs of boots tipped the ends.

It took three of them in coordination to stretch out the edges of the skirts-and-tunics panel, walk sideways around the base layer, and carefully lay it over the framework. Now it began to resemble the canopy of a peddler's booth on market days but with jointed legs coming out of the sides.

Kyrggh yanked the bear's skull and its pike out of the ground. He whispered a prayer drowned out by the windy gusts. After a reverential pause, he positioned it at the front of the puppet.

Aya thought it did not contribute to the illusion and had to say, "The creature does not have a face."

"It has two eyes, you said?"

"Well, yes..."

Kyrggh used two water bags and tied them onto the skull, threading a cord through the empty eye sockets. From a few steps away, the dark leathery cow bladders full of water wobbled and bobbed very much like the distended, external eyeballs of the monstrous creature in the cave below their feet.

Shadboyut flashed a bright grin. "My friend, you've got a talent for this!"

Beside him, Ula frowned and pointed out, "It's all the wrong color."

Shadboyut looked to Aya for a translation, and she said, "The cloaks and my skirts are dark colors. The crab is white."

"Ah yes but not to fear," Shadboyut replied. "We are surrounded by gypsum stone."

Kyrggh nodded and murmured quickly to Jurrid. The two men kneeled to scrape at the stony ground with their kindling hatchets. White powder bloomed puffs of grainy fog around their bare legs. Dorrith gathered handfuls of the chalky dust and rubbed it into the threads of the fabric.

"That won't last for long," Aya said.

Shadboyut told her, "It doesn't need to be durable. It needs to hold together long enough to capture the beast's attention."

Ula came to stand with them. Hands on her hips, she surveyed the creation. Utterly nude except for a cord of bone beads on her right wrist, the woman did not seem to be bothered by the frigid winds relentlessly streaming over the rocky ridge.

"Let's hope The One Who Screams has poor eyesight," Ula said.

"It's in constant agony," Aya told her. "It won't be seeing anything clearly."

"I know it could be better," Shadboyut responded wistfully as if he understood the mountain men's language. "If we had more time and more materials, we could do a more artful job. But given the circumstances, even I'm impressed by what we've built here. Someday, when the story is told of the six of us standing here naked on a mountaintop, we can say that it looked a lot better than it really does. That's what storytellers do, right? We lie... We lie, sometimes, when the truth falls short of what it should be."

Aya reflected on her dream of future days, of the illustrations and the figurines sold to the visitors who had come to hear their history. "Yes, Shad, the truth is not as pretty as the legends someday will make it be."

The four mountain men positioned themselves evenly spaced around the puppet's body. Kyrggh said, "We go together, now."

They hoisted the puppet contraption off the ground by the ropes and carried it forward. Kyrggh led the way, this time, not toward the open flat shelf where Aya and Shadboyut had walked with such difficulty to the cave's entrance. The recent landslide blocked that course. Instead, he led the group around the opposite side of the pinnacle's base. They crept along the precarious edge where granite boulders formed a lumpy irregular crust around the rim. They carried the unwieldly load carefully, slowly, their bare feet blindly seeking the way with each step.

They reached a vertical wall formed by a cluster of rock pillars. Kyrggh signaled to the group to put down their contraption.

Aya looked up and down the palisade of granite cylinders. She saw no entrance, not even a crevasse that a child might squeeze through, much less six people carrying the model of a creature the size of a peddler's wagon.

"Now what happens?" Shadboyut asked.

Kyrggh had given all his clothing to the effort of making the creature puppet, but he had preserved two things. He still wore his necklace of glass beads and a bear claw. He also carried a doeskin pouch hanging from a cross-body shoulder strap.

The other three bowed their heads in reverence as Kyrggh unhooked the pouch's flap. He brought forth two items wrapped in buan fleece. In his right hand, he held a two-pronged musical fork that was clearly Gerrawgon's handiwork. In his left hand, Kyrggh held a tarnished silver bell that bore engravings of intricate geometric patterns of interlocking circles and squares.

"Exquisite workmanship on that bell," Shadboyut said with appreciation. "It looks to be solid silver."

"But the metal's black," Aya responded.

"It hasn't been polished in a lifetime," he explained. "Perhaps a hundred lifetimes."

Kyrggh said solemnly, "These are the tools entrusted to our clan as guardians of the One Who Sleeps and who sleeps no more. These tools were held by the father before me, and his father before him, and for as long as our people have dwelled in this mountain. Our lore teaches that the spirits of the mountain's stones are appeased by their ringing song. May they come to our aid in this time of need."

The father extended his left arm and shook the bell in four banging claps. Silvery ringing pierced the winds in a tone so clean and so perfect and so out of place in the mortal realm. Metallic ringing pierced into her ears and filled Aya's skull with the sunshine of sound. It harmonized to the chime of the heavens, to the song of the stars, to the chorus of incinerated gods who had died long ago, to the screams of the creature trapped in the cave beneath their feet. The sound strummed Aya's veins and gushed through her in shivering waves like a sneeze.

"Oh!" Shadboyut coughed and cleared his throat. "Did you enjoy that too?"

"Yes," Aya whispered.

A spot of light shimmered on the rock wall brighter than a candle's flame in a dark room. Next, Kyrggh tapped the tuning fork's prongs and raised his arm overhead. Being a tall man with long arms, he reached easily to the bright spot. The rocky palisade flexed and shuddered. A vertical crevasse opened from that glowing spot, extending downward to where the pillars ended at the base of the ledge.

Impossible but it was happening. Part of the mountain's side broke away and sank inward as if pushed on rollers. A passageway opened before them, framed by a perfect semi-circular arch. The tunnel entrance appeared large enough for a whole peddler's canopy wagon to pass through.

"We give thanks to you, spirits of the mountain, who heard our prayers and answered." Kyrggh reverently re-wrapped the bell and the prongs in their kerchiefs and tucked them back into his pouch.

Beyond the archway lay a deep passageway of blue, green, and purple shadows that penetrated the core of the mountain itself. The four picked up the monstrous puppet. Without hesitation, they ventured forward.

A lump swelled in the back of her throat as Aya watched them enter the archway. She knew what they all knew from the legends and the lore. All four of them knew that to enter the forbidden cave was a death sentence. They knew they would be poisoning themselves and be doomed to spend the second half of their life in a wasting-away illness. They entered the toxic, glowing air with a spring in their heels and the hope of victory.

Shadboyut threaded his fingers in between Aya's and squeezed tight. "Let's finish it this time, shall we?"

Twenty-Eight

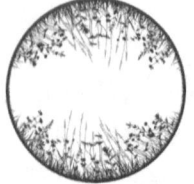

THE ROCKS OF GYPSUM, selenite, and alabaster were as white as ice blocks but not at all cold to the touch. Blades of translucent crystal clustered at the ceiling like whitefish fillets in a smokehouse. Pillars of milky opaque crystal lined the passageway on either side of them.

This is not a natural tunnel, Aya concluded. The floor was too level; the corrugated ridges that served as shallow steps were too regular and symmetrical. The passageway itself was of a uniform height and width in a straight line penetrating into the mountain's core. This tunnel hewn from raw stone was too expertly crafted to be the work of men's hands. Aya wondered if she could dream someday of the ones who built this place. Perhaps they were the kindred of her father's original form—a winged thing that was neither bird nor bat, who hatched from a golden eggshell in a crystal nest in the clouds. *There is more to this world than we think we know.*

"I hate tunnels." Shadboyut's hushed voice echoed all around.

The rocks themselves glowed a turquoise light from within. The farther they walked into the passageway away from the surface, the brighter the walls became. People's faces took on a strange glaze of mineral green.

"We must be getting close," Aya said quietly to the four walking ahead. "Be careful."

The air thickened and shimmered with an unnatural metallic ringing like a troupe of pipers whistling through their flutes at a festival's revelry. Aya felt rather than saw the passageway come to an end. The four stopped walking and laid down the monstrous puppet.

Shadboyut maneuvered ahead of the group. He hugged close to the wall and took care not to touch anyone along the way. Indeed, the passageway ended at an abrupt drop-off that was clearly not in the original design.

Part of the opening was blocked by obstacles of fallen pillars and broken stalactites. It looked like a lumberyard of felled trees if woodsmen had harvested a forest of gigantic white crystals. Aya looked down through the rib bones of the mountain's cavern. Amid the triangular gaps between the stacks of cracked pillars, she could peer into the green and violet chamber below.

The creature's slimy tentacles slithered about the chamber's walls and floors still searching for the trespassers from an hour before. Close to the glowing blue pool where it still squatted, half-submerged, a small faint orange light glimmered in the tin bucket.

Shadboyut grinned at the sight of the smoldering bark. "Who knew? We might actually succeed at this."

Kyrggh asked, "Are you ready, oh Shining Ones?"

"Yes," she said. "Are you?"

He nodded.

Shadboyut flashed the taller man a smiling wink. "May the show look good, my friend."

Aya ventured onto a log of white stone. Like crossing a felled tree to span a shallow creek, she balanced carefully with her bare toes turned outward. Shadboyut followed close behind and, though she could not see him, she sensed his nearness by the warmth at her nude back.

They found footholds along the white marble wall. Descending from log to log, straddling as if climbing down from a mighty oak tree, they managed to find their way down.

All too soon, the pair reached the floor of the cavern. Their bare feet crunched into gravelly silver sand. She looked over her shoulder to check that the monstrous crab, in the pool facing the other way, probably had not seen them.

Shadboyut squatted near the bucket filled with smoldering chunks of wood. The yellow-orange glow on the underside of his chin was the only warm color in the whole chamber. "Hello, little friends," he whispered. "Are you ready to play again?"

A few timid embers spurted upward and hovered in the air. *Yes, yes,* they hissed. *Yes, let's play.*

The pool of blue lava emitted no heat. If anything, it was the coolest part of the chamber. Fire that was not fire perpetually burned what did not burn. Stronger and brighter than the fiery pit beneath the funeral chamber; more intense and fearsome than the boiling lava of a volcano's heart. This was a volcano unlike any other. This was a beast that needed to be sent into oblivion.

The crab's outer shell floated like a scarf in a laundry basin, flat and wavering under the surface. Waves of blue-violet flames sloshed and licked around its edges. At the far side of the pool, opposite to where Aya crouched, the horns of eyes on stalks protruded, looking in the other direction. At any moment, the eyes might bend around and see them at its rear.

Come on, Kyrggh, she thought. *Time to start the show!*

High up on the marble wall, at the shelf of the promenade half-blocked by the crossbars of alabaster pillars, there appeared the shape of another monstrous crab.

Aya watched the puppet's appearance and even though she had lent a hand to its construction, she was impressed by the sight. Gypsum dust rubbed into the cloth glowed sky blue in the eerie ambient shine of the walls all around. The flimsy internal framework held its shape as an oval shell. The jointed tentacle limbs were supported by cords too thin to be clearly seen. The well-concealed team of puppeteers manipulated the strings to make it appear the claws moved under their own power.

The gigantic puppet crab waggled on its descent from the edge. The body expertly tilted left and right as either set of claws appeared to straddle the milky-white alabaster log. Bulbous eyes made from leathery water bags bobbed naturally as if looking around the chamber. The thing looked alive. If she had not known any better, she too would have thought that another monstrous creature had arrived.

Aya's throat went dry. *Come on, come on.*

The crab in the blue lava pool slowly rose. Its eyestalks turned upward to assess the new arrival. Its jointed legs extended from the crouch and like the poles of a tripod raised its body. The disc of its outer shell emerged into the air for the first time in centuries. Blue lava dripped like melting wax from the scalloped edges of its body.

Slowly, slowly, its tentacles unwrapped from the pool's edge. The beast raised its two forward claws, gray blades with serrated edges, and clicked the tips. Whether that gesture was to invite a mate or challenge a foe, Aya could not be sure. They had no way to gauge in the construction of the giant puppet if they were making the image of a male or a female, or if it were possible to know if such a creature had a sex, or which would be more appealing.

"Come now, friends," Shadboyut whispered. "Let's play."

He poised his hands above the bucket and lifted his arms in a carefully controlled motion like a potter at the wheel raising a pillar of clay. Fire spirits swarmed out of the embers smoldering in the bucket. The bucket's orange light grew brighter. Fiery eyes flew in from all around, from the sparkles of the crystalline sand and from the ambient glow of the turquoise stones.

Then, with his left palm outstretched, he pointed at where they should go.

In a mirror image, Aya also extended her hand with palm outward. She recalled the pleasurable feeling that had vibrated and reverberated into the core of her soul when Kyrggh's silver bell had clanged against the mountainside. The ever-present chime that had been whistling inside her inner ear for the past several months grew louder and louder, in harmony with the memory of the bell's tone radiating inside her skull. She called up the power that sang in her blood and bones—the same power that could split her flesh from her soul and send her spirit soaring into the cosmos.

White-orange flame gushed out of Shadboyut's outstretched palm. The spear of fire streaked to the beast and collided at the underside of the shell. Its tentacles thrashed wildly. The beast screamed in a voiceless hiss that Aya felt rather than heard and rattled the stone walls of the chamber. Stalactites cracked loose from the domed ceiling and dropped to shatter on the sandy floor.

Its scream pierced into Aya's core. She felt overcome with a rush of passions—love, fear, anger, pain, and most of all, loneliness. In that moment, she knew that this beast was the last one—or the only one—of its kind. They had deceived it by preying upon its despair and pain. It was not at all sad to die; in the end, its last quivering feeling was frustration that it took so long for death to come.

Shadboyut strained to push the stream of fire harder until sweat dribbled down his cheeks. He held his arm outstretched until his hand trembled.

The crab's shell crinkled and curled up like a parchment tossed on the fire. It popped with the sound of chestnuts roasting. Its claw legs turned to blackened sticks. An aroma of roasted salty flesh, both delicious and terrible, filled the chamber.

Every color turned white. Aya's sight blurred. Her blood ran cold. Her ankles went weak. Reeling sideways, she smacked her hand down to the sparkling sands.

Shadboyut collapsed on his side. His long black hair was a sweat-drenched veil. Still, he kept his arm aloft, kept his palm facing forward. With the joyous squeals of fire sprites dancing in revelry, he kept up the ever-narrowing stream of orange fire, blasting into the shell of the creature that was clearly dead.

"You can stop now," she said hoarsely.

He grunted and dropped his hand.

Fire sprites whirled away to the domed ceiling. Still giggling in fading voices, they glittered one final time before they vanished in puffs of smoke.

Aya closed her eyes as silence ached inside her skull. All the strength leaked from her limbs, and she could not move her smallest finger. Did she faint? Perhaps. Time passed, measured by the rapid irregular patter of her heart.

"Victory!" Kyrggh bellowed the word and howled like a wolf.

The gigantic puppet crab fell from its perch, discarded in a heap as so much fabric, sticks, and string. All four jumped off the stone pillars and landed tumbling in the sand. They grasped each other by the shoulders as they sprang to their feet. Smiling and laughing—no longer seized with pain from the touch of each other's skin—they squeezed their nude bodies together in a wild tangle of joyous arms.

"We've done it." From where he lay on his back, Shadboyut weakly rolled his eyes to look at the four in their delirious celebration.

Aya dragged herself the short distance across the sands and reclined, exhausted, beside her companion. "I almost felt pity for it at the end. It was so alone for so long."

Shadboyut turned his head to the side. "I don't see my papa's body. Do you? Do they?"

"He's buried under all that rock." She pointed across his naked chest, past the celebrating group. A pile of broken crystal pillars lay beyond the creature's charred carcass.

"Then, by the mercy of the gods, this is where he's meant to be. May his spirit find peace. This is where it all began. I'm just..." Shadboyut choked up and took a moment to clear his throat. "I'm going to miss him so much."

"I know." She stroked his long hair away from his eyes. "I know."

The blue pond still glowed with its cool lava from within but no longer had the crab monster squatting in it. The pool seemed strangely cleaner and calmer. It no longer bubbled like a cauldron of soup but had settled down to a smooth sheet of liquid glass. Its surface mirrored the spiderweb veins and flecks of golden pyrite in the marble. *So beautiful,* Aya thought. *Such a beautiful place to be the scene of such suffering.*

Kyrggh broke away from his group and approached the charred carcass of the creature. He pulled off a spike from its mandible. Raising his trophy overhead that was either a tusk or a horn, he proclaimed, "This is a day of victory! Our clan will sing the songs of this day for as long as we have voices to sing."

Jurrid and Ula stood with their hands clasped, gazing at Kyrggh, as they whooped all together in triumph. Their voices echoed throughout the chamber so that three sounded like thirty.

Dorrith trotted over to where the pair of Shining Ones lay on the sands. He dropped to his knees and smiled as if welcoming a friend after a long time apart. He laid his palm to rest on Shadboyut's chest.

"Good fire," Dorrith said in the language of the valleys.

Shadboyut returned the smile. "Good puppet show."

Aya laid her hand on top of Dorrith's knuckles, the first person in months that she had touched other than her companion. His skin felt coarse, weathered, his knuckles chapped. There was a fuzz of soft hair on the back of his wrist.

It was too soon to see the effects of the toxins, she knew but her joy dwindled the longer she watched the four of them laugh and smile and celebrate their victory. A certain indefinable hue had begun to taint their skin. Subtle, barely noticeable, an illusion of the peculiar ambient light that emanated from the glowing rocks all around, but Aya only perceived it from having seen the hue of their complexions from the moment they first entered the passageway. It would be many years before they began to feel the effects, and many more years before their strength and vigor wasted away until finally they succumbed to the illness.

They had known that the cave was toxic; at this moment, they had no regrets.

Twenty-Nine

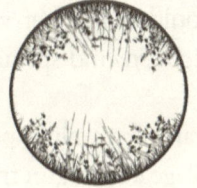

THE GROUP DISASSEMBLED the monstrous puppet as best they could to recover their boots, their cowls and cloaks, Ula's quiver full of arrows, and walking sticks. From the base floor of the cave, they ascended the slippery pillars of white crystal up to the promenade's edge. From there, they made the short trek out of the passageway to emerge into the afternoon's light.

Treading upon the mountain's ledge no longer hurt. The vibration in the stones had now ceased. Shadboyut closed his eyes and drew in a deep inhale of the high-altitude breeze. Aya saw in the others' serene expressions that all of them no longer suffered the constant ringing in the ears. For the first time since that day in early winter, the air sounded clear and quiet. A flock of migrating geese honked passing overhead at such a height that Aya would not have heard them before.

The six descended the mountain back the way they had come. Aya felt drained and weakened in her legs. Oddly, the longer they walked downhill, the more of her strength returned to her numb and tingling legs. She focused on plodding one foot in front of the other as the afternoon dimmed and white clouds turned pink.

They reached the tree line as sunset turned the sky to the color of raw terra cotta clay. The land below was all hues of gray and blue with granite rocks and white bark birch trees. It looked as if the entire world had turned upside-down and tiny humans clung to the underbelly of it all.

Aya gazed outward to marvel at how enormous the world appeared to be from this height. She thought of all the people she had met along the way and wondered how they were celebrating this moment. For years to come, everyone would remember where they were, and what they were doing, on this night in mid-spring when the chiming blight ended.

She imagined the caravan of traveling peddlers. Had their wagons reached their destination village and begun trading their wares at market days yet?

She imagined the neighbors she had known in her home village but now it no longer felt like home. It was a faraway, strange place. Already, she was forgetting the details of the faces that she had known for her entire life. For now, she did not feel the urge to return to Lisshardra Valley.

She thought of her sister Dimylse and her husband, and of her vision of a future time when they still shunned her and knew nothing of the heroic deeds she had performed. She thought of her younger sister Feianthe and her paramour who had never given up hope of the seasons changing. The Keeper of Books and his new apprentice could now consummate their marriage after sharing a roof for several months. The midwife's widower... The barley farmer who lost his wife Nuriasha along with a third child... Would they ever know what she and Shad-boyut had done to ease their suffering? Would they believe her story if she returned to tell them that the fearsome mountain people were honorable, not wild brutes, who had sacrificed their lives to save the rest of the world?

She wondered about her immortal father Gerrawgon, where he was, what he was doing, who he stood with, who he might embrace on this joyous night. Surely he knew what they had accomplished but he would forever keep it a secret. In her vision of a distant future, he was still with-holding his secrets.

"Mercy on my feet but I need to smoke a pipe! How much farther!"

Shadboyut exclaimed this sentiment more than once in the several hours that it took to descend the hillside.

Soon, torches shined through the sparse trees. Small wings of yellow-orange flickered from oiled wads of cloth wrapped around the tips of walking sticks.

"My people!" Kyrggh called out.

Dozens of people wearing trousers and hooded cowls rushed up the steep incline. Voices cried out in joy to the staggering group. "Father! Father, you return in triumph!"

Kyrggh smiled broadly enough to show all his teeth. "We are victorious!"

Several people patted him on the back and chest. They cried out exclamations of joy and celebration, hailing him with praise for leading his clan to deliverance from their suffering.

Dorrith's wife rushed into his arms. The two embraced and kissed with limbs intertwined so tightly as the branches of two sapling trees growing together. It seemed they might never separate again.

A young man rushed into Jurrid's embrace. The two men caressed and kissed like familiar lovers. Aya briefly blinked in surprise at their unabashed, open affections. She had never seen such behavior of men in the valley, or if it had been there, the villagers kept it hidden from view. More lies. More secrets. More innocents feeling shame and being shunned. Her surprise soon passed, melding in with all the new sights and ideas that she had experienced since leaving behind the home where she had lived in a box for her entire life.

Kyrggh hugged all the people clustered around him that he could reach. Across the shoulders that surrounded him, his fingers extended and tried to touch more. "The glory and praise go to the Shining Ones who summoned the spirits of fire and wielded the elemental powers."

"Praises be, praises be," the crowd murmured while smiling reverently in the direction of Shadboyut and Aya.

"The One who Sleeps, the source of the world's misery, has been vanquished and is dead!" Kyrggh held up the trophies of a couple of mandible spikes, twice as large as oxen horns. "Henceforth, the beast of the mountain shall be known as The One Who Rots!"

The group let out a unified, open-mouthed cheering roar. Aya cried out, "Ha!" in her best effort at imitating their full-throated cheers.

Shadboyut lit up his pipe from the flame of a nearby torch and puffed-up clouds that swirled around his dark hair.

They continued the descent although not as swiftly as they could have gone. The narrow trail was meant to walk single file, but the people could not refrain from hugging each other in pairs or groups of three or four in a cluster. They stepped over tree roots and rocks in the path that they could have crossed more easily if not for holding onto each other so tightly. Darkness and the chilling wind meant nothing when hands touched hands once more. Skin pressed against skin, and no one felt pain.

A few of them broke away and sprinted downslope to spread the news. Ula clutched her quiver of arrows under one arm and jogged alongside them. Her strong legs opened wide. Her heels kicked out behind her. Ula pulled ahead of the others and laughed in challenging the others to catch her. *Like my mother in her youthful days*, Aya thought with a tear rising to the corner of her eye.

Shadboyut walked ahead of Aya but slightly off to the side on the narrow trail. He spoke to her by looking back over his shoulder. "Can you politely explain to the boys that I'm exhausted? I know they'll want to celebrate and sing and revel all night and for days to come, but I need sleep. Just sleep. Will they be offended?"

Aya looked to Kyrggh and the others whose grins could not be dimmed. They walked with a bounce in their steps. Their eyes glittered brightly with joy, unafraid of the falling night. Once more, a wave of melancholy overtook her to know that they were poisoned by entering the forbidden cave. They would slowly be wasting away the second half of their lives in an illness that had no cure.

"They don't have politeness, Shad. Be honest with them. Speak the truth plainly and they will respect your wishes. How could they deny you any request?"

He looked at her meaningfully as he inhaled the last of his pipe's smoke. "How about you? Are you going to sleep tonight? Are you going to dream?"

She shrugged. "I don't know yet what I will do. I'm hungry but my stomach is filled with too many flutters to eat. I'm weary but my thoughts are too jittery to sleep. Perhaps I will sit beside you and watch *you* sleep for a change of habit?"

He smiled and held the empty pipe against his chest. "I'd like that."

Thirty

SEVERAL DAYS LATER, Aya accepted the invitation of Kyrggh to meet in the Chapel of the Ancestors and bring the urn of her mother's ashes. She carried the bundle in the shoulder sling she had used since the village. She recalled standing here only a few days earlier with the volunteers. It felt as if a whole cycle of seasons had passed.

Aya looked at the man close by her side and felt as if she were seeing Shadboyut again for the first time. But for his darker complexion, he appeared as a man born to the mountains. He was shirtless in brown leather trousers and clan-style boots. His long straight hair partially veiled his chest, leaving his taut belly exposed.

"Mamma would be glad that you're with me, Shad," she said.

When he smiled, his black eyes glittered by catching a bit of candlelight.

Kyrggh stood alone at the center of the round chamber. Barefoot, he was nearly nude but for the cloth that knotted around his loins. Braided cords encircled his forearms in concentric rings that spanned from his wrists up to his elbows.

Beeswax candlesticks added light to the sunbeam shaft that pierced through a single crack in the ceiling. As before, multi-colored gemstones and iron pyrite encrusting the walls glittered rainbows in every direction.

"Welcome home, spirit of Aho," Kyrggh said solemnly. "As Father of the Clan, I declare that you are no longer shunned. Your bones shall rest here in the belly of the mountain where you were born. Forever more, may your spirit be at peace."

Kyrggh used a nearby candlestick to light a bundle of herbs wrapped in sycamore bark. Bright eyes came awake in the growing flame. Aya frowned at the fiery sprites to behave. He slowly waved the burning bundle of herbs to spread the fragrant smoke throughout the room.

On cue, Aya approached the center of the round floor. A ring of marble blocks encircled a bottomless shaft.

"I bring home the ashes and bones of my Mamma. It is one year since the breath left her body. I come beseeching you, oh Father of the Clan, to... to, uh..."

Shadboyut tilted his head, curious as to why she faltered in the recitation but unable to inquire in the foreign language.

"The ancestors will forgive you if you do not know all the words of the prayers." Kyrggh spoke softly in a fatherly tone "You plead for the overwatching gods to receive her ghost into the bliss of paradise?"

"Yes, I do." Aya unwrapped the bundle in her arms and allowed the sling's fabric to drop away.

The ceramic urn was glazed a pea-green color with random speckles of blue and brown. Wax sealed the lid. Holding it now, it felt so small in her hands. Aya blinked at tears threatening to well up in her eyes. It was hard to imagine that her mother's tall and strong body could be reduced to a handful of bone dust in a jar.

Kyrggh inhaled deeply before exhaling a long, single note. One quick gasp for breath and he chanted rhythmic lyrics on that droning tone. *Your bones belong to the mountain. The mountain receives your bones. Be at peace, oh blissful spirit. Aho daughter of the Black Bird, you are home.*

This was the song that Aho had known since her childhood, taught by the former Father of the Clan and every father who had come before. *This is the song*, she thought with a shiver, that Aho had begged on her deathbed for her daughters to sing.

He paused reverently to allow the echo of his deep bass voice to finish reverberating up to the dome.

Aya gazed down at the hole in the floor. Murky, purple darkness penetrated deep into the core of the mountain. Unafraid, she stood at the rim of the bottomless shaft. Perhaps one day she would dream. Her soul's wings could plunge to its depths and see if any other monstrous creatures lurked below their feet or not.

"Goodbye, Mamma." Aya extended her arms and held the ceramic urn over the gaping hole.

"Is this all there is to their funeral customs?" Shadboyut asked. "Burn some weeds, sing a rhyme, and drop her ashes into a hole? I'm sorry, Aya but it seems a bit... A bit, uh... A bit too quick. Shouldn't we be allowed to say a few things? Tell our favorite memories of her, or cook a meal of her favorite foods in her honor?"

Kyrggh furrowed his brows in trying to follow the man's rapidly spoken words.

"I understand how you feel, Shad," she said. "But this is what she wanted."

Aya dropped the ceramic urn into the chute. It plunged into the shadows. All three held their breath until the faint crash of the ceramic urn shattering at the bottom of the shaft.

"Her soul is free." Kyrggh stepped away from the hole's rim.

"Mercy be." Shadboyut pressed his palm over his heart.

I don't feel any difference in the air, Aya thought. *Was Mamma's soul ever truly in that jar of ashes and bones? Has she already been gone all this time?*

Kyrggh briefly swayed on his feet. Shadboyut caught him at the elbow and held him steady. "Feeling all right, big fella?"

"My head..." The father rubbed the bridge of his nose. "I am well now."

Aya noticed a jaundice hue passing over his pale cheeks. She exchanged a meaningful glance with Shadboyut who also saw it. The poisoning of the forbidden cave had no known cure. They both knew it was the beginning of a lifetime ordeal.

"Let's share a meal?" Shadboyut suggested.

"Another time," he said. "I am not hungry."

Kyrggh turned away and trudged on sluggish feet to the archway entrance of the chamber. The two hopped to either side of him. He waved off their hands offering to grasp his elbows.

"With all respect, oh father," Aya said. "We are all going in the same direction."

They still attempted to lay helping hands on his back, so Kyrggh raised the volume of his voice. "I said, leave me! I can walk on my own feet without help. I am not dying today."

Together, they stayed and watched Kyrggh from behind. He ducked the apex of the archway and disappeared into the outer passageway. His pale form blended into the darkness.

"Can't you dream of something to save them?" Shadboyut slid his arm around her slender waist and hugged her tightly to his side.

Aya blinked at the tears dribbling out of her eyes. "I will try. I won't give up trying. As he said, he's not dying today. It's a long, slow, wasting-away illness. We have time for me to search everywhere, in every yesterday and every tomorrow."

Thirty-One

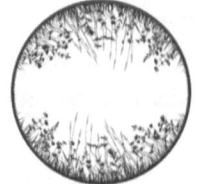

SPRINGTIME POURED out its warm showers until the sky brightened and dried up for the summer months. Aya and Shadboyut dwelled in a sod brick cottage built at the edge of the mountaintop meadow. They had carefully chosen a spot near the entrance to the Black Bird Clan's home cavern—but not too close. Shadboyut had measured the distance in walking paces, as he described it, within shouting range on a warm day if the breezes flowed in the right direction. But he refused to live in a hole in the ground where he could not see the sky or the stars.

One day in early summer, Aya returned from gathering a variety of mushrooms in the wild woods below the tree line.

"You're back early."

"It helps when I already know where to go," she said.

Shadboyut straddled a workbench in the open yard of cleared dirt. He often spent his hours in that patch of wild grass off to the side of the cottage's flagstone step. Early afternoon sunlight shined on the roof's golden straw thatching. A narrow bar of shadow crossed the cottage's foundation of blue and white river rocks. All around, the grass was bright green. Mountain peaks blocked off half the sky.

While smoking a pipe that hung from the corner of his mouth, he worked at sculpting the ceramic face of a new puppet. Nearby on the ground was a bucket of water and a tarp-covered pile of raw clay.

"I made some flatbreads and a porridge of boiled beans," he said. "Are you hungry?"

"That sounds good," she replied. "But perhaps I will eat later."

"Later?" He looked up from the half-finished head of the figurine.

Aya placed her basket full of wild mushrooms near the cottage's doorway. Then she withdrew from the shady doorstep and emerged into sunshine. "I want to go again and see what I can see."

"Oh." He spared one hand to extract the pipe from his mouth. When the lavender smoke finished billowing around his face, his jaw sagged into a frown.

Aya came to stand at his right-hand side, blocking the sun overhead. Her body cast a shadow over his hands. "Is there something you wish to say?"

"You know what I wish to say," he mumbled.

"I'm doing too much? I'm over-exerting myself?"

"Be honest with me. If it's taking a toll on you, then pause. Stop and rest for a while. It's not giving up hope to find a cure for them, but you're useless to everyone if you're exhausted."

I'm looking for him. Aya parted her lips, but the words would not come forth. Too many times had they argued about her wish to speak with Gerrawgon once more. Too many times had they run out of breath after speaking for hours but failing to change each other's opinions. Too many times Shadboyut had advised her to let the selfish clod go find his own way in the world. She had not yet found a good time to confess her secret that Gerrie was her father.

"The headaches are easier to tolerate now with the remedies I've made," she said. "It's no more of a hardship on my body than it is for you to sit here in the hot sun and sculpt your puppets."

He shrugged. "The sun is not so hot."

She leaned over to kiss him. He lifted his chin to receive her. Aya inhaled against his cheek and savored the taste of his latest meal and the odor of burned lavender on his breath. While their faces stayed connected, her spirit dislodged and withdrew. Dizziness washed over her mind, the sensation of reeling off balance but falling in two different directions.

Every time, it got easier for her soul to fly free of its flesh. Every time, she felt more in control.

In her thoughts rang the memory of the well-known folk song and lyrics spoken by Eiyallandra and her faithful companion the Man of the Forest. *We are children of the light, the begotten of the spirits of our ancestors who haunt the silver clouds. We will always find each other. You and I, one and one, two as one... we are one...*

As a spirit, she soared upwards to the cloudless sky, unafraid to be away from her own skin, knowing that his feet anchored her body to the ground.

* * *

The dream's winds carried her spirit westward to the seashore. Villages of rickety shacks on stilted platforms faced the wide, gray ocean. Small boats bobbed on the waves. People stood waist-deep in the surf to haul nets and wicker baskets into the shore. Seagulls squawked as they circled overhead.

She glided onward on the drift of a northwesterly wind. A hidden cove of white sands nestled in a hollow crescent of brown cliffs.

One man waded into the lapping waves of the ocean, making ready to launch a rowboat. A cedar chest, burlap bundles, jugs, and several baskets overloaded the boat. Aya saw little room for anyone to sit at the center of it all.

Even viewed from behind, Aya recognized the man by his height and his broad frame. His muted beige clothing dripped with fringe strings at every seam. Gerrawgon had trimmed his long brown hair short to the collar.

Are you a fisherman now? her spirit asked in a voiceless voice.

Gerrie stopped standing ankle-deep in the water. He held onto the prow of the rowboat that remained mostly secure in the beach's white sands. The sea's waves continued to lap at the calves of his boots.

"You are a most persistent child." He spoke to the open sea before turning around to face her.

Will you come back to the trading post and meet me there for a visit? Will you spend the autumn holidays with us? There is so much I want to share with you and learn from you.

"You don't need to learn anything from me. You're doing quite well."

We cured the world!

"I figured as much. We all felt it pop loose. So, you and Shad exterminated the ol' pest? Well done, child."

It was as you showed me.

"I did? When?"

I had a vision of future days. You spoke to me.

"Oh, I see, and of course my future self gave you instructions for exactly how to deal with the problem?"

No, you were unclear.

Gerrie tilted his head. "That's terribly sloppy of my future self. When the fate of the continent depended on your success, I was no more specific in telling you how to vanquish a primordial beast?"

We figured it out by ourselves.

"Indeed, you did. Once again, I'll offer my congratulations and praises for a job well done."

The mountain people who helped us were poisoned in the cave, though. Do you know a cure?

"There is no cure," Gerrie said. "It's one of the reasons why I refused to accompany you. That place would poison me too! If a few decades are unbearable for a human lifespan, imagine suffering a debilitating illness for thousands of millennia."

What about Fless?

"Why mention her?"

Shad's mother is like you, isn't she? Fless dropped out of the clouds too? Is she immortal like you?

"Yes, of course. You 'Shining Ones' are the hybrid children of fallen immortals like me, like Fless, like the others whom I avoid." His voice rang with irritation. If Aya were not in spirit form, she might have blushed in embarrassment for not deducing it sooner.

Would she know of a cure?

"I doubt it," he said. "For as old as Fless and I may be, there are things much older than we. Nonetheless, you are welcome to seek her out and inquire for yourself."

Please help us. Tell me where to seek out the others like you? Please do something!

"I'm sorry, child. You will hear the same answer from the others of my kindred, if they will even deign to speak with you. Humans are frail and short-lived. They die. It's very sad but such is the way of things."

A person's head rose out of the water not far offshore but too deep to be standing in the shallows. The face had narrow, feminine cheekbones but it was certainly not a woman. Her stringy hair was blue-green and thick like algae. Her skin dotted with purple freckles had the pasty hue of rendered pork lard.

Who is that? What is that?

Gerrie cocked his head in the direction of the sea creature. "I met a bog blythe in the wetlands. She's going to help me journey across the ocean."

As he shifted his grip on the prow of the rowboat and made ready to continue with the launch, Aya's spirit called out. *Why are you leaving me?*

His grip tightened on the wooden post. "I'm not leaving you, child. I'm leaving all of this! I have walked this continent from one shore to the other for almost a thousand years. I'm weary of it all."

Haven't you ever been in love? Enough to stay?

"Yes, I've loved," he answered somberly. "But it does not matter if I stay or not, for the mortals always leave me in the end. Five years or fifty years or five hundred years, what's the difference? Mortal humans always die too soon, and I always go on alone... Even in bed with a lover, I am always alone."

Will I ever see you again?

"You're seeing me now. You can see me whenever you wish."

But in the flesh?

"Probably not. But then again, you're the one who can view the future, not me." On that word, Gerrie pushed his rowboat into the waters and hopped aboard to the bench at the center.

The bog blythe reached up from the sea and took hold of the rowboat's prow. She reclined backward with her head aiming to the west. Under her guidance and power, the little rowboat floated away from the shore and set its course for the distant horizon.

Goodbye, father. The sentiment in a wordless language pushed her spirit away in the opposite direction. She soared eastward merging into the cool breezes of a golden afternoon. Fields of wheat and barley streaked beneath her translucent feet. Soon she soared beyond the tree-tops of the evergreen forest. Clouds drifted alongside and beneath her.

For a moment, she felt a temptation to remain as a milky specter floating in the sky forever. How easy it would be to remain in the clouds, free of weeping or pain. Alone but not alone, the air sprites tickled her mind and whispered temptations. *Stay with us. Be with us. Join us. Play with us.*

The scent of burning lavender leaves wafted in the mists of the sky. Aya remembered the taste of him, the warmth of him, the softness of his hands, and his prickly stubble when they kissed. His soul's chiming gong called for her return. The music of his voice rang into the deepest core of her mind.

Her spirit grew heavier and heavier. Clouds floated farther away. Ground rushed up to catch her. Aya's spirit splashed back into her cold, stiff body that reclined in the grassy meadow by her lover's feet.

"Welcome back," he said while puffing on his pipe. "What did you see this time?"

The End

About the Author

Denise B. Tanaka has a lifelong passion for writing stories of magical beings and faraway worlds. Her father inspired a love of art with his landscape paintings, portraits, and photography.

Her mother inspired a love of books by reading aloud The Gingerbread Man and Mrs. Tittlemouse, so from a very young age Denise believed that cookies run away and mice can talk. She is sometimes sidetracked by nonfiction biography and true crime projects. A graduate of Sonoma State University, she pays the bills by working as a paralegal in immigration law.

She has dabbled in genealogy for many years and is very grateful for the internet.

www.ingramcontent.com/pod-product-compliance
Lightning Source LLC
Chambersburg PA
CBHW031100020726
47495CB00007B/1970